BEYOND
Poetry

ABOVE & BEYOND

Wendell,

Thank you for your support. I'm grateful you found this series compelling. I hope to share more of my works with you in the near future.

One love,

Paperback ISBN: 978-1-7362248-3-0
eBook ISBN: 978-1-7362248-4-7

Interior Design: The Book Designers
Interior Images © Shutterstock

Editor: Katie Zdybel

Exterior Design: Robin Johnson

Cover Photography: Murat An, Viktoriia Hnatuik,
MimagePhotography, Francisroux

Author Photography: CL Tyson Photography

BEYOND

Poetry

ABOVE & BEYOND

NATHAN JARELLE

Washington, D.C.

Nathan Jarelle strives to publish books that promote conversation. Although the world has changed since 1999, the topics of yesteryear remain the same.

Life is A Picture Book

Storied experiences for us to share

with faces that ache from laughter.

Make a wish if you dare.

Share a kiss.

See the world while it still exists.

Write a song to sing.

Turn a nightmare into a dream.

Find a soft spot in one's heart.

Now, that's the best place to start.

Speak a love language others can interpret.

Keep a secret that keeps the birds chirping.

Be a picture book while there's still time.

NATHAN JARELLE

Author's Preface

Dear Reader:

Follow me as we embark on a new path, *Above & Beyond*, the sequel to its ancestor novel, *Beyond Poetry*. In the first book, we followed Junior (a.k.a. Leonard Gerard Robinson Jr.) on his quest for perseverance. We laughed, we cried, and we cheered on a 14-year-old African-American boy from the fictional neighborhood in Philadelphia known as Brooke's Rowe. We stood on a filthy street corner and watched through Junior's eyes as his younger brother, Lawrence, was killed. We saw what it did to him and his family.

During my writing of the first book, I aimed to capture the art of combining fiction with poetry. The feedback was unbelievable. I gained more readers than I could've ever anticipated, and the traction on social media was just as plentiful. Readers sent messages, some with teary-eyed emojis thanking me. It was an honor to tell Junior's story and a privilege to share. It broke my heart, and it healed it all at the same time. I landed in a few bookstores here at home. I went from driving an ugly, blue Jeep with my head hanging down, to driving an ugly, blue Jeep with my head held high. My wife bought me a pretty ink pen with *Beyond Poetry* engraved on it. Now, I use it to sign all of my books, and in the very back, I always try to write "thank you" along with the reader's name. World, thank you for making *Beyond Poetry* special.

Early on, I knew that if *Beyond Poetry* would be any good, its sequel, *Above & Beyond,* would need twice as much time to complete. It was one of the toughest books I've ever written. In the sequel, Junior returns in the hope of re-discovering his identity and purpose. Junior is 18 and on the verge of adulthood; the year is 1999. For many of us, it's the hardest transition to make. There are so many things pulling you by the coattails: love, peer pressure, alcohol, drugs, sex. For Junior, the soft-spoken scholar from Brooke's Rowe, the pressure of living in the big city is more than enough.

When I think of 1999, I'm reminded of the Y2K scare along with the many breakthroughs in technology. We went from carrying brick phones to smaller devices (still with antennas) that allowed users to play games like "Snake" or even tennis. Video game consoles were better and faster. Cassette tapes were on their way to extinction as CDs came in. We bought blank CDs and used them to download music from file-share services like Napster. Finally, after years of hopeful wishing, you could talk on the phone and use the internet at the same time! We still hadn't broken ground on the latest iPhones—and Facebook wasn't yet a thing. Hell, we didn't even have

MySpace yet. The Y2K crisis was the biggest scare. It took us two decades to realize that the real crisis was COVID-19.

In 1999, I was nearing the end of high school and juggling the decision to attend college or enlist in the army. I didn't wanna hang around doing nothing since that's typically what led to trouble. Where I lived, you had to be careful as a Black teen, driving through the city in a nice car with other Black kids in it. My brother owned a Toyota with tinted windows. He later added a custom radio which came with a detachable CD face. He kept it inside of a black case which made my mother flip because the case could've been mistaken for a handgun.

About junior high is when most Black parents have "the talk" with their kids. You have to. My brother and I were fortunate to live in a decent neighborhood. However, because of that, it was imperative we understood that although we grew up playing with white children from time to time, we were not the same. When you're Black, a detachable CD face inside of a black case is a dangerous weapon. For a white kid, it's a detachable CD face. It was what it was.

Mom was serious about making sure that her Black boys understood perception. I was learning to drive that year and becoming more independent. I needed to know what to do if I was stopped by the police. I met my first girlfriend that same year. Young love is the best love going around because you live in the moment. My girlfriend and I would stay on the phone until late—even on school nights. We'd save our dirty chat for AIM or Yahoo Instant Messenger. I got a webcam that Christmas, but the quality was snowy so I barely used it. When mom would call me to the dinner table, I'd type "brb" which is millennial slang for "Be Right Back". My girlfriend and I would talk about sex, but I was deathly afraid of bringing a baby home. The two stand-out rules in my house were: don't bring a baby home and don't bring the cops to our door. I had friends that did both. Another kid I knew went a step further and got himself "kilt" over a girl. I learned from that experience that who you date is just as important as who you choose not to date.

At the time of writing, it's the summer of 2021, and I'm faced with the arduous task of preparing a new book for the world to read. I hope this title lives inside of you and that you find the characters as recognizable to your own worldly experiences. Similar to the first novel, the poetry is finessed throughout the book to soothe the cruel blow of life happening before your eyes.

To you and yours, thank you for your support and for reading *Beyond Poetry: Above & Beyond.* God bless you and your family.

Sincerely,
Nathan Jarelle

Prologue

PICTURE PERFECT

Picture the perfect romance. Two souls together as one—
withstanding the hands of time.
You and I are sand of the same kind. A love that's divine.
I can think of 1,000 different ways to say
I'm happy that you're mine.
You make a city, a city. The sky is bluer when you're around.
The sun is a little brighter.
You make my soul feel a little lighter. You put the "K"
in a kiss. Let's make a motion flick.
On my heart, or on my sleeve. Girl, I can't believe
this is reality and not some silly dream.

—LEONARD G. ROBINSON JR.

The way the sun illuminated New York City during the summer mornings made it hard for Junior to get out of bed. The big city was his home away from home. He'd linger at his windowsill before the start of his day and take in the golden arch as it emerged beyond the horizon. Its radiant beam glared warmly over the Twin Towers which loomed in the background. To the north was the Empire State Building which overtook the city's skyline. Below that was the bustling sound of city racket. For "The City That Never Sleeps", noise was its mantra. Junior was proud to be one of the seven million residents who lived there. One whiff of his adopted hometown was enough to keep him there an extra weekend. Before starting his day, Junior reflected on his journey thus far.

Most mornings, he'd start his day with a love poem inside of his journal. What else does a college freshman dating the baddest girl in all of New York write about? Junior's poetry still shone the way; just as it had when it once rescued him from a neighborhood in peril. Shy and subtle, he still wore his turbulent past on his sleeve. The traumatic death of his brother, Lawrence, forever shattered his world. Five years had passed since that dreadful day. Though Junior's anger remained, it had subsided somewhat throughout the years as he fostered a new life beside Vanessa Bailey, his first love and graduating classmate at Langston High. With their winsome smiles, they fulfilled each other.

Vanessa's soft, brown eyes were hard to refuse. To keep her smiling, Junior would lie to his parents so he could stay the weekend behind in New York. "Well, I am kind of busy this weekend, Ma." He'd wink over at Vanessa as the two lounged near Times Square. "Can I visit next weekend?" Often, the two would spread out an old, flannel blanket in

Central Park as they overlooked the city. Some days, Vanessa brought a bottle of wine inside of her purse for them to share which she took from home. Initially, Junior didn't think much of Vanessa's drinking. It seemed to be in check. She'd bring along her portable radio and play some of her favorite artists: Billie Holiday, Ella Fitzgerald, Miles Davis, Louis Armstrong, or her all-time favorite, Nina Simone. If not contemporary jazz, it was R&B: Lauryn Hill, Mary J. Blige, SWV, Aaliyah, Total. Vanessa would remove her sandals and rub her toes in the grass, bobbing her head. She loved music but had decided to study African-American history her freshman year of college. Since Junior was a hip-hop head, the two often discussed the conspiracies surrounding the recent deaths of Biggie Smalls and 2pac. The recent demise of other rappers like Big L and Freaky Tah only fueled the debate.

Other days, Vanessa would bring a bottle of her favorite burgundy polish and allow Junior to paint her nails. "Yo, who needs a salon when I got you?" she once said. Junior would carefully paint each of her toes as if he was writing lines inside of his journal. If not polish, it was lunch, a nap in the shade, or the two would lie face-to-face, gazing into each other's eyes.

"So, what are you thinking about right now?" Junior once asked her.

"Uh, you. Duh!" Vanessa replied in her cute, New Yorker accent. "Who else? You're so wack, J." Vanessa grinned before leaning over to kiss him.

If not Central Park, they'd wander around town or

overlook the city from the top of the Empire State Building. When that became monotonous, they'd bicycle across the Brooklyn Bridge, catch a play on Broadway, or hit-up a movie theatre. A billboard for *The Matrix* starring Keanu Reeves enthralled them. They'd also visit the many museums scattered throughout the city's five boroughs. Vanessa carried a cheap Polaroid in her bag. With her arm extended, she'd snap a selfie of the two of them together. The flash always caught Junior by surprise.

Yo!" she'd bark, startling him into an awkward pose. *Click*. "Ha-ha. Got ya."

"Another one, V.?" he'd chuckle. "Man, gimmie that fuckin' camera. C'mere!"

"No, get your own!"

Vanessa would then take off as Junior chased her through a mob of passersby, laughing.

Days later, she'd show up with a new picture for him to add to his shrine at home. Tacked on his wall back at Casey's was an archive of captured memories. Junior's favorite was Vanessa's senior class photo from Langston. He also had other photos of Vanessa that he kept hidden inside of his drawer next to his bed.

Junior had never seen a girl as alluring as Vanessa Bailey. Originally from Bed-Stuy, she lived with her mother and stepdaddy in a small, suburban town in Wilshire, New Jersey. At 5'8, she had a cute mole above her corner lip which complimented her foxy face and delicious frame. Vanessa was naturally beautiful, and she seldom wore makeup except for her burgundy shade of lipstick. She had a Kodak smile and a cute laugh that was addictive. Some days, Junior would run his fingertips a long Vanessa's tender soles just to hear her giggle. She'd squirm under his wrath in good fun. Junior once tried the same childish act to his sissy, Casey, while she was watching TV at home. She quickly jerked her foot away and punched him on the arm so hard that it bruised for a week.

Back in high school, most, if not all of the girls, passed on Junior. Vanessa found him adorable, though. He'd leave sweet notes inside of her locker or roses on the front seat of her car. Using his favorite pen, he'd stencil poetry along her forearms, thighs, back or wherever she allowed. "Ugh! Yo, how much longer? I'm dyin' over here—hurry up!" She'd wiggle with a pleading smile. Vanessa would show off Junior's work to her jealous friends. They'd all swoon over his penmanship and the fact that Vanessa was so happy with him. Whether Junior wanted it or not, he was king of Langston his senior year, and Vanessa was his beautiful queen. The two earned Langston's "Cutest Couple" and "Always Together" superlatives in their class yearbook. They were also voted King and Queen at their prom and interviewed by a writer from the *New York Times*. Before long, Vanessa was teaching Junior the ropes beneath the sheets.

Lying naked, Junior let Vanessa touch and kiss him in places he never experienced. He liked it... a lot. She guided his green hands along her shapely pastures and down to her thriving sex. He noticed that she shivered as he rubbed it in

5

a circular motion. Meanwhile, Vanessa licked and caressed Junior's engorged flesh until sap seeped from its canal. "Mmmm, stringy," she moaned, licking it from between her fingers before mounting him.

Junior panted with anticipation as Vanessa lowered her love-well onto him. Her cushiony walls gripped and released him as he groaned and shifted under her assault. Her jiggly cheeks slapped against his thighs as she rode him. "Shhhh," Vanessa whispered, quieting him. "Just try to relax." Vanessa placed Junior's hands onto her perky breasts. His subtle grip changed as he felt himself on the verge of spasming. He held back, urging Vanessa for a break as he felt himself on the verge of erupting. She grabbed his handsome face and kissed it. "I'm on a pill," she whispered. "You can make a mess."

On cue, Junior's mind went dark. The euphoria of Vanessa's cove overpowered him as he sprayed her insides full of warm cream. "Fuck-fuck-fuck-fuck-fuck—oh shit—oh shit!" Electricity swam throughout Junior's body as Vanessa stripped him of his soul. She reached between her legs and rubbed herself to a weeping orgasm as she cried out bliss-fully. Weary and weak, Vanessa collapsed into Junior's arms as the two cozied into an afternoon siesta.

When it came to love and affection, Vanessa had a heart of gold. She was a giver who expected the return of her investment paid with interest. At times, however, Vanessa's expectations often superseded her reality.

During their senior year at Langston, Junior was on the Poetic Youth Team where he'd perform spoken word on stage.

He'd started the year before and had gotten so good that the director sent his name to a talent agency. Junior's name landed on the desk of a gentleman by the name of Russell Simmons. Simmons had been working a major project and prowling for talent. "Keep grinding, son," the director encouraged. "You never know who might show up one night."

Junior spent hours in front of the mirror working on his voice, facial expressions and body demeanor. He'd practice in front of Vanessa as she sat on his bed inside of his room. When he messed up, she'd give him a thumbs down. Everything else was a kiss or better. At school, his involvement with PYT consumed his time, albeit worth the risk, considering the light at the end of Junior's tunnel. He wrote and performed "Brooke's Rowe" in front of a packed house which included both his parents, Casey, his best friend, Mel, and Vanessa.

A street corner coated in red. An innocent child
hit with hollow point lead in his head.
Drugs and corrupt feds could care less.
A mother's biggest stress
is the day she has to lay her own child to rest.
Nobody sees a thing. That's how it always is.
It's the cold code of the neighborhood where most
disadvantaged kids live.
Failure is imminent. The city forgot to mention it.
At the townhall
where they passed the buck on the last call.

They said it was for the betterment.
To keep the hood from the good
by ensuring that the system was unjust
in these low-income neighborhoods.
If they could they would leave us for dead.
No child deserves a bullet in their head.

—LEONARD G. ROBINSON JR.

It was gritty, but honest. The attendees celebrated Junior's creativity and coarseness. He didn't cuss or use the word "nigga" like some might have suspected he would. Many didn't know he had just told the story of his brother's gruesome death. Junior won first place that night. His folks congratulated him backstage. His name gained traction amongst his peers as a prolific rhymer and spoken word artist. To keep him sharp, the director of PYT upped Junior's involvement in the program his senior year.

For three nights each week, he'd practice his craft until it took a toll on his relationship with Vanessa. It was bad enough he worked nights down at the Grocery Mart. Feeling dejected, she began complaining. "What about me?" she asked him one night after a show. "Every other day you're on the stage or at work. What about *our* stage, J.? Don't I matter, too?" So, to make Vanessa happy, Junior limited his participation in the program. Eventually, he dropped out altogether and stopped showing up. The director was stunned. When Junior told his momma he quit the program, Sandy shook her head at him. "You gotta do what makes you happy, and Vanessa gotta do what makes her happy," she said. "Then, y'all supposed to meet in the middle—both happy people. That's usually how it works." The scars on Vanessa's heart from her abandoned childhood, however, commanded Junior's attention.

For years, Vanessa grieved the absence of her biological daddy. According to her, he had a drug problem. When Vanessa was ten, her momma left her daddy and re-married a man named Steve. Vanessa hated Steve because he wasn't her real daddy, but Steve had done more for Vanessa in eight years than her real daddy had done in eighteen. He'd buy her nice clothes which Vanessa would give away or sell from the trunk of her car. The apparel was exceptional: Jordan sneakers, Donna Karan New York bags, Parasuco jeans, jean jackets, leather jackets, Timberland boots. The cash Vanessa made from her sales, she'd use on Junior. She'd buy him expensive gold watches, shoes or fitted caps. She'd also write him love notes that went with his gifts. It made Junior's family suspicious, of course. One day, he showed up at his parents' house with a pair of fresh "butters", a Cipriano-style watch, and an Avirex leather jacket. Junior's parents accused him of selling dope. They ripped him the moment he walked in.

"Where'd you get this shit from, huh?" Senior growled as he looked him over. "Dem boots? Dem jeans? That fancy goddamn leather coat—what's all this? Whatcha been doin' up there? You sellin' that shit, ain't ya? Lemme find out! I'm gonna break you in half. Hear me?"

"I ain't slingin' no dope, Daddy!" Junior protested. "Vanessa gave this stuff to me."

"Well, where's she gettin' the money from?" Sandy inquired. "You ain't makin' that kind of money workin' at no damn grocery store. You explain yourself right now, Junior."

Junior's sissy showed similar concern for Vanessa's pricey kindness.

"I'm worried about y'all," Casey told him one night. "Look, J., I love Vanessa—we all do. She's a sweetie. But I just feel a little funny about her droppin' all this dough on you. Just the other week, she was bitchin' about PYT. I agree with your mom; it's too much."

"She just wants to show her love, Sissy," Junior argued. "What's wrong with that?"

"Yeah, but all *this*," Casey rummaged through his closet. "This shit is expensive, man. Look at this stuff. Look at this coat, for example. I saw this the other day down in Manhattan—for $700, Junior. This Triple F.A.T. Goose, yo, this shit is like $250. Three pairs of Jordans? Silver Tab jeans. Guess jeans. Timberland boots. Eddie Bauer—give me a break. Vanessa can buy this stuff when y'all are married. Dial it back some."

"But she doesn't want to dial it back."

"Well, I'm tellin' you to dial it back," Casey laid down the law. "What are you even givin' this girl in return for this stuff?"

"What else? Love. Dick. Affection. Understanding."

"You don't understand shit." Casey closed his closet. "You don't need all this stuff, J. You ain't no superstar. You can keep one outfit. The rest goes back."

10

"C'mon, Sissy!" Junior threw a tantrum. "What the fuck? What's the big deal?"

"Boy!" Casey raised her fist at him. "I will knock you out in here—don't be buckin' at me like that. You crazy or somethin'? Take this shit out of my house!"

"Yes, ma'am." Junior lowered his head before cleaning out his closet.

The next morning at school, Junior showed up with several black bags full of Vanessa's gifts packed inside. She looked through the bags with worry.

"I don't understand." She shook her head. "If I'm giving it to you, what's the issue?"

"V., you don't have to buy me this stuff just for me to love you." Junior held her hands. "I love you anyway. Are you buying me this stuff because you think it'll make me love you more than I already do?"

"…Maybe," she said. "I just want you to be happy."

"Well, what makes you think I'm not?"

Vanessa looked elsewhere, refusing to look at Junior. He lifted her by her sweet chin so that she was facing him. He lowered his voice to a soothing ambience.

"So, are you gonna tell me?" he kissed her, placing his head against hers. Her eyes teared.

"…I just don't want you to leave," she told him.

"What makes you think that I'm gonna leave you? C'mon, V. That's silly."

The sun highlighted her beautiful face as her lips started

to quiver. Junior thought she might cry, but she didn't. She replied with a solemness in her eyes that made him feel guilty for giving her back the stuff she got him.

"I love you, V."

Vanessa closed her eyes to marinate in Junior's words. A tear rolled down her tender cheek.

"You better," she sighed.

One

She had a shattered heart when I first met her.
She was broken. My little token.
Overrun by the cruelty of life—
hoping to outrun the cruelty of the night.
Her world was covered in darkness. I just provided the light.
I showed her a path and she never looked back.
I offered her a better image but she couldn't picture that.
I touched her heart. I kissed her lips.
I caressed her soul. I ate her clit.
I fell in love. She fell in love. We fell in love.
Stars shined above.
My first ever love.

—LEONARD G. ROBINSON JR.

Junior couldn't stop his hands from twitching as he stepped to a microphone inside a shabby nightclub in District Heights late one August evening. A year had passed since he last performed on stage at Langston High. There, the bar was low for a skinny kid known for carrying journals and wearing headphones everywhere he went. The fear of being judged worried him; to make it in New York City in front of an audience, you had to be greater than great. It took charisma, passion, and the conviction that to fail on stage was a compliment to one's journey. Junior had none of those things. He was just a damn good writer who was encouraged to give spoken word a go.

Junior had gotten the call that night from a gentleman named Luke who was somehow connected to the director at his alma mater. He had originally planned to go with Vanessa to a going-away party in honor of his best friend, Mel. Junior got the call hours before the party began. "Well, I'm not doing that kind of stuff these days—not since Langston," Junior told the man. But when Luke offered to pay Junior to perform on a weeknight, he jumped at the chance.

"It's a weekday crowd, I'll even give you the opening act so you can get it over with," Luke explained. "I just need the slot filled until my other acts get in. I'll pay you twenty bucks."

Twenty dollars was everything to a broke student. Not to mention, Junior hadn't got his paycheck yet from the Grocery Mart, his part-time gig. He decided to accept the job.

Luke's Lounge was a decent hole-in-the-wall spot for newcomers hoping to get their feet wet on stage. The inside was moderately clean with subpar food and customer service. Album ads covered every wall, dating as far back as the days of Grandmaster Flash and the Furious Five. There were boxing posters so old that Larry Holmes was still heavyweight champion of the world. On the manager's door down the hall was a coming-soon poster for The Roots' fourth studio album: *Things Fall Apart*. The aging poster was held upright by thumbtacks. Next to that was Junior's favorite album of that year *I am* by Nas. He noticed the golden poster on his way into the club.

In the theatre was a blue light which illuminated the crowd from the ceiling. To the right of Junior was an old, Magnavox TV attached to a wall with his picture on it. Astonished, he waved at the box as the restless crowd gave him hell.

"Yo, ya fuckin' dead up there, bro!" a man shouted from the crowd.

The crowd snickered at Junior as he turned to look for the culprit. The heckler's rudeness brought him back. He reached inside his back pocket for his poem, reviewed it and returned it back to his pocket. He cleared his throat.

"Th'fuck you waitin' on, kid? New Year's Eve?" another voice shouted.

Junior tapped the microphone with his finger. *What am I doin' up here?* He thought to himself. He looked around for a familiar face in the crowd but struggled; it was hard to see anything through the thick black. He surveyed the crowd again and found Vanessa's beautiful face sitting near the bar. She smiled at Junior warmly, melting his heart as he suddenly remembered what he had come for. He spoke into the mic, keeping his eyes glued on Vanessa throughout.

"Love the air you breathe. Love the way you walk.
I hear the way the city talks and the fluorescent moon
as it gawks. Your body is art.
Your spirit is sincere. Your soul is paramount.
Your essence I revere.
I cherish your earth and the way it revolves around me.
You absolve me.
Wherever you are is where I want to be.

—LEONARD G. ROBINSON JR.

Junior closed his eyes and slowly opened them, one at a time. There was nothing to see. No standing ovation. No Russell Simmons there to sign him to a fat contract. Nothing. Vanessa clapped her hands, hoping to entice the crowd to join her. Although a few did, the rest carried on in typical auditorium banter. Junior couldn't tell if the minor cheers he received were for him or the fact that his clown act was over. He exhaled with regret and plodded off stage to Vanessa. She wrapped Junior in her arms and held him. *Never again*, he thought.

"Yo, fuck this crowd," she told him. "I loved your poem! These folks wouldn't know a great poet if Maya Angelou smacked 'em clean in the face. You good, J.?"

Junior shrugged.

"I guess I don't have it anymore," he said. "Maybe if I got some more practice in, I could've done a lot better—I don't know. I should've listened to you, V. You were right."

"Deadass. This place is wack!" Vanessa kissed his long

face. "You'll always be my favorite poet, J. No matter what. I love you."

Junior returned a sweet kiss to her tender lips.

"Love you too, V. Whoa! Is that Hennessy I taste?"

"It was only one drink. That's it."

"C'mon, V."

"I couldn't wait!" Vanessa laughed. "Yo, the guy didn't even card me. Can you believe that?"

"Yeah, I can believe it," said Junior. "Man, these folks don't care about a girl being under 21. It's all about the almighty dollar, V."

"You know the vibe," she said. "C'mon, let's bounce."

Holding Vanessa by the hand, the two quietly exited the theatre and headed to Luke's office down the hall. Junior left Vanessa out in the hallway and went in for his money. He walked in to find Luke on the line raising hell about a performer who apparently was late getting there. Junior took a seat in front of Luke's desk and waited for him to finish. The club's manager looked like a cheap rendition of the character Dollar Bill played by Bernie Mac in *Player's Club*. "Look, I need the bitch here in the next hour!" Luke cussed into the phone. "Th'hell am I supposed to do now?"

Junior grimaced at Luke's harsh dialect. The owner was a middle-aged man with a graying horseshoe for a hairline. While waiting to get paid, Junior surveyed the man's office. Behind him was a *Born Again* poster for the late rapper, the Notorious B.I.G. The album was slated for release in December of that year. It was Biggie's first posthumous album since his death two years earlier. Next to Biggie was a poster for *Unleash the Dragon* by singer and songwriter Sisqó. Beneath Sisqó's poster on a wooden table was a nasty-ass coffee pot that looked as if it hadn't been washed in ages. There was a raggedy couch in the corner of Luke's office. The room was stuffy and smelled like crack sweat. After the manager finished his call, Luke reached inside of his desk and handed Junior a wad of one-dollar bills. Junior counted the money to ensure the manager didn't try to stiff him.

"So, when are you comin' back?" Luke asked him.

Junior folded his money and placed it in his pocket.

"I'm not," he said. "I'm done with being up there, man. I ain't got it no more."

"Whatcha mean you ain't got it no more? You're just gettin' started at this."

"He said he doesn't wanna do it anymore," Vanessa said as she entered the room. She took a seat beside Junior in front of Luke's desk and interlaced her hand with his. "Besides, with school starting in a couple weeks, J.'s not gonna have the time."

"Well, I thought you did really well, Junior," said Luke. "You've got an incredible gift—I've seen you perform at Langston. You know I'm friends with your old director, right? You really ought to come back and give it another go. Look, being on the stage is a perishable skill, son," he explained. "I've seen all of the greats have a bad night. Eddie Murphy. Martin Lawrence—you name it. Shit, I was there when Eddie bombed his first night. It happens. You just gotta dust yourself off and keep going, Junior. I know you got it."

"I just don't think it's for me anymore," Junior spoke up. "Besides, my girlfriend's right. I've got school comin' up in a few weeks. I really should focus on that."

"But you could do school and pick up a night or two each week. I'm always in need of artists—and I'll pay you. It won't be much, but it'll be somethin'—and you're gettin' the experience under your belt. What'd you say, son?" Luke bargained.

"Well, actually—"

"Sorry, he's not interested," Vanessa crossed her arms. "He won't have the time, and it's too much work and the crowd didn't seem all that receptive to him."

"Well, that takes time, young lady. Y'all are not at Langston anymore. It's the real world now. It's like playin' ball in college. The NFL is a lot of different. And from the way I see it, Junior has a real shot at this if he continues to practice. He's just a little rusty, that's all." Luke looked over at Junior. "C'mon, Junior. How can you expect to get better if you don't practice, man?"

Junior looked over at Vanessa and noticed her staring back at him.

"She's right, man." He shook his head. "I don't have it anymore. I appreciate the bread, Luke, but I think I'm gonna pack it in."

Luke cut his eyes at Junior with disappointment.

"Oh well—what the hell, I'm just a club owner. Here, take this." Luke handed Junior a business card. "You're the one with the talent. If anything changes, let me know."

Junior reached for the card.

"Thanks." He looked down at the card and sighed. "I, uh… I'll keep you in mind."

Afterward, Junior and Vanessa left Luke's office and pushed open the metal door which led them out into the city night. The two locked arms as they crossed the lot together. Up above them was a beautiful crescent moon loitering in the sky. Junior looked down at Luke's card again. He tapped it against his palm, unsure if he should keep it.

"I'm proud of you," Vanessa told him.

"For what?" he asked.

"For standing your ground. You don't have anything to prove. It's okay to let it go."

"Yeah, but I feel like if I practiced more, I'd be better. I probably could get as good—if not better—than I was at Langston. I mean, what's one or two nights a week?"

"That could be a lot, J. Like Luke said, it's not college ball. It's like the NFL out here. The expectations, the demand," Vanessa continued. "It's just too much."

"Yeah, you're right," said Junior.

As they neared Junior's car, Vanessa stopped him.

"Hey!" She lifted his face by his chin. "You'll always be my favorite spoken word artist."

Junior leaned in to kiss her.

"Thanks, V. I needed that. Yo, thanks for havin' my back in there."

Vanessa reached down for Luke's card and shoved it into her purse.

"Of course," she said, beaming back. "C'mon, we ought to get to Mel's. I need my medicine!"

Junior unlocked Vanessa's door for her and closed it as she slipped inside. He looked up to notice Luke standing near the back exit. The owner shook his head at him in disgust. Junior pretended not to see it. He climbed into the driver's seat and left.

Too Much to Drink

When they arrived at Mel's, Junior parked and shut off the engine. Before he could react, Vanessa quickly kidnapped his keys from the ignition. She dropped them inside of her bag as Junior gave her an evil glare. "Sorry, J.," she teased him. "I know you; you'll get in there and then wanna leave before all the fun starts. Not tonight."

Junior pouted all the way up to the door as he followed Vanessa from behind. He was *not* the party type. He liked to hangout, talk a little shit (maybe one drink) and leave. Vanessa liked to stay out all night, sometimes until early the next morning. Although Casey had never issued Junior a curfew when he started hanging out, he tried to be reasonable.

"Not too late, V.," Junior warned her. "You know how Sissy is when she worries."

"Casey ain't hardly worried about you, J. Nice try!" she laughed. "Besides, she's probably at home studying for her exam, anyway. When does she take it?"

"Few weeks, I think," said Junior. "Yo, don't be drinkin' too much and shit when we go inside of here. You already had one cup at the club."

"Son, that wasn't even a good cup; the bartender didn't know what he was doing."

"One drink, V."

"Two, J. Trust me. For real, I'm good."

"One and a half."

"Junior!" She whacked him on the arm. "Look, Mel's my friend too. Don't you trust me?"

Junior didn't answer. It was hard to go against her pretty brown eyes and she knew it. Vanessa winked at Junior and pressed the doorbell. She jiggled her purse at Junior, teasing him.

"That's why I got the keys!" she taunted him.

"Oh yeah? Bring your ass here!"

As the two playfully wrestled on the stoop, Mel answered the door with a red solo cup in his hand and a hair pick in the other. The pick had a black fist at the end of the handle. Mel's puffy afro was split with bald tracks extending across his cranium. With the military on his horizon, he'd plucked out his cornrows for a fresh cut the next morning before heading down to Parris Island.

"What up, y'all?" Mel greeted them.

"Oh, my God! Son, look at your hair, yo!" Vanessa laughed.

Mel reached his cup behind Vanessa to hug her as Junior waited his turn. Mel stuck his pick inside his squiggly fro and dapped him.

"What up, you bum-ass nigga?" said Mel.

"Fuck you," Junior chuckled. "What you got to drink? I don't want no Colt 45 either."

"Colt 45? Man, that's old school shit, Junior. Don't nobody drink that shit no more but old heads. Ma'fucka, it's 1999. You like Steel Reserve?"

"I don't want that shit either. You got any Henny?"

"Ooooh—yes," Vanessa co-signed. "Please tell me you got the Henny, Mel. I gave you ten dollars!"

Mel raised his cup for Vanessa to take a whiff. She took in the fumes and smiled with elation before bypassing him at the door.

"Good man." She patted his chest.

As Junior entered behind her, he stopped Mel at the door.

"Yo, man," he muttered. "Take it easy tonight. You know how she gets when she drinks."

"Junior, let the girl have a little fun," Mel whispered back. "College is in two weeks. Don't be such a fuckin' stickler. It's our last weekend together. Everybody's leavin' and doin' different shit. C'mon, J. This might be the last time we even see the crew from Langston, baby. Loosen up."

Junior let out hot breath through his nostrils.

"I know, man, but just...watch that shit—just a little. That's all I'm sayin', Mel. Remember graduation night? I don't want that shit to happen again. Man, Casey's car still smells like Taco Bell when you turn the air on. Every time I'm in her car, I gotta hear about that shit."

"Word? That was in May!"

"Yeah, I know. Now, it's August," Junior laughed. He draped his arm around Mel's neck.

"Aight-aight. I'll take it easy," Mel conceded. "I'll add extra ice to all of her drinks."

Junior patted his friend on the chest as he walked inside. "Good man. Good man."

Mel was a military brat, no doubt. His daddy was in the Air Force and had moved the family there in '93 after his promotion. The Roberts family did well for themselves, better than the Robinsons. They owned a single-family home in East Kennebec, and both earned substantial incomes. Mel wasn't a writer like Junior, and he didn't have a passion for history like Vanessa. Instead, he was a gifted engineer. Mel's true genius was his comedy. His father, however, nipped his ambitions to follow in the footsteps of his idol, Chris Rock, and sent him to Langston. Junior met Mel during freshman year after transferring from Medgar High.

Aside from Junior, most of the kids who went to Langston had mommas and daddies with decent careers. They had trust funds or bread for college already set aside. Most of them got cars as gifts for graduation. Vanessa's best friend was a girl named Shannon. She got a brand-new Mercedes Benz to take her upstate to Syracuse where she was going to study law. Mel got a fully-loaded '98 Nissan Pathfinder. Vanessa's gift was an investment property her parents would transfer over to her after college. Junior's graduation gift was a Visa gift card for $100.

Hell had nothing on the heat inside of Mel's house that

night. His proper send-off felt like an invitation into the abyss. His parents had left him the house for the night and allowed him to invite his classmates over. Mel's momma had gone the extra mile, frying up a batch of chicken wings for his guests. What Mel's momma didn't know was that her son and his underaged classmates had access to alcohol. Add weed and loud music into the fray, and things got fucked up quickly.

An hour into their visit, Mel's house was packed with kids from their school. Damn near everyone had a red cup in their hand. Kids played *Tunk*, *Spades*, or Dominos. Junior played none. He floated from room to room, bobbing his head to whatever rap music emitted throughout the house. Occasionally, he'd glance down at his watch to check the time.

Like every other kid there, Junior had a red cup but he knew his limits. Vanessa didn't. He watched as she continued to sip beyond her two-drink max. When he tried to save Vanessa from herself, her best friend intervened.

"Yo, lighten the fuck up," Shannon blocked him. "Let her have fun, J. We got her. She's good. You ain't gotta babysit her. Vanessa's a big girl." Irritated, Junior returned across the room. He'd never cared for Shannon when they were at Langston together. She'd interfere in his and Vanessa's relationship and would try to give them advice even though she was single. No guy in their right mind would fuck with Shannon—not even Mel, who would smash anything that walked.

As the night went on, Vanessa kept drinking and Mel

allowed the alcohol to keep rolling in. Soon, kids were rolling up marijuana. Concerned, Junior carted Mel into the kitchen to talk some sense into him.

"Son, I thought you were gonna take it easy?" he asked him.

"Man, fuck that." Mel swayed like a palm tree. "Why do you always gotta be so fuckin' responsible all the time, Junior?"

"It's not like that, man. I can't let Vanessa go home tonight all fucked up."

"Well, y'all can spinnanight here, J." Mel jabbed his arm. "It'll be like one big sleepover."

Junior shook his head and walked off. Meanwhile, the show went on. One kid was so plastered that he urinated on himself. The stench of piss and summer musk made Junior gag. Vanessa continued to drink. To take his mind off of her, Junior retreated to the basement to play *Madden* on PlayStation. He had given up on trying to save Vanessa and convince Mel to dial it back.

By midnight, Mel's party was still jumping as more students from Langston High showed up to celebrate. Even underclassmen were there to participate. Junior was halfway through a competitive Jets vs. Giants game when he heard kids cheering loudly from upstairs. He leapt from the couch and went to investigate. When he got there, he saw Vanessa with her head down at the card table. They were playing *Strip Spades*. She was sitting in her bra and was so drunk that she could barely lift her head. Her partner, another classmate, was completely naked and out of it. Their male opponents were fully dressed. Junior picked up Vanessa's T-shirt from the floor and covered her chest. As he tried to cart her away, Vanessa fought with him. "No! I can win!" she argued. A line of sloppy, slobbery drool hung from her mouth. Kids were laughing and cheering the bullshit on. Before long, Mel staggered his way down the steps. He was wearing jeans with no shirt, and his zipper was undone.

"Th'fuck is this shit, Mel?" Junior barked. "Yo, where were you? Where's Shannon?"

"How am I supposed to know?" said Mel. "C'mon, I'll help you get her out."

With Mel's help, the two carried Vanessa outside to Junior's car. During the walk, her sneakers dragged along the pavement. None of their graduating classmen volunteered to help the two; they carried on as if nothing had happened. As her deadweight torqued Junior's neck and back, he grunted with frustration. At one point, Vanessa's belly ripped in half as she belched and vomited Hennessy and wings down onto her legs. When they got her to the car, Junior freaked out when he couldn't find his keys before remembering Vanessa had them. He reached inside her bag and unlocked the passenger door as Mel tried to keep her from falling. Together, the two placed her into the passenger seat. Vanessa cut loose again as she vomited onto the floorboard of Junior's car. She clutched her belly and whimpered as Junior fished for a rag inside of his trunk to clean her up. Mel stood there like a useless lump.

"So, uh... you think she'll be ok?" Mel asked him.

Junior threw the rag at him.

"Fuck you!" he shouted. "Man, I told you to take it easy."

"Son, I was upstairs! How was I supposed to know?" he asked him.

"Upstairs with who, Mel? Who were you upstairs with?"

Mel lowered his eyes. Junior knew right away.

"Nigga!" Junior growled through his teeth. "Th'hell is wrong with you—you know damn well that Shannon wouldn't fuck with you if her life depended on it. That's rape, Mel!"

"Son, I ain't rape no-goddamn-body!" Mel shouted. "She asked me to take her upstairs, Junior—don't come at me with no rape shit—you know that ain't me."

Junior eyed Mel with distrust. "Man, I don't know who you are right now."

Mel's eyes grew wide with fury. "Fuck you, Junior. Look, it's not my fault you ain't got no control over your girl. To me, it seems like Vanessa's got control of you, and—"

Wham! Down Mel went. Blood streamed down his nostrils. Above them, a dingy streetlamp shined into Mel's face; he covered his eyes as he rolled over, trying to get up. As Junior went to help up his friend, Mel pushed him away. "Th'fuck off me!" he yelled. Blood trickled from his nose and down through his teeth. Mel rose to his feet and spat blood onto the ground. He wiped his face and looked down at his hand.

"My bad, Mel," Junior pleaded. "I didn't mean to swing on you, man."

"Fuck you, Junior," he said. "Fuck you and Vanessa. Y'all are dead to me."

Junior watched as Mel turned his back and went inside. He looked over in the passenger seat at Vanessa and saw she was slumped on her side. He couldn't drive her home, not like that. Out of options, Junior drove her back to Casey's.

Two

What should I do? I'm inebriated
by the very thought of you.
I can barely stand when you're around.
My heart skips at 'hello'.
My soul departs inside your well. It isn't hard to tell. Whether
I stumble, trip, fall, or if I fell,
without you near, all that's left
is this empty shell.

—LEONARD G. ROBINSON JR.

It was 1 a.m. when Junior parked behind Casey's blue Toyota in Fort Foote-Brooklyn with Vanessa inebriated beside him. She was out with her head propped against the window, snoring. He glanced up at the house and noticed the living room light was on. *Shit*, Junior thought. Casey was still awake. He unbuckled Vanessa's seatbelt, walked over to the passenger side and opened her door. She fell into Junior's arms, knocking him backward onto the pavement. His frail arms wobbled as he struggled to get her back in the car.

Lucky for him, Vanessa awoke just to vomit. He moved just in time to avoid getting splashed with a face full of her bile. "C'mon, V. Lift yourself up," Junior told her. Straining, the two worked together to get Vanessa back into the car. She fell over onto the driver's seat for a quick nap. Aggravated, Junior slammed the door and dialed Casey from his cell. She picked up without a greeting.

"Hey, uh…you busy?" Junior asked her.

"I am, as a matter of fact," Casey told him. "I'm trying to study. What do you want?"

"Come to the window."

"For what? I just told you I was busy, Junior. Now, what is it?"

"Can you please come to the window, Sissy?" Junior pleaded.

Junior could hear the annoyance in Casey's voice as she walked over to the window of her brownstone house. Her wide silhouette stood in front of the shade as she peeked through the vinyl. Junior waved at her.

"Okay, I see you." Casey waved back. "What's up?"

"Can you come outside for a second?"

Junior moved so Casey could see Vanessa slumped across his seat. Casey hung up on him immediately. She burst through the door out into the night wearing a hoodie, basketball shorts and house slippers. Her hair was in a messy bun with her glasses propped on her head. She marched down the steps and into Junior's face with her arms crossed.

At 34, Casey Haughton was still in Junior's corner. She

had strings of staggered gray on her head and had gained more weight since the two first met. Casey claimed the gray and extra package was Junior's fault—some of it was—but it was largely due to her poor diet. Her arched eyebrows were slanted in wicked anger. She bopped Junior on his stupid forehead with her palm.

"What did we talk about before you left earlier?" she asked him.

As Junior hung his head, Casey lifted his chin.

"Boy, look at me when I'm talkin' to you!" she raised her voice. "Now, how much did y'all have to drink?" She glared at him. "Tell me!"

"I had about a cup and a half, I swear!" Junior raised his hand to the heavens. "I'm not sure how much Vanessa had."

"Really, J.? You *know* y'all are not supposed to be drinkin'. Y'all are barely eighteen. Yo, I got an exam I'm tryin' to prepare for, I don't need this shit right now."

"I know. Look, I'm sorry," Junior pleaded. "Can you please just help me get her in?"

Casey looked over at Vanessa's slumped body and back at Junior. Her pretty green eyes were like daggers. The muscles in her face were tight with displeasure. She manhandled Junior, pushing her brother from one end of the car to the other.

"Move, before I knock your teeth down your throat—go away!" she fussed. Junior moved.

When Casey opened the door, Vanessa awoke, looked at Casey, belched in her face, and went back to sleep. Casey ran her fingers through her hair and gripped it.

"I'm sorry, Sissy."

"Oh, shut up!" she snarled at Junior. "C'mon, help me get her out. Help me get her inside before someone thinks we're trying to kidnap the poor girl—hurry up. Let's go."

Together with Casey's help, the two carried Vanessa inside the house and laid her on the sofa. Casey sent Junior off to get a cold washcloth. She placed it against Vanessa's forehead and pressed it. Next, she placed a garbage bin beside Vanessa's head in case she vomited again. Junior looked on like a medical student watching a doctor perform open heart surgery. Once Casey had Vanessa secure for the night, she grabbed Junior by his ear and dragged him upstairs to his room and closed the door. He shrieked the entire way.

"What were you thinking tonight, letting that girl get fucked up like that?"

"Man, I told Mel—"

"You're supposed to know better. I'm responsible for you, Junior. Me." She patted her chest. "This looks bad. If you're not gonna do what I tell you then pack your shit and get out."

"C'mon, Sissy, why do we have to take it there?"

"Because you're a smart kid, and it pisses me off when you do dumb stuff like this. I'm having a hard enough time studying for this stupid placement exam. I don't have time for this bullshit tonight! It's selfish and it's inconsiderate, J. Next time, go sleep it off in a park. Got it?"

As Casey turned to leave, Junior stopped her.

"I apologize, Sissy." He held her hand. "I promise, I'll be more careful."

Casey lowered her eyes at Junior. She walked him over to his bed and motioned for him to sit down. Casey sat beside him and placed her hand on his shoulder.

"Junior," Casey sighed. "Look, I know things happen once in a while. I know y'all wanna have fun. Just use your head, J. What if someone put somethin' in Vanessa's drink tonight or something worse happened? Just be smart about your shit—that's all I'm sayin'. We good?"

"I got it," Junior told her. "So, what do we do about Vanessa?"

Casey sprung from Junior's bed and over to his door.

"I've done enough. You figure out the rest," she told him. "I've got an exam to prepare for, Junior. When Vanessa gets better, she can go home."

"Thanks, Sissy. I owe you one."

Casey rolled her eyes at Junior

"Go to hell, Junior, alright?"

Together, the two returned downstairs to Vanessa. To accommodate her overnight stay, Casey gave up her study space. When Junior asked his sissy where the remote to the TV was, she looked at him balefully before heading upstairs to her room. She slammed her door so hard the ceiling lights flickered. Junior removed his shoes and cozied next to Vanessa on the sofa spooning her from behind. His right hand ached as he draped the blanket over them. He thought about Mel and shook his head. What a night, Junior thought. As he snuggled beside Vanessa, he closed his eyes. Above him, he could overhear Casey stomping across her bedroom floor. Junior felt guilty knowing he had upset his sissy. She'd gone through fire to bring him to New York, saving him from a troubled life in Brooke's Rowe. With his hellacious night coming to an end, Junior reflected back on their humble beginnings, four and a half years earlier.

The City That Never Sleeps

When the world turns cold, and I feel close to my very end,
I think about my friend and everywhere we've been.
And every night before I say 'Amen',
again, and again and again, I say 'thank you' for my friend.

—LEONARD G. ROBINSON JR.

In 1995, Junior's neighborhood was ranked the sixth most violent in the country, according to the city's paper. His family had moved from the northside shortly after Lawrence's death. For a year, Junior struggled to make new friends until he found poetry. A fan of his gift for words was a woman named Casey Haughton. Born white as snow with crinkly orange hair, the two met at Medgar Evers Secondary School while Junior was in exile. Believing she was white, Junior stereotyped her initially, before learning she was Black. "I'm albino, you dummy!" Casey had told him. "My skin might be white, but my soul is Black." Holding Junior's poetry book, Casey found herself immersed in the young boy's talent. Eventually, Junior moved to New York with Casey and her sister, Courtney, for school.

Despite his grand opportunity, Junior's first several weeks were hell. He cried himself to sleep most nights. On the weekends when he'd returned home to visit, he'd tell his parents he wanted to stay in Brooke's Rowe. His parents scoffed at his pleas. "Nope," his daddy, Senior, told him. With his head hanging down, Junior climbed into Casey's car and returned to New York.

The classes at Langston were tougher than what Junior had faced at Medgar. His test scores were the lowest in all of his classes. He tried to participate during lectures but felt stupid for answering incorrectly. He spoke very little. At lunch, he felt ashamed for not knowing what bison was. Kids laughed at Junior when he asked if Langston served Kool-Aid as a soft drink. "I don't think they serve that here, Leonard," a girl laughed in his face. Embarrassed, Junior kept quiet.

His first real smile came at the hands of a wannabe comedian whom he recognized from his math class. The kid's name was Mel Roberts. Mel was worse in math than Junior was. When Junior got his test score back from the teacher, he saw she'd marked a big fat "46%" in bold, red letters on his paper. Junior's eyes were misty. He looked over at Mel, his neighbor. Mel looked back at him.

"What'd you get?" Mel asked him.

When Junior showed Mel his test score, Mel showed him his. He had scored a pathetic 14%.

"At least you got an 'F'. I got a 'Z' on my shit," he laughed. "I didn't even know they gave those out at Langston."

Junior cracked up all day.

The laughs were few and far between, however. When an English instructor handed Junior back his fifth failed assignment, the school's dean placed him on academic probation. Distraught, he asked to withdraw from the program. The dean laughed. "You can't withdraw—you're only fourteen!" the woman told him. "Just hang in there, it'll all come together soon." Junior trudged back to class where he failed another assignment.

Later at home, when Junior failed to show up at dinner, Casey went looking for him and found the boy weeping in the dark inside his room. "Don't turn on the light!" he exclaimed, startling her as she opened the door. Casey turned it on, anyway. With his hoodie pulled over his face, Junior sat with his knees in his chest, sobbing.

"Junior!" Casey gasped, kneeling beside him. "What's wrong?"

Junior was so upset he could barely talk. Casey put her arm around the boy, allowing him to cry as the pressure finally broke him.

"I want to go home!" he whined. "I can't do nothin' right up here, man. I'm already on academic probation. What next, Casey?"

Seeing Junior snivel tore Casey apart. Her eyes filled with tears. She pulled Junior's hoodie from off his head as he leaned onto her shoulder. She gently rocked him.

"C'mere, little brother." She held him. "You're not gonna fail, Junior. OK? I won't let that happen. Just keep fighting this thing. Don't give up. You got it, J.?"

Junior stared up at Casey with admiration.

"OK, Sissy." He wiped his eyes, sniffling. "I'll keep going."

Casey lifted the boy onto his feet. Noticing a smudge of crud next to his eyelid, she dabbed her finger onto her tongue and flicked it away. Junior let her.

"Shit, sorry," she giggled. "That was kind of gross. Come down and eat soon, OK?"

Casey touched Junior on his biscuit nose and left. Junior followed her out.

It wasn't only the pressures of the school work that added to Junior's stress; the cost was a burden on his family and he knew it. Financing Junior's education took a village. The Robinsons had to take out a second mortgage on the house. Until Junior became old enough to legally work, he made money detailing the neighbors' cars after school. From freshman through the middle of Junior's sophomore year at Langston, Casey worked two full-time jobs to make ends meet. She worked as a senior admin assistant at a law firm during the day. At night, she worked as a custodian at a high school in East Bronx. Her car was broken into three times, and once, a man robbed her coming home from work.

By the end of her long week, she'd be so exhausted she'd crash onto the couch. Junior would come downstairs from studying and find her asleep still in her clothes. He'd remove Casey's shoes and socks for her and wrap Casey in her favorite blanket. The bottoms of her feet hurt her so badly some nights, she'd cry. Unbeknownst to anybody but the two of them, she was also battling Stage 1 breast cancer at just thirty years old. "I can't believe this shit!" she sobbed one night after learning of her diagnosis. "I don't care if I go all the way to Stage 8. I'm not stopping. I'll just work the cancer off, I guess—but I won't quit."

Junior laid his head on Casey's shoulder.

"I don't think it goes that high, Sissy. Only four stages, I believe."

It made Casey laugh. So, Junior laughed too. It was much needed. Junior placed a pan with hot, soapy water down at her feet as she smiled at him. "You're worth it, OK?" she said. "You're always worth it. You're gonna graduate and I'm gonna beat this cancer shit."

Junior never forgot that. Invigorated by her loving support, Junior fought on too. Within a few weeks, his world began to change, and so did his grades. He tutored right alongside Mel on the weekends until the next test date. The first grade Junior got back was a 72%—he passed by the skin of his teeth. Mel came in just under him at 70%. The two boys had been close ever since. Going into his sophomore year, Casey had beaten her cancer, and Junior earned a top-ten grade point average at Langston High. By eleventh grade, he was top five of his class. He walked with his head high and enlisted himself onto the Poetic Youth Team. Junior's penchant for poetry eventually attracted the attention of a girl named Vanessa Bailey.

Junior didn't think much of Vanessa when he first saw her. She was pretty but had a shitty attitude. Where Junior was from, people like Vanessa got their asses beat. Vanessa could pick a fight inside of a room all by herself, she was so nasty. He'd heard stories that she was stuck-up and how she'd motherfuck the boys who tried to get at her. He thought to himself that if Vanessa ever side-talked him that way, he'd cuss her out in style. As luck would have it, he got his shot.

One evening, Junior was late getting down to the library when he spotted Vanessa Bailey. Coincidentally, the two happened to be headed in the same direction. As Junior went to hold the door for his classmate, she bypassed him with her nose stuck up her ass. Fed up, Junior unleashed.

"Umm, thank you!" he shouted.

Vanessa turned around to challenge him.

"What? Yo, who are you?" she said in her New York accent. "You ain't nobody!"

"I just held the door for you, and you didn't say shit."

"First of all, I was gonna say it." She bobbed her head at him. "You don't know me like that. Don't be talkin' to me like I'm some ho!"

"Well, next time learn to be more polite with your stupid-ass." Junior walked off.

"*Fuuuck* you, aight? How 'bout that?" Vanessa howled. "I can use bad words too!"

Lucky for the two students, no one was around to hear their fiery debate. If either had been caught using profanity in the hallway, both would've been suspended on the spot.

Later, when Junior walked into the library to study, he cringed when he noticed Vanessa sitting at the main desk.

The two cut their eyes at one another; they were stone ene-mies. Vanessa gave him shit all night, and Junior gave it back. Once when he went to get up, his seat scraped against the floor causing a shrieking sound. He looked over to notice Vanessa glaring at him. She put down her book and hastily raised her finger to her lips. Junior raised his middle-finger back at her. Later, when he tried to check out a book by James Baldwin, Vanessa scoffed at him.

"Hmph. Surprised you even know who that is," she said.

Junior rolled his eyes. "Just gimmie the damn book."

As Vanessa handed Junior the book, he snatched it from her hands. She went off again.

"Yo, don't be snatchin' nothin' from me!" she whispered. "I'll go Bed-Stuy up in this piece—I don't play that shit."

As Vanessa went back to reading her book, Junior closed it.

"Bed-Stuy that!" he told her before walkin' off. He hated her guts.

That night, after the library, Junior performed spoken word on stage in the auditorium. His latest masterpiece, "Fall", was a poem he had written earlier during the day when thinking about the elusive concept of love and its meaning. He was new in the program but with serious potential as a young artist. Nervous, he stumbled onto the stage to a chuckle or two from his fellow club members. Junior may have been clumsy, but there was nothing clumsy about his talent. The words appeared inside of his head.

Fall in love. Fall out of love. Fall for love.
Some just enjoy the fall of love
because it gives them something new to dream of.
Some fall in love. Some love to fall.
Few ever truly give their all.

—LEONARD G. ROBINSON JR.

To a few claps and a cough from the audience, Junior bowed gracefully at the program's director seated in the front row and walked off stage. He went to take his seat in the audience and noticed Vanessa watching him from the door. He turned his back toward her. After his program ended, he left to wait for Casey to take him driving. Junior had just got his learner's permit.

At his locker, he tossed on his headphones to drown out the world around him. With Outkast vibrating through his headset, he failed to hear Vanessa sneak up to him from behind. She tapped him on the shoulder. Startled, Junior turned around, saw it was her and went back to shuffling inside his locker.

"Um, excuse me? Junior, right?" Vanessa laughed, touching him again. "That was a really nice poem. I was impressed. Did you write that?"

"What's that supposed to mean?" Junior stood erect. "You think I stole it?"

"Son, I'm just askin'."

"Son?" Junior screwed his face. "I ain't your son. Don't call me that."

42

"It's a New York thing, aight? Chill out."

"Well, I ain't from New York," Junior growled. "Find another son to kick it with. I'm out."

Vanessa's smile went cold as Junior closed his locker. He threw on his hoodie and walked off. Halfway up the hall, Vanessa appeared in front of him again.

"Look, I'm sorry about earlier. You were right, OK? I was being rude. For real, though. Where'd you learn to write like that?"

"None of your business," Junior told her.

As he tried to leave, Vanessa blocked him again.

"I'm being sincere, Junior." Vanessa touched his hand. "So, are you gonna tell me where you learned to write or not?"

Junior looked into Vanessa Bailey's hazel eyes and felt himself give way.

"I taught myself over time. Look, I'm not from around here. I stay with my sister in Fort Foote. I'm only here during the week. On the weekends I visit my family in Brooke's Rowe. So, do you write, too?"

"Niiiice. Philly? Wow!" Vanessa smiled. "I write some-times but not a lot. I'm not as good as you." She touched his arm. "You got a girlfriend, Junior?"

"Who? Me?" Junior turned red. "Nah, I ain't got no girlfriend."

"OK, well I guess you don't mind if we go out for ice cream, then? I wanna hear more of your poetry. I think that's really dope."

Taken aback by Vanessa's boldness, Junior grinned at

her. He couldn't help himself; he liked Vanessa Bailey a lot. Lucky for him, Vanessa liked him, too. He blushed terribly, unable to hide his giddiness.

"Uh, sure," Junior said. "I'd love to have you scream—I mean have you for ice cream—I mean… you know what I'm sayin', right?"

"I got you," Vanessa laughed. "That's so cute—you're nervous, I can tell. You're so handsome, yo, and you got a nice smile."

Junior cheesed even more. "No, I don't!"

"Yes, you do! See, you're doing it again." She pointed at him. "It's a good thing."

"Well, if I'm smiling it's because you made me smile. So, it's all your fault."

The two chuckled sweetly together. It was the first time Junior had ever got any play from a girl. His heart strobed inside of his chest like a disco ball. He agreed to meet Vanessa after school the next day for ice cream.

Junior and Vanessa fell fast for one another. They hung out every day after school and even on the weekends. They'd talk on the phone two or three times each day despite seeing each other at school. Eventually, she began hanging out with Junior at the house. Casey thought it was cute, initially. Vanessa would stay as late as 9 p.m. some week nights and would even eat dinner there. If Casey was in a good mood, she'd let Vanessa stay until 9:30 p.m. They'd snuggle together watching *America's Funniest Home Videos* hosted by comedian Bob Saget. Junior would show off his poetry books to her. They'd kiss, and she'd smile so wide, melting the boy's heart. At night, they'd talk out on the stoop overlooking the golden sunset while listening to music. Casey would then flick the porch lights, bringing their night to an end. "Damn, son!" Vanessa would chuckle. "Aight-aight, so how 'bout I come back tomorrow night? You busy?"

Junior would drive Vanessa home with Casey lingering behind the two in the backseat. "Two hands on the wheel, please!" Casey would say when Junior tried to put his arm around Vanessa. When Casey would sit back in her seat, Junior would place his hand over Vanessa's hand.

The Robinsons also liked Vanessa when Junior first introduced her. "How do you do, Miss Lady?" Senior shook Vanessa's hand with his big bear claw. He reached across her to jab at Junior's chest. "What's up, Sucka?" Sandy was who Junior worried about, though. She'd been overprotective of him since he had inherited her old Buick after passing his driver's exam. She sat in her favorite chair, sipping from her wine glass as she reviewed Vanessa's application to date her son. Junior and Vanessa held hands throughout the meeting.

"So, Vanessa, Junior says you grew up in Bed-Stuy?" Sandy asked.

"Yes." Vanessa smiled. "I lived in Bed-Stuy until I was about nine and then my mom re-married and we moved to Wilshire."

"Do you like Wilshire?"

"It's OK, I guess. A lot of white people, but it's not bad. They're cool."

Senior walked inside to kidnap Junior. "Junior, run with me down to the store for a few minutes."

As Junior went out the door, Sandy smiled devilishly at him.

Senior pulled his ugly truck into the shopping center's lot and walked Junior into the pharmacy. He led Junior down the aisle and stopped in front of the contraceptives shelf. "Somethin' you ought to think about," Senior laughed. "Here's ten dollars. I'm gonna grab a beer next door. Get yourself a box, and I'll meet you back at the truck." Junior shopped through the section and picked out a box of Lifestyle condoms and took it to the register. Afterward, he climbed inside of his daddy's truck.

"You get you some?" Senior asked.

Junior unbagged his box and held it up for Senior to see.

"Very good," Senior told him. "I don't know if you are or not—and I don't wanna know. But if you do…use 'em. Hear me?"

"Thanks Daddy," Junior told him.

Junior was ashamed to tell his daddy that he was still a virgin. He hadn't even told Vanessa by that time, nor had he tried to put on a condom or seen one up close. Curious, he tore open the box in front of his daddy, unpackaged one and held it up to get a closer look. When Senior realized what he was doing, he smacked the lubricated ring out of Junior's hand. It rolled down onto the floor of his truck. The two were sitting at a red light.

"Nigga, put that motherfuckin' shit down." He wiped his

hand against his shirt. "Don't be holdin' that shit up for people to see! Th'hell is wrong with you?"

"I just wanted to get a closer look."

"Well, get a closer look with Vanessa, Junior," he barked. "Not in here!"

"Well, can you tell me how to put it on?"

Senior glared at Junior.

"OK, fine. I'll figure it out."

"Yeah, you do that!"

As the light changed, Senior shook his head and drove off.

Junior's stomach boiled the first time he met Vanessa's family at their house for dinner. They were an awkward bunch, all of them. Vanessa picked at her food, barely speaking. Meanwhile, Steve, her stepfather, grilled Junior on a number of taboo topics, including his living arrangements with Casey. Vanessa's mother, a great cook, was no help at all. She began and ended almost all of her sentences with "...according to the word." Growing up, Sandy would take the boys to church some Sundays but not every weekend. After Lawrence died, she stopped but still worshipped in her own way. Senior was up in the air, and Casey was an atheist. Steve lost his shit when Junior explained his family dynamics. Vanessa had nicknamed Steve "Mad Midget" due to his angry, short stature. At 5'4, he was shorter than Vanessa's mother who was five inches taller. Vanessa said her momma married Steve for his money. Hearing him speak, Junior couldn't find much more in terms of substance.

"So, Casey isn't really your sister, is that correct?" Steve asked him.

"Casey *is* my sister, sir," Junior corrected him. "I don't see her any differently because she's older or that we don't have the same parents. She's my earth sister."

"Yeah, but," Steve folded his arms, confused, "I guess what I'm trying to understand is this whole living arrangement you two have—that's where I feel a bit befuddled." He raised his brow. "You're a kid living with a single, white woman who's in her thirties. And your parents are OK with this? It just seems strange, that's all."

"Casey's not white, Steve. She's Black; she's albino," Vanessa said, not taking her eyes off her plate. "What does it matter, anyway?"

"Well, it should matter, and this whole church thing is pretty concerning, too. The Lord says that a solid foundation begins with a strong involvement in the church."

"Some foundation. Didn't you have a kid out of wedlock before you got with Mom?"

"Vanessa!" Her momma interjected. "How *dare* you disrespect your father like that in front of company, young lady?"

"Fuck him! He is not my father!" She stood on her feet like Godzilla. "C'mon, J., let's go to Burger King. You shouldn't have to sit here and listen to any more of this."

Junior happily followed Vanessa out of the door.

Vanessa played tough at the dinner table, but she broke loose in the car. She sobbed again when they got to Burger King.

She hated her life in Wilshire. The two picked a corner seat in the back of the restaurant where she cut up often. "Sorry about that." She wiped her eyes. "I hate that place sometimes. I can't wait until I get the hell out of there." Junior left from his chair and walked around to sit next to Vanessa. He pulled her pretty face to him and rocked her.

"You don't have to apologize, V. Man, your stepdaddy is rough, though."

"Sonnnn, Steve brings the devil out of me!" Vanessa giggled.

Junior stayed out late that school night. He arrived home just after midnight smelling of Burger King and a good time. In her bag, Vanessa had a small bottle of E&J she had taken from Steve's bar. Junior couldn't say no. When he got in, Casey was waiting for him in the living room. It was the first of many times Vanessa had got Junior into hot water with Casey.

"OK, I'll let it slide this time, J." Casey shook her head. "Steve sounds like a real asshole. But yo, from now on, young man, you're to be in this house no later than 10:30 p.m. on a school night. You got that, mister?"

"Yes, ma'am," Junior straightened. "Sorry, Sissy. I'll be more mindful of the time."

"You better. One last thing." She crossed her arms. "Have you been drinkin'?"

"What?! No way!"

Casey lowered her eyes and walked away as Junior continued up to his room. He closed his door, changed and crawled into bed. He turned off his lamp and lay in bed, thinking about Vanessa. Junior rolled to his nightstand and grabbed his cell phone to call her up. She answered on the first ring.

"Hello?"

"V., what up? It's me," said Junior. "Yo, what you doin'?"

The rest was history.

Three

If you were my heaven, I would die happy
knowing my soul would glow.
I swear to God, I would die in your paradise
knowing the sacrifice.
My lover's eye would never die, even if it tried.
Even if I was stubborn and full of pride,
my soul would depart into her arms
high in the sky.

—LEONARD G. ROBINSON JR.

"Boy, if you don't come out of there!" Casey pounded on the bathroom door on a Sunday afternoon. A week had passed since Mel's party. Junior had managed to play it safe by wisely staying out of Casey's crosshairs until then. He'd been in the bathroom for over an hour which angered Casey. She'd gone through a pot of coffee earlier at breakfast and was on the verge of springing a leak. "C'mon, I got to go. What are you doing? What's taking you so long?" She pounded again.

"Yo, go downstairs," Junior told her. "Why do you have to use this bathroom?"

"You know why," she fussed. "There's spiders down there."

"So, take the bug spray with you."

"Ugh!" Casey exhaled in disgust. "I hate you. You get on my damn nerves."

As Casey disappeared down the steps, Junior peeped out into the hallway to ensure she was gone. He closed the door and went back to examining the eerie, dark lesion beneath his penis. It first appeared the morning after Mel's party and had bothered him since. It later manifested into a blister that itched like crazy. When Casey wasn't looking, Junior logged onto the internet and researched photos of people with STDs. He found a picture of a man with genital warts and gasped in shock. The worst photo he saw was of a man with full-blown AIDS. His eyes widened with terror at the sickly images he found throughout AOL's web browser. A photo of a 25-year-old woman on her deathbed from the virus gutted him. The woman, who according to the article, had contracted the virus from unprotected sex was skin and bones. Junior read further and learned that the young woman had died. When Casey knocked on his bedroom door, he turned off his computer.

Rusty and brown, the pus-filled mark was inflamed and painful to touch. Using a Q-tip, Junior prodded the odd lesion until its scab broke off. A trickle of dark blood dripped between his legs onto Casey's beautiful, white rug. Casey was crazy about that damn rug, he remembered. Panicking, Junior tried blotting the mess with toilet paper but ended up smearing it. He threw the mat into the bathtub and tried to rinse it. When that failed, he grabbed a bottle of Ajax next to the toilet and tried to scrub it out. It turned yellow before his eyes. He grabbed the plunger beside the toilet and circled it as if it was in the wash. He tapped the pole against the side of the tub as if he was serving soup at a shelter. Tink-tink-tink. Before long, Casey returned to the door to check on him.

"J., are you alright in there?" Casey asked him. "Sorry about earlier. I realized I didn't even ask if you were OK. You good? Stomach botherin' you again?"

Junior rushed to the door.

"Uh, no, I'm actually in the uh… shower," Junior told her.

"Cool. Well, I need a comb. So, I'm gonna grab it and leave."

"No, don't!" Junior held the door. "I'll get it, uh… what does it look like?"

"I've got about 10,000 combs in there, J." Casey fiddled with the knob. "OK, J., quit playin'. I need the comb, open up. I got some errands to run. Let me in."

Junior watched as the knob rattled under Casey's grip. Annoyed, she began pounding on the door like the cops. Boom-boom-boom!

"Junior," she raised her voice. "Look, I ain't playin'. You open up this door, right now!"

"You promise you won't hit me?"

"I promise I will hit you if I don't like what I see. Now, open the door."

Junior's stomach tightened as he anticipated Casey's reaction to seeing her mat. He slowly opened the door, exposing his head to her. Casey busted her way into the bathroom, knocking Junior backward into the sink.

"See, I didn't even hit you," she said. "Now, what the hell is goin' on in..."

Casey walked over to the tub and stood in front of it. She turned off the hot water and reached into the tub to pull out her now yellow rug. Junior watched her face through the bathroom mirror. Her fangs showed like a vicious rottweiler. Casey turned around and baptized Junior on his forehead. She swore at him worse than Joe Pesci in a gangster movie.

"Th'fuck outta here!" She bopped him again. "What are ya? Fuckin' stoopid, Junior? Hah? Th'fuck happened in here? Hah? What happened to my bathroom?"

"I can explain, Casey. Just calm down—"

"Calm down? Look at my bathroom." She gestured. "What were you doin' in here? Yo. Yo!" her eyes widened. "What is wrong with you?"

Before Junior could explain, Casey threw one of her flip-flops at him. The first one hit Junior square in the chest. The second one, he ducked. It hurled over his head and down the steps. Casey picked up her rattail comb and held it as if it was an ice pick.

"You're fuckin' dead, yo, I swear God, J. I can't believe you'd do that—Jaaaay! What'd you do? Blow your nose with it or somethin'?"

"Well, it was—you see—I thought I had—I was gonna..."

"Spit it out!" she snarled. "What possible excuse do you have this time?"

Junior said the first thing that came to his mind. "I uh… I got AIDS, Sissy. Yeah. Real bad—don't come too close! I would've told you sooner but… that's what it is. See, there's this spot right next to my—I went to check it and then… I don't know. It like… exploded, or some shit. I'll buy you a new rug with my next check."

Junior's explanation was so ridiculous, Casey laughed at him.

"So, you got AIDS? That quickly?" Casey raised her eyebrow at him. "Sure, I believe you."

"It's the truth. I read it on the internet."

"Lord, child." She shook her head. "I'd bet my life that Vanessa didn't give you AIDS. You can't believe everything you read online. I told you that, J. AIDS doesn't work that fast."

"How do you know? Have you ever had it?" he asked. "I saw another article last night talkin' about the Y2K crash. We probably should get a new computer soon. Man, everything's gonna shut down. I probably can't get any medicine 'cause my insurance won't show in the system."

Casey bent at the waist, laughing at him. He sounded so fucking stupid. Meanwhile, Junior believed all of what he was saying. He was serious about his health and the Y2K crash expected to happen once the year 2000 hit.

"Man, I could die from this shit, Casey, and you're sittin' there laughin' at me."

"You're damn right, I am; you sound ridiculous." She pinched his cheek. "Look, I used to volunteer at a clinic years ago. AIDS doesn't work like that. It's probably just a boil or maybe a bad follicle infection. It's not AIDS, J. I'll prove it."

Casey left Junior momentarily. She went down to the kitchen and returned with a set of rubber dishwashing gloves. Junior's eyes widened with trepidation.

"Alright." She popped her gloves. "Dr. Haughton is in the house now. Let's have a look, Junior. Drop your shorts."

"What?!" Junior's voice hoarsened as he backed off. "Th'fuck out of here—hell naw!"

"Look, I've seen a dick or two in my day. One more ain't gonna hurt. Now, stop being such a pussy and let me see your AIDS."

"Man, don't be callin' me that," Junior fussed. "I ain't no pussy, Casey!"

"Well, stop acting like one. C'mon, I'm your sister. Let me see."

"No, man! You ain't no doctor!"

"I am tryin' to save you a co-pay at the doctor's office, J. Trust me, I've got better things to do than to be concerned about a college wee-wee. If you're worried about me seeing how small it is, just use your hand or a towel to cover it."

"Whatever, my shit ain't small."

"Fine, J. Look, I really don't give a shit. Just let me see the damn spot, already. I swear to God, man. Men, ugh!"

Junior lowered his shorts and showed Casey the scabby lesion beneath his crotch. He used a hand towel from the rack to conceal his goods as Casey examined it.

"See, just like I said." She removed her rubber gloves and

tossed them into the bin. "It's folliculitis—stop lookin' up random shit on the internet. Now, was that hard?"

"Follicu—what?" Junior asked. "Th'hell is that?"

"It's an infected hair follicle, and it's not AIDS," she told him "I've got an over-the-counter antibiotic you can take. I hope you learned your lesson, Junior." She crossed her arms. "I should've let you believe it was. Maybe then you'll listen more. I got you those condoms for a reason."

"Well, we use 'em… most of the time. Besides, Vanessa said she's on a pill, anyway."

Casey punched Junior on the shoulder.

"Ow, Casey!" Junior grabbed his arm. "Yo, what was that for?"

"I don't give a fuck if she's on the pill or not, J. Use 'em! Don't gamble with your health like that. It's not worth it, OK? I'm not kidding. We straight?"

"Yeah, we straight." Junior rubbed his arm. "Thanks, Sissy."

"Thanks, my ass. What about my rug?"

"I'll buy you a new one."

"When?"

"My next paycheck."

"Hmph. I forgot you still had a job. I could never tell the way you call out so much. I'm surprised they haven't fired you yet. Didn't you call out sick yesterday? You better get your shit together, homie. You know your boy E.T. don't play."

"His name is Mr. Wilkinson, Casey."

"Well, he looks like E.T." She shrugged.

Casey reached beneath the sink for an old, dingy bucket

and handed it to Junior. Inside was a container filled with Clorox wipes, Lysol, and a bottle of Mr. Scrubby. She shooed Junior back into the bathroom.

"I want it spotless in here. I'm not joking. You got to start learning how to clean up after yourself. Once you finish, the hallway needs to be vacuumed, and there's potato chip crumbs on the floor in the dining room."

"C'mon, Casey," Junior fussed. "Look, I got to work this afternoon."

"Well, you better hurry up." She pulled the door shut. "Spotless, Junior. Not a stain."

After she left, Junior dropped Casey's bucket down onto the floor and kicked it. When she opened the door, Junior quickly picked up the bucket and began to work. Casey cut her eyes at Junior and closed the door again.

When Junior's chores were complete, he returned to his bedroom. He took a seat at his desk to read through a poem he had written days earlier. The urge to return to the stage had been on his mind since he'd bombed at Luke's club on the night of Mel's party. Lyrics in hand, he walked over to the mirror and gave it a go.

We're in a league all on our own. You and me. Together, so happily, we could withstand the…

Dissatisfied, Junior swiped through his journal for a new page to read.

We were meant to happen.

The way our world revolves around the sun with a galaxy others couldn't imagine. I was destined to…

Junior looked down at his journal with discontent. Frustrated, he exhaled in anguish of his seemingly lost art. He tossed his journal down onto his bed. It was all over. He grabbed his work apron from the closet and headed down to the Grocery Mart.

Part-Time Blues

When Junior walked into his part-time job down at the Grocery Mart later that day, his colleagues all sneered at him. Unsuspecting, he carried on as if nothing was wrong. "Hey, Judy." Junior nodded at one colleague. "Mary, how are you?" he said to another. Nothing. Confused, he continued toward the back, pushing through the strip of plastic barrier and into the warehouse. While on his way to punch in, Junior ran into another colleague. He put out his fist for a bump. "Mike, I didn't forget about you, I got caught up tryin' to…" Mike bypassed Junior and went through the plastic, leaving him hanging. Scratching his head, Junior headed down to the manager's office to sign in. When he got there, his boss, Mr. Wilkinson, was reading from a clipboard through a cheap pair of reading glasses. Junior greeted him as if they were homeboys.

"Yo, Mr. Wilkinson! What up?"

Junior's boss glanced at him and went back to reading from his clipboard. He cleared his throat and reached for a cup of coffee at the edge of his desk. He took a sip. Afterward, he removed his glasses and placed them on the table in front of him.

"You stroll into my store late and then ask me 'what up?'," Mr. Wilkinson asked him. "Not a damn thing. What up with you? Homeboy? Here's a question for you. Why are you late?"

Junior looked down at his watch and back up at his boss. It was 4:04 p.m.

"I thought you had me comin' in by four?" he said. "It's Sunday."

"I know what day it is." Mr. Wilkinson lifted up his glasses for the kid to see. "These do work, you know? If there's anybody here who needs glasses, it's you—maybe new ears to go with those eyes might help too. What did I tell you last week about this Sunday, Junior?"

Junior closed his eyes. "Oh, shit."

"*Oh shit*, is right," Mr. Wilkinson mocked him. "You were supposed to be in today at eleven to help with inventory. We had a big shipment of stuff. Somethin' wrong that you can't follow directions like everybody else, son?"

"No, sir." Junior straightened.

"Then why are you showin' up half a century late to work? Tell me why I shouldn't fire you right now? You did it last week and the week before that. If I needed you in at four, I would've asked you to come in at four. Don't go around makin' shit up, Junior."

"Sorry, Mr. Wilkinson. It won't happen again. I promise."

The boss walked over to the time clock on the wall and pointed at a memo he'd left the prior week for his store

60

employees. He stuffed his glasses onto his face and read the words out loud.

"Attention all employees," he turned to look back at Junior. "Don't forget, next *Sunday*," he emphasized, "is our final inventory for the end of August. Please be here at eleven. Also, be sure to check your schedule daily. Hours are subject to change."

Mr. Wilkinson removed his glasses and placed them into his breast pocket. He took a seat at the corner of his desk. His big, bald head glistened like an eight ball on a pool table. At 67 years old, the skin on his face sagged like a French bulldog. He was a funny-looking man with a long, bald head that extended backward like E.T. Casey nicknamed him that the day Junior got hired at the Mart. After his first night working there, Junior arrived home to find that Casey had left a trail of Reese's Pieces by the front door.

Despite his laughable appearance, Mr. Wilkinson was all business. Beneath his buttoned work shirt was a gold chain with a medallion that was barely visible through his hairy chest. For work, he wore a pair of bubbly, all-black New Balance sneakers. The shoestrings were pulled so tightly, Junior wondered how he could even walk. He sat at the corner of his desk, swinging his long foot, scowling at Junior the way his daddy would. Behind him on the wall was an old, rusty fan. The fan looked older than Junior, as its wheezing winds levitated a pile of invoices atop the boss's desk.

"Time is runnin' out on you, Junior," he told him. "I don't wanna have to fire you, but I will. You wouldn't want that, would you?"

"No, sir," said Junior. "I'll try to be better about my time from now on."

"I don't need you to try—I need you to do it," he said. "Would you like me to try to pay you every week, or do you want your money?" he asked him. "One man doesn't carry the whole ship, but all it takes is one man to kill everybody on board. You're just like everybody else here, Junior."

"Yes, sir."

"Any more problems, I'm writin' you up. You know if you get three in six months, that's a termination on the spot, Junior. This is my last warning. After this, I gotta put paper down."

"Yes, sir." Junior nodded. "It won't happen again."

"Puttin' paper down" was Mart slang for the boss issuing a written reprimand. Junior had never had paper put down on him before. He almost did once when he first started. He had just turned 17 and had lost a crate of dairy that cost the store $200 to replace. Junior was a rookie back then. Innocent and sweet, he offered to surrender his paycheck to help cover the lost dairy, but the boss cut him slack. "We'll figure it out." he told him. "Try to be careful with that stuff, alright?"

By senior year, the sweetness was gone as Junior became… a teenager. He strutted in late some days. Five minutes. Ten minutes. Fifteen minutes. Realizing it was his senior year, Mr. Wilkinson cut the boy slack. He gave Junior more leeway than he'd normally give out. The more serious Junior got with Vanessa, the more his nonchalance grew. He hated his gig down at the Mart but needed the extra change and couldn't afford to lose his job. He had received a partial scholarship to attend Steny College of New York, but it didn't cover books or all his tuition.

Sundays were terrible down at the Mart. The cashier lines extended to the back of the store. Customers were cranky and moody. Plus, the store was already understaffed which made work unpleasant. Colleagues were short and snippy throughout their shift, and during the summer months, Mr. Wilkinson was too cheap to run the A/C inside the break-room. A few months back in May, he'd fired his assistant manager, Felicia, for cussing loudly in front of customers. It happened on a Friday. Rushing to the front of the store with her till halfway unzipped, $180 worth of quarters fell from her bag and exploded across the floor of the Mart. Felicia lost it. "FUCK!" she bellowed. Everybody laughed, including Mr. Wilkinson. Unfortunately for Felicia, the store's District Manager was in that day. So, to save his own ass, Mr. Wilkinson fired her later that night. She went on a tirade as her voice echoed throughout the warehouse.

"You bald-headed, Black motherfucker!" Felicia shouted at her ex-boss. "How dare you fire me? I been with you nine years—for you to do some shit like this?"

"Look, Felicia, it's over my head!" Mr. Wilkinson explained, sweat trickling across his globe. "I gotta let you go. Otherwise, it's my ass!"

Felicia left shortly thereafter—but she didn't go quietly, Junior remembered. She screamed and cussed on the way out. She pulled down cans of sardines from the shelf and tossed raw vegetables into the aisle over. Felicia busted open a box of cereal and threw it high into the air, sending pieces of Cap'n Crunch cereal raining down onto the floor as her ex-colleagues watched with amazement. Up until July, every time Mr. Wilkinson turned on the store's fan, cereal would blow from the vents onto the floor. Junior didn't envy Felicia, and neither did his colleagues.

The Longest Break Ever

"Why would you even *think* about going back there after what happened?" Vanessa questioned Junior on the phone during his lunch break. "You saw how those people treated you, J. Besides, we got school comin' up soon. I thought we talked about this already?"

"I just wanna see what I got left, V., that's all," Junior explained. "I'm tired of this journal bullshit. I just wanna make the best out of the talent that I have. I wanna get the most of me."

"We will, Junior. We're gonna do a lot of things together."

"I know, V., but that's not what I meant. I'm talkin' about…me."

Vanessa got quiet whenever Junior talked about his own mission, he noticed. At times, she acted as if the only mission was the two of them.

"I hear you, J."

"Why do you get like that whenever I bring that up?"

"Bring what up?"

"Things I wanna do for myself. You're part of the package too, V. You know that."

Vanessa snickered into the line. "You're so good to me, J. I don't know why I be buggin' like that sometime. We still gettin' together later?"

"Where you wanna go?" Junior asked.

"Somewhere—I don't know. I'll call up Shannon and see if she knows where there's a party. She might roll with us. Son! Did you know she and Mel hooked up? She told me the other day. Wack-ass bitch. I can't believe she fucked that dude. Mel's disgusting. Makes me wanna vomit."

Junior suddenly went cold. "Fuck Shannon and Mel."

"Will you get off that shit, J. That was last week!"

"Last week. Last month—it doesn't matter," he fussed. "Don't you remember anything about Mel's party, V.? Man, I had hell gettin' you out of that house. My back still hurts."

Vanessa laughed at him.

"It's not funny, V. Man, Casey was pissed. She threatened to kick me out if it happened again. For real, V. You got to check that drinkin' shit. I ain't tryin' to go back to Brooke's Rowe."

"I'm sorry, J.," Vanessa apologized. "You're right, it's not funny. I'd be so hurt if Casey kicked you out. You're the best thing that's happened to me in a long time. I'll be more careful. I promise. You still love me, don't you?"

"You know I do," Junior pouted. "You can pay me back later."

"Mmmm. I can't wait," she moaned into the line. "Guess what I'm doin' right now?"

"Something I wish I could be a part of, I'm sure."

Anticipating their night, Vanessa's honied voice excited Junior as the two talked recklessly over the company phone. Boo-loving and giggling, Junior talked all kinds of trouble to Vanessa, unaware that Mr. Wilkinson was standing behind him. With his hands on his hips, the boss reigned on Junior's parade.

"I hope you got a hard-on for this work we gotta get done in here!"

Junior ducked and hung up the phone.

"C'mon, Mr. Wilkinson. You know how it is, man."

"Son," he said. "I haven't known how *it* was in a long time." He crossed his arms. "First, you come in late. Now, you're on the lunchroom phone for an extended amount of time, and you're late getting back on the floor? You're taking advantage of me, Junior. I can't let this slide. I gotta put paper down."

"For what?" Junior raised his voice.

"Insubordination. Tardiness. Extended phone calls in the breakroom," his boss continued. "Need I go on? Hopefully, this write-up will straighten you out."

"Why do you have to write me up? Why can't you just give me a warning?"

"You got enough warnings for one day. Now, get out of this breakroom and get back on your floor before I throw you out of here. Go!"

For the rest of Junior's shift, he sulked and frowned as he loaded and unloaded dairy products on the main floor with his boss breathing over his shoulder. When he finished, Mr. Wilkinson sent him outside to sweep up trash in the parking lot. Junior caught an even grander attitude when he learned of his new assignment for the night.

"Why do I have to clean up after other people?" he questioned. "That's not my job. I didn't mess up the lot, so why should I have to clean it?"

"Your job is whatever job I give you, young man." Mr. Wilkinson stepped into his face. "You think you're too good to sweep up trash? Since you've been giving your co-workers trash lately then maybe you should spend the shift cleaning up other people's trash."

Mr. Wilkinson handed Junior a broom and dustpan and shooed him off. Junior threw a tantrum when he got outside. He slammed the broom against the pavement. Before long, Mr. Wilkinson came after him.

"If you don't pick up my broom, Junior, I'm gonna lay you out next to it," Mr. Wilkinson threatened.

As the boss returned inside, Junior ripped the broom from the ground and began to sweep.

Debris was everywhere on that lot. With Junior's luck, it just so happened to be windy that evening. He gagged as he swept the remnants of a runny diaper. As it rolled into the dustpan, Mother Nature blew a whiff of its lethal gas through his nostrils. The smell was death. Curious, but not curious, he lifted the broom to examine its yucky contents. Coated throughout its straws was a thick, slimy brown wax. It seeped onto the asphalt like ice cream on a hot day. Traumatized,

Junior dropped the broom. Disgusted, he walked it over to the nearest dumpster behind the shopping center. As he went to throw it away, Mr. Wilkinson appeared at the backdoor. His furious, bald head looked like a Goomba from *Super Mario Brothers*.

"You will not throw my broom away, Junior," he shouted at him. "If you need to, there's a hose for you to rinse it. You throw my broom away, I'm gonna throw you out with it!"

Junior yanked the hose from the side of the building. Three rinses later, he encountered his fourth wash when a customer backed over a pigeon. The fifth rinse was a bloody tampon wrapped inside of a napkin. He shuddered as the pad slid down from the dustpan leaving a smear of blood. The remaining debris was typical: napkins, straws, shattered beer bottles, and cans. When Junior returned inside the Mart, Mr. Wilkinson walked over to the store's window to inspect his work. He shook his head and ordered the boy back outside.

"I said you're to clean the entire lot," he told him. "Not just near the store."

The boss shooed him off again.

"I want that asphalt so clean that the mayor of New York wouldn't mind sleepin' on it. Off you go. Don't come back 'til it's clean."

Junior could give a damn about the city's mayor and where he slept. With the hose turned on, he rinsed away a patch of yellowly vomit on the pavement right outside the store. The patch exploded onto his pant leg from the hose's pressure.

As night fell over the lot, Mr. Wilkinson came out to inspect Junior's work. Of every employee there, he was the last to leave. His work shoes squished and slushed with water as he followed Mr. Wilkinson around the lot, waiting for the boss's approval.

"Mmhmm." Mr. Wilkinson checked his work. "Looks like you missed a spot right over there near the lot's entrance, but I guess you did alright. The next time you come into my store late, I'm gonna make you re-tar the roof."

Junior rolled his eyes as he walked away.

"Junior, hold up a minute," the boss called to him.

Junior turned around, annoyed. Mr. Wilkinson walked over to the kid and placed a hand onto his shoulder.

"You might think I'm being an asshole, but I'm tryin' to help you. I know you're upset that I had to write you up, but I had to. Aren't you startin' school in a couple days?" the boss asked him. "It's cold out there, son. You think Mr. Wilkinson is bad? Wait 'til you start workin' for those snobby-ass white folks downtown. You got two strikes already, Junior—three if you count how smart you are. The last thing one of those crackers wanna do is give a young, Black man a chance to bypass 'em. Do you understand?"

"Yeah, I guess." Junior flattened. He looked down at his spongy shoes. "I did it to myself."

Mr. Wilkinson began to laugh as Junior shrugged.

"You look like you've been out in the rain," the boss chuckled. "Listen, don't worry about that write-up. It's only paper; it'll go away. Don't make me be an asshole to you, Junior. I like you," he told him. "You're a good kid."

"Thanks, Boss."

"You're welcome." Mr. Wilkinson winked back. "Oh, and for God sakes, Junior, don't use the company phone to talk that crazy shit to your girlfriend. Jesus Christ," he laughed. "Use your cell phone the next time, OK? Be smart!"

"My bad. I'll keep that in mind next time. Have a good night, sir."

As the boss went back into the Mart to close for the night, Junior continued to his car parked in the lot. He turned back to wave at his boss. The boss shook his head at the boy affectionately and disappeared inside. Junior sighed in relief; his long day was finally over.

Junior didn't tell Vanessa, nor Casey, but before returning home from work that night, he tried to redeem himself at Luke's Lounge. He wanted to know if he could still do it, and he was short on cash and could use the extra bread. Open mic nights paid spoken word artists twenty dollars for five minutes of stage time. The really good ones earned thirty or even forty dollars. Junior parked his car in the lot and reached beneath his seat for an old journal filled with poems. He turned on his dome light and rummaged through his book for something to read. His phone rang on the passenger seat next to him. It was Casey calling to see where he was. Junior let it ring. He went back into his journal for something halfway decent to perform. Satisfied, he tore out the paper and headed inside to look for the manager.

When Junior arrived at the door of Luke's he noticed a long line ahead of him. He decided to use the extra time to rehearse, but the line moved faster than Junior had hoped for, which allowed him to get a view of the stage. A current went through his stomach as he became nervous for the person performing. The woman on stage, Sydney, claimed that she was from Flatbush. She looked to be older than Casey from what Junior could tell. "Yo, it feels good to be back with y'all tonight, Brooklyn. Thank you all for havin' me." The crowd soared in appreciation of Sydney but turned its back on her the moment she strung together her first few lines.

Check it—check it, I might be depleted,
but I'm also undefeated.
My baby daddy ain't shit. Nigga went out and cheated...

They booed the shit out of Sydney right away. It came as a shock to Junior since Luke's was one of the more forgiving and easygoing places to get a decent pop from the crowd. "We ain't tryin' to hear that shit, bitch—shut the fuck up!" Someone yelled from the crowd. Onlookers threw things on the stage at her. They heckled the poor woman and even mocked her as she stumbled through her lines. They tormented her so badly that she ran off stage and out of the club. She ran right by Junior and up the street. Junior looked down at his lines and back up at Sydney as she hustled into the night. He had never been propelled off stage in such a way, nor did he have any intention of doing so that night.

Vanessa was right all along. Th'hell with it. Junior looked at his lines again and back inside the lounge as the club's owner attempted to soften the crowd for the next sacrificial lamb. No *way* was he going back up on a stage ever again. Not even if his life depended on it. Junior crumpled up his poem, tossed it in the bin and left.

Four

The drive down to Steny College the following Monday was unnerving to Junior as he prepared for his first day. Before leaving that morning, Casey had met him down at the door. She wrapped her brother inside her arms as if it was his first day of kindergarten. "College, I can't believe it!" Casey straightened his collar for him. She cheesed with delight. "Have a good day, J." The moment was surreal to Junior. *College? Me?* he thought to himself. Once upon a time, Junior didn't think he'd make it out of Brooke's Rowe alive.

Steny's enormous campus appeared forbidding from the main roadway. The closer Junior got, the more he shrank. Three times, he thought of turning back but couldn't bring himself to do it. Too much was on the line. Senior had dropped out of school as a young child. Sandy had a high school diploma and "some" college, but for years, Junior had watched his momma come home fussing and cussing because someone with a degree had beaten her out of a job. Meanwhile, Casey's G.E.D. only went so far. She too had "some" college, but a felony conviction provided its own set of challenges. Lucky for her, the federal government offered a placement incentive down at her job. If successful, the feds would pay for her to return to school. It was Casey's dream to practice family law. She was lucky to have a good job despite her conviction.

On the lot at Steny, Junior parked his scruffy Buick far in the back where no one could see him and stood near the door, taking in the view. Hundreds, if not thousands, of kids ambled on the college's grounds. His heart warmed as he looked on. The boys were playing flag football while the girls lounged on blankets with their friends. Kids were rapping, painting, or singing. Some on bicycles. One kid played guitar on the hood of his Dodge truck in the lot. Junior dropped a quarter into the kid's case. The sights and sounds were unfamiliar to him, but he liked it. Junior hooked his bag onto his shoulder and headed down the lot to begin his first day.

The main building where Junior's first class was had so many steps that he could've gone to heaven. Students rushed by him as he stood in the center of the main hallway and looked around. The enigmatic clothing trends wowed him. Long hair. Short hair. Cornrows. Braids. Haircuts with designer styles. Facial tattoos. Tattoos that covered the neck, arms, legs or eyelids, piercings. It was nothing like Langston's dress policy. Kids wore flip-flops, and one student didn't wear any shoes. There were T-shirts with colorful language, or quotes. "Fuck the police." "I'm with stupid." "Weed is from the earth." "By any means necessary". Students were unapologetic about their taste in fashion. One kid wore a shirt with a Confederate flag on it. The girl who wore it had a shaved mohawk that was painted the color of a rainbow. Her partner was dressed in all black with matching lipstick, eyeliner, and boots with metal chains. Further up the hallway was a kid performing spoken word poetry on the staircase. The young artist lured students and passing faculty members to him. Fascinated, Junior weaseled through the crowd to get a closer look.

They say go to college if you wanna get paid,
or else you'll flip burgers makin' minimum wage.
It's called the American Dream, but it's really a scheme.
To hustle people into debt, now that's really the dream.
Because you gotta be asleep just to see the results.
Of all the useless-ass electives that the students get taught.
Because the cost of one book can feed a family of those crooks.
Then when you try to sell it back, it won't even get took.
The American Dream
in the City That Never Sleeps. We are the sheep.

The performance put Junior's Dollar Store poetry to shame. The kid rhymed with a cadence that was unmatched. His lines were barbaric, yet powerful and beautiful in the same breath.

Students were clapping and pumping their fists in support of him. The boy then picked up his bag and vanished up the staircase. Even his exit was epic, Junior noticed.

"Yo, does anybody know that kid's name?" Junior asked around. "Anybody?"

"Don't know, but he calls himself the 'Trolling Poet'," one

student blurted. "I've seen him a few times; he's good. He never signs his real name. He writes Trolling Poet on everything."

Curious, Junior walked over to the bulletin board on the wall to search for events by the Trolling Poet. He sifted through a collection of student ads, pyramid schemes and found a flyer with the Trolling Poet on the front of it. He copied the information down into his journal before realizing the event was dated for last year. Discouraged, Junior headed down to his first class, Introduction to Human Anatomy.

Introduction to Life 101

Junior arrived to class early with minutes to spare and noticed the professor hadn't come in yet. His curiosity led him to check out the laboratory and display shelf in the back. Behind the glass was a replica human skull. Next to the skull was a mini-version of the human body showing the different muscle and nerve groups. Junior carefully pushed back the glass to get a closer look, unaware that the professor was standing behind him.

"*What* are you doing?" The man scared him. Junior's feet left the floor. He turned around to notice his straggly professor standing there. According to his campus ID, the man's name was Mr. Freemont.

"Gotcha, you little rascal," the man chuckled. "Leave my stuff alone and take a seat!"

With unkempt and electrocuted hair, Mr. Freemont

showed up in jeans and a suit coat that looked like it came from a yard sale. He strutted throughout the class in high-top sneakers and a cup of Dunkin Donuts coffee in his hand. He looked like a cheap version of Marc Summers from the gameshow *Double Dare*. He placed his suitcase onto his desk and yawned, moaning like an elephant having an orgasm. Junior could tell he was a jerk.

"When you hear your name called, please say 'present' or just say something—anything." Mr. Freemont then called from a list of students' names from his coffee-stained roster sheet. To Junior's surprise, his name was never called.

"Excuse me, sir." He raised his hand. "My name didn't get called. Leonard Robinson?"

Mr. Freemont flipped through a stack of papers on his desk. Junior watched as he scratched his hair, muttering to himself. "Leonard Robinson. Leonard Robinson. Leonard Robinson. Where are you? Hmph. Where the fuck are you, Leonard Robinson?"

Junior's classmates laughed but Junior didn't.

"Ah! There you are! Leonard Gerard Robinson Jr., got it! Yup, you're on here."

The class laughed again. Right after his blunder, Mr. Freemont asked the class to pull out their textbooks and turn to page 107. Junior reached inside of his bag and pulled out his *Introduction to Anatomy* book. He placed it onto his desk and went to adjust his chair. The book slid off and landed flat against the floor, loud. BAM! Everybody jumped, including Junior.

"Holy shit, man! What the hell was that?" the teacher shouted.

The kids laughed at Junior again. Red with embarrassment, he returned his thick book to his desk and apologized.

"My bad, everybody," he said. "My book fell."

"Dude, next time say excuse me!" said Mr. Fremont, putting Junior on blast once again.

The man couldn't help but to mess with him. Junior's young, worried face was easy pickings.

For much of the morning, Junior sat through his first class with his eyes emboldened, unsure if he'd ever make it out of Anatomy 101 alive. He hated science. As his teacher breezed through the lesson plan, Junior's book hit the floor again. BAM! As he returned his book to his desk, he noticed his laces were untied. He reached over to tuck them inside of his sneaker. The damn book fell a third time. BAM!

"Dude, seriously?" the white boy behind him said.

By now, Mr. Freemont was not about to let up. With his hands behind his back, he slowly walked over to Junior's desk and stood in front of him. Junior slouched in his chair.

"If you need a bigger desk, I can order you a Fisher Price set from Toys R Us." The class all snickered at the teacher's sarcasm. "The next time you interrupt my class, you're gonna be my new display back in the glass case over there. You know, the one you love so very much? You got it?"

Mr. Freemont picked up Junior's book to get a closer look. He shook his head at him.

"No-no-no! What is this—c'mon, man!" he fussed. "This is the wrong damn book."

The kids laughed at Junior once again.

"What are you talkin' about?" Junior asked, fed up with his teacher's crudeness. "It says *Introduction to Anatomy* right there on the cover, man. See?" he pointed.

"Yes, but this is from last year! I clearly put in the syllabus to buy the newer version. What the hell is—where's your syllabus, pal?"

Junior looked around confused. "I must've misread it."

The class all groaned, including his teacher.

"Forget it, guys," said Mr. Freemont. "I'm afraid we've lost Leonard to the wild. Will somebody please help this poor kid before I write a big fat 'F' on his *forehead*. Please!"

"I can go exchange it if you want?"

"No, do it later. With your luck, you'll probably come back with a fucking sports almanac from the 1920s and that will make noise too! If you need another syllabus, you can have my copy. It's on the desk up front."

As Junior went to get it, Mr. Freemont fired at him again.

"Why don't you wait 'til after break? Th'hell's your problem, man? Jesus, kid. You're already up there, now. Go'on take it."

Fuming, Junior returned to his seat. His peers snickered at his misery. Sitting beside him was a goofy-looking, white girl wearing braces and thick glasses. Junior could tell she liked him. Before asking, she scooted her desk close to him… too close. She leaned over to whisper into his ear.

"You better get your shit together, dude," the girl said. "There's a reason they call Mr. Freemont the 'F' bomb."

"Is it because he says 'fuck' a lot?" Junior guessed.

"No, because he gives out a lot of F's. Almost everybody here has failed his course at some point. I failed him twice in one year, but I'm prepared this time."

The girl placed her book between herself and Junior. She then grinned at him.

"I'm Rachel," she smiled, showing wedges of peanut-buttery cracker stuck between her metal braces. "Don't be shy, Leonard. I don't bite...not unless you want me to."

When anatomy ended, Junior was the first student out of the door. His next class was a downer: Sociology During East London's 16th Century Period. Minutes into the professor's lecture, Junior began to nod. The instructor alone was Ambien. He talked in a dead, monotone voice that reminded Junior of the guy from the Clear Eyes commercial, Ben Stein. One kid was so bored, he placed his jacket over his head and went to sleep. Another kid packed up his belongings. "You're boring! I'm out of here!" the kid called as he walked out. Junior's teacher continued, never missing a beat. To keep from passing out, Junior pulled out his Nokia phone and played Snake. When that got boring, he challenged himself to a game of Tic-Tac-Toe. Within the first half hour of lecture, the professor had killed seven students and made four of them leave. The rest were either on life support or engaging in something else besides his class. His name was also too damn long. On the board above his contact information was his full name: Dr. Robert Emil Zeulerickbastargen. "Can we just call you Mr. Zzzs?" a kid asked. It was the first laugh Junior had all morning. For once, he was on the right side of a joke.

When Mr. Zzzs' class finally ended, Junior continued his tour of the college while waiting for Vanessa's classes to let out. To kill time, he roamed throughout the concourse level to see if he could track down the Trolling Poet from earlier. He peeped through the glass of Ellington Hall, a theatre, and noticed a group of young dancers hanging out near the stage. Junior pulled on the door handle, but it was locked. On the wall next to the door was a sign. "Auditions underway, please do not disturb." Junior released the handle and continued to watch. He wasn't a fan but enjoyed the elegant moves of his peers as they flipped and twirled across the stage. His phone began to ring.

"What up, freshman?" Vanessa asked him. "Yo, where are you?"

"What up, V.?" Junior said back. "I'm over here by the Ellington Theatre watching these kids dance. Man, you ought to see 'em. Yo, have you seen the Trolling Poet?"

"Trolling Poet? Ellington Theatre? Oh! You're on the concourse level. I think I might be close—wait a minute. I see you! OK, I'm hangin' up."

Vanessa hung up the phone and hurried over to Junior as he turned around to greet her. She ran into his arms, teary-eyed.

"Sorry," she sniffled. "It's times like these, I wish my daddy was still around."

"Well, wherever he is, I'm sure he knows that his little girl is doing big things." Junior lifted Vanessa's face and kissed her. "College freshman."

"Exaaaactly. So, whatcha takin'? Anything good?"

"Shit, I wish," Junior sighed. "I could barely stay awake in sociology, and my anatomy teacher is a trip. Man, he fucked with me the whole class, V. He kept on gettin' on me about my book. Apparently, I got the wrong one. I had to share with a neighbor."

"Word? Yo, bet, let's get you the right book. C'mon."

Junior and Vanessa headed down to Steny's library. The line went to the back of the store. Junior stopped at the door as Vanessa shoved him inside. "Go, J.!" she laughed at him. Steny's library not only had books but school memorabilia as well. A coffee mug with the school's insignia cost $18, and if you added a $45 hoodie, it was 5% off both items. The two bypassed the overpriced merchandise and headed over to the sciences section to grab Junior's book. He looked at the price.

"Man, what the fuck?" Junior said loudly. "$220?"

"Shhhh!" Vanessa flapped at him. "You need it, don't you?"

"I don't even make that down at the Mart, V. I can't afford this book."

"That's why we're gonna exchange the other book first, Junior." She took it from his hands. "C'mon, let's get in line. Son, didn't you read this stuff in your packet from orientation?"

"What packet?" Junior asked.

Vanessa pulled him by the hand. "Just forget it, yo. C'mon, J."

Despite his discontent, the line inside of the store moved swiftly as Junior and Vanessa waited for an open register. One kid had eight books, a mug, sweater, and a hat inside of his shopping cart. The kid's total came to $586.27. The boy handed the cashier his credit card. Junior shuddered at the thought of paying that much. He was already on the hook for $30 to replace Casey's bathroom rug.

At the register, Junior placed his new book on the counter and handed the old one to the cashier. "I'd like to return this," he told the cashier. Junior had originally paid $150 for the older version. The cashier scanned the barcode and showed him the screen.

"It's gonna be $27.85," the man said. "Would you prefer cash or store credit?"

"What? How's it only worth $27.85?" Junior argued. "I just bought the book the other week. Man, that's highway robbery. Y'all can't do that!"

"It's last year's version, buddy. Th'hell do you want from me?"

"I want my $150 back—that's what I want from you."

As Junior went tit-for-tat with the cashier, Vanessa handed the man her credit card.

"Here you go, sir," she told the man. "Just put it on this for now. We'll keep the old book."

Junior's mouth hung open.

"Yo, I can't believe you just did that," he said. "No, V., that guy is a con artist. He's trying to rob us. Don't pay him! I'll just share with my neighbor. The guy's a crook."

Vanessa ignored Junior. She reached across the counter to take Junior's books and carted him out the store. Junior complained all the way out into the parking lot. When they got outside, Vanessa handed him the two books.

"Here, J., will you stop lookin' so evil?" she giggled. "You needed it, right?"

"That's not the point, V.," Junior went on. "These fuckin' people— $220? For a book?"

Vanessa grabbed his angry face and kissed it. Her sugar kisses always calmed Junior down when he got hot. She petted his handsome face.

"I don't know what'd I do without you sometimes. Thanks, V.," he exhaled. "I'll pay you back when I get my hands on some money."

"Don't worry about it," she told him. "Consider it payback for Mel's. Actually, hmmm. There is another way you can pay me back. So, you working later?" She rubbed between Junior's legs. "You know I need my meds, J."

Junior put his arms around Vanessa's waist.

"I'll put an extra dose in for you at the pharmacy. Would you like extra strength?"

"I need all the strength I can get, Doctor."

The two kissed again before Vanessa ripped herself away.

"OK, I gotta go, I got an appointment," she giggled. "Oh, don't forget about your webcam appointment this afternoon with your mom. Don't be late, yo. 1 p.m. Try to be on time so you don't get in trouble."

"How'd you know about that?" he asked.

"Son, you told me on Instant Messenger last night, duh! You said your parents just got a new webcam and that your mom was gettin' on you 'cause you hadn't been there in a minute. Yo, you are seriously buggin' today, J. Don't you remember anything we talked about?"

"Nope. I need another kiss to help me remember better."

"Bye, Junior!" Vanessa laughed. "I'll call you later, OK?"

As Vanessa walked off, Junior watched as her rump bounced beneath her shorts. He was lucky to have her in his life, he thought. He looked down at his new book and back up at Vanessa's curves; he was extremely lucky to be studying human anatomy, for sure.

Little College Man

"Hold on, give your mom a second—you know I ain't used to all this stuff." Sandy wrestled with a wiry webcam on her end. The screen was dark as Junior waited for Sandy to troubleshoot her newest add-on to the family computer. Sandy said she'd use the computer to pay bills and that it'd be a good addition for Junior—whenever he decided to visit more often. According to her, Senior was afraid to go near it. The computer's talking navigation and dancing baby on the screensaver confused him. Senior raised all hell when the computer warmly greeted him. "Uh oh," he said. "Them god-damn gubment peoples are in the house now!" He left Sandy all on her own to put it together.

The noise behind Sandy's microphone sounded as if she was out in the wind. To save time as he waited, Junior prepared for work. Junior's momma was out of commission for so long that he was able to drop a full basket of clothes in the wash downstairs. He returned upstairs to find Sandy still struggling to diagnose the problem. He pulled up a chair to help. He could hear his momma's voice but couldn't see her on screen.

"Ma, go into your settings and click on the video icon," Junior suggested. "There should be a little man holding a camera. Do you see him? See the little man in the corner?"

"What damn little man, Junior? I don't see no little man!" she fussed.

Junior threw up his arms and returned to the basement to finish washing his clothes. Not long after, Junior over-heard Sandy calling to him and ran back upstairs to his room. He walked in to find his momma's cheesy face on screen. Junior took a seat in front of his camera and waved. Sandy waved back. She had a steady streak of wintery gray blended into her hair. Her mouth was still slightly crooked from a stroke she'd suffered a few years earlier. Behind Sandy, was Junior's old living room exactly as he remembered it. The ugly wallpaper and the huge wooden spoon set used by David and Goliath. The fireplace. The old TV and the ancient VCR that Junior's parents refused to switch out for a DVD player. Above on the mantel was his enshrined diploma from Langston High—the family's most notable achievement to date. At times throughout their virtual visit, Sandy's huge bug eyes blocked the view of his childhood home.

"There's my little college man." She waved again.

"Ma, move back some," Junior laughed. "You don't gotta be so close!"

Junior waited as Sandy readjusted her webcam.

"Is this better?" she asked. "So, how are you today, my son? And how was your first day of college at Steny? You know, you're the first Robinson to ever enter a university."

"I know, Ma." Junior cheesed. "It was good. Takes some gettin' used to. Where's Daddy?"

Sandy rolled her eyes. "You know how your daddy is when it comes to learning new things; he ain't about to learn nothin' new when it comes to a computer. Not Leonard Robinson Sr.," she laughed. "He doesn't want *nothin'* to do with this machine. He's outside somewhere, I think. Probably cussin' at the old, broken-ass lawnmower of his. So, how's that poetry comin' along? Are you still writing?"

"Here and there. Not as much. I'm tryin' to work myself back on stage. It's hard, though."

"Well, you should've never left in the first place." Her face straightened.

"Just tryin' to balance things with Vanessa, Ma."

"Don't lose sight of your goals up there. You're a student first and a boyfriend last, Junior."

"I know, Ma." Junior told her. "I won't."

"Good. Well, I miss havin' you around. I'll try to get your daddy on screen next time. Have a good shift at work and an even better week at school, son. Love you, Junior."

"Love you too, Ma. I'll be home soon."

Five

Love is colorblind. Love has no color.
The day is white. The night is black.
Kisses help us to link. The vagina is pink.
You got a skin tone. I got a skin tone.
We got the same color bones.
You make me scream. I make you scream.
We both scream. Beyond our wildest dreams.

—LEONARD G. ROBINSON JR.

By the end of Junior's first week of the real world, he laid in bed waiting for his sissy to leave for work. Casey had a sinister routine which started at 4:45 a.m. every morning followed by a loud slap to end her alarm clock. She'd snooze until 5:05 a.m., then her box spring creaked as she got up to take a shower. She'd return to her room afterward to meditate or listen to music. Around 6:10 a.m. she'd dress for work, have a cup of "caw-fee" (sometimes with bacon or "saw-sage") with Frosted Flakes, fruit, and a granola bar. She'd go back to her room after breakfast to read. After that, she'd peep through Junior's door to tell him goodbye before catching the 7:00 a.m. bus into Manhattan. She'd leave Junior a list of chores for him to complete. That day was no different.

"I'm out, J.," Casey told him. "Don't forget it's trash pickup day."

"Aiiight," Junior groggily replied, his face mashed into the pillow.

"I'm expecting a package to come in from JC Penny's. Can you bring it in for me? It's shoes. I think we might get a shower or two."

"Aiiight."

"J., I left some envelopes on the table, OK? One's for the cable bill, and the other is for the mortgage. Can you drop it off at the mailbox sometime today?"

"Aiiight."

"Bye, punk."

"Aiiight."

That was their morning routine.

As Casey left that morning, Junior rushed to his window to ensure Casey's bus swept her away. She was dressed like an everyday work commuter with business attire and sneakers, as she climbed onto the bus and left. Junior grabbed his phone from his nightstand and called Vanessa. She was waiting up the road nearby.

"She's gone. Come up," Junior told her.

Vanessa's car appeared on his street shortly after and Junior went down to let her in. With Casey gone, the two had the house to themselves. Vanessa showed up in a hat, T-shirt, nylon shorts, flip-flops, and a change of clothes for later. It was Friday. Her black Nike hat was pulled tightly over her ponytail head. Junior lit up as she made her way up the walkway with her bag slung over her shoulder. She looked like a college student. Her nylon shorts revealed her soft, toned legs. Vanessa wasn't into sports but had good family genes. Junior swelled with excitement; Vanessa Bailey was a work of art. He unbolted the latch and let her in.

"Hey, you!" She kissed him as the two embraced.

Vanessa gave the best hugs. She had long, double-jointed arms that wrapped around Junior and she'd hold him tightly. Junior ran his hands down Vanessa's back and grabbed her backside. When he stroked her vulva from behind, she stood on her tippy toes, moaned and returned to the floor. He noticed right away Vanessa wasn't wearing any underwear.

"Damn, you come prepared." He beamed with glee.

Vanessa eyed him devilishly. "What's the point? We're grown. We both know what we want," she said.

Vanessa slid her hands inside of Junior's trunks and grabbed his raw flesh. Her soft hand made Junior grunt with gladness as Vanessa excavated his boneless limb. She rubbed Junior's head in a delicate grabbing motion as he groaned with pleasure. With the door still open, the two began to strip each other before realizing they were putting on a show for an older woman out walking her dog. The woman covered her mouth in shock.

"Sorry, Granny," Vanessa laughed. "This one's mine."

Vanessa closed the door. It had just started to rain.

It didn't take much for Junior and Vanessa's clothes to come flying off. It also didn't matter where, either. In the backseat of their car while parked in the lot at a movie theatre. Inside the movie theatre. At a park. In a public restroom. On the couch. On the floor. Inside the coat closet at Mel's house, once upon a time. They even did it inside the library at Langston, back when Vanessa was getting her community service hours in. Their clandestine operation was smooth. They talked in perfect code.

"Excuse me, I'm looking for a book." Junior would wink. "You wouldn't happen to have anything on Frederick Douglass, would you?"

Vanessa would lean over the counter, batting her hazel eyes at him.

"Well, we have quite a bit of those books on hand." She'd eye him tastefully. "I've been holding on to 'em for a quite a while now. Would you like to see 'em?"

Bingo. Junior and Vanessa used every prominent name they could to get back there: Marcus Garvey. Malcolm X. Stokely Carmichael, Rosa Parks, Harriet Tubman. One day, their luck failed when the school's librarian, Mrs. Harper, changed the lock. When they tried to get the key, the woman cut her eyes at the two lovebirds. "What's the name of the book? I'll go look for it," Mrs. Harper offered. Junior's and Vanessa's rendezvous at school ended, but it didn't stop them from finding other ways to get it on.

A change of clothes wasn't all that Vanessa had brought along inside of her bag, Junior soon discovered. She had a zest for experimentation. In her short bag were a set of scarves, essential oils, a massager, and a quill's feather. She emptied her eerie devices onto Junior's nightstand next to his bed and sprawled across his mattress. Confused, Junior looked on. "Tie me up," she told him. "I wanna try somethin'." Shrugging, Junior bonded Vanessa to his bed, securing her wrists to his headboard. "OK, grab the oil… not that one— that's for later—the other one. *Deadass*. Now rub it on me." Junior squirted some of Vanessa's magic oil into his palm and rubbed his hands together. Right away, his hands began to pringle. Junior looked down at his hands, concerned.

"Are my hands gonna fall off with this shit, V.?" he asked.

"No, J.," she laughed. "OK, put some on me. C'mon, rub it on my chest and put the rest around my vajayjay—not too much."

Junior rubbed Vanessa's naked body with the odd oil. He cupped her breasts, flicking her sprouted nipples as she jolted with excitement. "Ooh!" she bounced, giggling. Junior did it again. Next, he rubbed the oil between Vanessa's moistened sex. Her legs squeezed together as she pulled against the headboard, bending her knees and straightening them. As the oil worked its magic, Vanessa began to pant as she struggled to keep her composure. She giggled and shifted from side to side.

"OK, listen to me, J." She took a deep breath. "I want you to use the feather on me—but you *have* to stop when I tell you! You know how sensitive I get when you play with it."

Junior picked up the quill feather and looked it over. He

dragged its lenient bristles across Vanessa's neck and between her breasts. She jerked against the headboard.

"What if I don't want to, V.?" he teased her, twirling it in her belly button.

"Then payback's a bitch!" Vanessa giggled, wriggling under his torment. "C'mon, yo, stop. I want to try somethin'. I saw some girls talk about it on *Taxicab Confessions*. I wanna try it out."

Junior laid beside Vanessa's plumb desire and kissed it. Vanessa's backside clutched and cleared the bed. The oil had taken affect. He moved back her wet lips, exposing her clitoris and brushed it with the tip of the quill feather. Vanessa yanked against Junior's headboard so hard, one of the planks creaked under her protest. When Junior did it again, Vanessa struck the headboard with her head. "Ooooh shit! Wait-wait-wait-wait-wait!" Vanessa stopped him. She took short breaths as if she was in labor. "OK. Aight. Go."

"You sure you want me to go again? What's it feel like?" Junior asked.

"I'm wildin', yo. I don't even know. It's like nothin' I've ever felt. Grab the massager. I want you to use 'em both now—remember, you gotta stop when I say stop, J.," she giggled devilishly. "I can't believe I'm even doin' this crazy shit with you."

Junior returned to Vanessa's candy and went back to teasing her. He stroked her love button with the feather and turned on the massager. It buzzed like a set of hair trimmers. When Junior placed it onto Vanessa's throbbing sex, she thrashed wildly, begging Junior to hold her steady. Junior held her in place, allowing the massacre to go on. Before long, Vanessa's right leg began to seize as she climaxed with earsplitting frequency. Her fingers wiggled above her and her toes curled tightly against the sheets. Juices dribbled from Vanessa's fruit and onto Junior's bed as her body contorted awkwardly. She climaxed again as fluid squirted from her prickly body. "J., turn it off! Turn it off!" she screamed. Junior grabbed the massager and threw it. It banged against his closet door, leaving a nasty dent. The device vibrated across his floor like a Motorola pager. Vanessa groaned with relief as the two laughed at her erotic misfortune.

"I'm so fuckin' dead, J.," Vanessa laughed. "That shit was crazy, son!"

"You can't be dead, yet," Junior kissed her bits. "I need a turn now."

Junior untied and mounted Vanessa with her ankles resting high on his shoulders. He stuffed her pre-heated oven full of meat, stroking Vanessa as her eyelids fluttered. Her wrinkled soles curled inward, fusing behind Junior's head as he penetrated her insides with smooth fury. She held on for dear life. "Ah…Ooh—ooh!" Vanessa sounded. Before long, her right leg twitched again as Junior emptied his cannon inside of her and convulsed with abrupt depletion. He collapsed onto Vanessa as she wrapped her soft legs around him, kissing Junior on the side of his head. The two were still merged together.

"I'm cold, J.," Vanessa complained. "Can you pull the blanket over us?"

Half-dead, Junior pulled his blanket from off the floor, covering their damp bodies.

Later in the shower, the two washed each other before drying off and continuing their evening. Vanessa borrowed Casey's hairdryer from beneath the sink as Junior returned to his room to get dressed. By then, the rain had subsided over New York, but a new storm was on its way through Fort Foote-Brooklyn. Unbeknownst to either of them, Casey had just walked in from work and was headed upstairs.

Junior didn't realize it because he was too busy pumping Casey's *Capital Punishment* CD by Big Punisher. He rapped and danced as he put on his clothes. He sang into his hairbrush, brushing his wavy hair. Junior lip-synced, line for line, to "I'm Not A Player", not missing a beat. He took three steps backward and backed right into Casey. He could tell it was her without looking, based on her unmovable mass. Embarrassed, he shut off his stereo and turned around. She stood there with her soggy shoebox in her hand. Junior had forgotten to look out for it.

"Hey, Sissy!" Junior said awkwardly. "Uh... how was your day?"

Casey glared at Junior. She looked down at her shoebox and back at him. With her eyes still focused on him, she opened her wet shoebox and dumped it onto his floor. Water and two wrinkled, leather boots hit the wood. Junior looked down at the shoes and back at her.

"I was gonna get those, Casey—I'm sorry. I forgot all about it," he said. "How much did they cost? Can I pay you back?"

"You sure can. Thanks for nothing, J."

Casey turned to look at the dent in Junior's closet door. She went over to get a closer look.

"So, what the hell happened here?" she nodded at the door.

"Well, I had a little accident, but I was gonna go to the hardware store and—"

Before Junior could finish, Vanessa showed up in the room wrapped in a towel. She was holding Casey's hairdryer in her hand. Her curly hair dripped onto Casey's wooden floor.

"...Oh, hey...uh...Casey," Vanessa laughed clumsily. "Listen, I hope you don't mind, but I borrowed your hairdryer. I think something might be wrong with it. Here you go."

Vanessa placed the dryer into Casey's hand. Casey looked over her broken device and back up at Junior. She shook her head and gave it back to Vanessa.

"Why don't you keep it, sweetheart?" Casey smiled sarcastically. "In fact, help yourself to whatever else you want inside of my house. Mi casa es su casa." Her smile faded. "I'll be in my bedroom if you guys need anything else. And Junior." Casey lowered her eyes at him. "Fuck you for leavin' my leather boots out in the rain."

Casey stormed down to her room and slammed the door. Wham! Junior splashed onto his bed and hung his head. He picked up one of Casey's shoes and dropped it to the floor. Vanessa joined him right after.

"I'm sorry, J.," she apologized. "I didn't mean to get you

into trouble. The hairdryer worked for like three seconds and then it cut off."

"It's not you, V." He shook his head. "Listen, why don't you get dressed and I'll meet you outside? I gotta go smooth this shit out with Casey."

As Vanessa dressed and headed out, Junior slowly made his way down the hall to Casey's room. He tapped onto her door. "Come in!" Casey growled through the door. She sounded like Senior. Junior's hands trembled as he turned the knob. He entered Casey's room and stood near the door in case she decided to attack him. On Casey's bed was a pile of wrinkled clothes. On her nightstand were bottles of empty Heineken, coffee mugs, and two-day-old fast-food wrappers. The trash can in her room was piled high and shoes were strewn throughout. Her room looked as if she was about to move out. She walked over to her door and pushed it shut.

"Are you fuckin' kidding me right now, Junior?" she whispered. "What the hell was that?"

"She didn't mean to break it. I'll get you another one," he offered.

"I don't care about the stupid hairdryer. I don't even care that you guys were in here all day having sex—I don't care. But I asked you to do some very specific things and you didn't. I said get the trash, drop the mail, and get my shoes—you did none."

"I apologize; I dropped the ball."

"You're damn *right* you dropped the ball!" She jabbed his chest. "You see I'm strugglin' tryin' to keep all this shit together around here—and tryin' to get my ass back into school. Help a sista out once in a while." She hit him again. "You do me so dirty sometimes, J. You might not mean to, but you really do."

Junior looked on pitifully at Casey. He watched as she walked over to her window and stood in front of it. Junior could tell she was upset and went over to comfort her. Before he got halfway, Casey stopped him.

"Don't come over here, J. If you do, I'm gonna hit you again."

Junior stopped in his tracks. He looked on as Casey leaned against her windowsill. Dejected, he slogged out of her bedroom and closed the door behind him. He slumped outside to where Vanessa was waiting for him by the car. She went over to Junior and held him.

"Is everything OK?" she asked him.

"Nah," he sighed. "Listen, V., why don't we catch up later?"

Vanessa held Junior by his sorrowful face. Her hands felt warm and tender against his skin. She pulled Junior's face down to hers and placed her head against his.

"You know I'm not leavin' you, J. Not this way," Vanessa told him. "Why don't we take a ride uptown to Shannon's and give Casey some time to cool off? Maybe then, we come back, you guys can talk. If you want, I'll be there too. You didn't fuck up by yourself. We both did. Aight?" She eyed him.

Junior looked up at Casey's curtained window and stared. He hated when he disappointed Casey—which he seldom did. Vanessa grabbed him by his stubbled chin, moving his eyes back on her. Her gaze captivated him.

"Yeah, I guess you're right," he sighed in defeat. "Just give her a little time. Right?"

"Casey loves you. Y'all will be fine."

"OK." Junior nodded. "Yeah, by the time I come back she'll be better and we can talk."

Junior walked Vanessa over to his car and opened her door. He stopped to look up at Casey's window again, then shook his head and left.

Uptown

The drive into Harlem was only the third time Junior had been since moving to New York. The ride was numbed with traffic which allowed Junior time to sulk over Casey. Also weighing on his heavy mind during the drive was his parents. Junior hadn't seen them in weeks. Meanwhile, Vanessa continued to talk, unphased by his silence. She blabbed on about life in the big city, and how her daddy used to take her into Harlem as a little girl. "Ooh-ooh-ooh!" Vanessa chopped Junior on the arm as she pointed across from him. "Do you know what that building used to be?"

Junior swiveled his head left at the ugly, dilapidated structure. Clueless, he shrugged.

"Oh, my God, yo! Son, are you kiddin' me right now? That used to be the Audubon Ballroom, Junior. That's where Malcolm X was assassinated—I can't believe you didn't know that. Ugh, your momma would be ashamed of you!"

"Look, I ain't from Harlem, V.," Junior snapped. "I rarely come up this way."

Vanessa was quite the historian when it came to African-American history in the big city. It was one of her key attributes which got her over with Sandy when Junior introduced them. Vanessa was an intelligent, young, Black woman with a fondness for her people's history. By the time they reached 125th Street, Junior's arm was sore from Vanessa's trivia questions.

For a weeknight, 125th Street was lit. Folks lingered near a strip of popular night clubs. Traffic was bumper to bumper both ways as drivers stopped to take in the lively atmosphere.

The women dressed fly. Some styled in tops with their toned bellies exposed to complement their summertime outfits. At one upscale nightclub, the women dressed classy. One woman had a black, leather skirt with matching wedges, a fancy white blouse and a stripped zebra bangle to match. She was lauded by a group of men. Lucky for her, outside was a bouncer that looked like Deebo from the movie *Friday* to keep the dogs in line. The men dressed just as smooth as the ladies did. Cats wore slacks with fedoras, gator shoes, and Hawaiian shirts as if they were dressed for Easter. Some wore suits with their collars unbuttoned, flicking gold watches on their wrists.

Further up the block, the dress code was less dapper. Brothers were dressed in long white T-shirts with jean shorts, sneakers, and white slouch socks. Guys had one pant leg down and the other rolled high like LL Cool J. Folks rocked F.U.B.U., Phat Farm, Sean John, and other apparel Junior couldn't afford. Women wore Reebok "Princess" sneakers and shorts. Girls were dressed like the late singer Aaliyah with red-and-white Tommy Hilfiger and jeans. Cars were everywhere, extravagant ones too. One guy had a convertible, green Ford Mustang that sat on gold wheels like Caine from *Menace 2 Society*. Eventually, Junior and Vanessa made it past the Apollo Theatre. It's showy, red letters made Junior smile as his brother came to mind. Lawrence loved *Showtime at the Apollo*.

By the time they arrived at Shannon's house on Coleman Street, Junior was all Harlemed out. He lumbered behind Vanessa with his hands inside his pockets as they walked to the door. Junior rolled his eyes as Vanessa rang the doorbell. He didn't like Shannon, not even a little bit. After what took place at Mel's the other week, he had nothing for her. As Shannon answered the door, Junior scowled at the aspiring lawyer. The two girls screamed and hugged each other. Junior looked down the street; he couldn't wait to get out of there.

"I can't believe you, girl," Vanessa cried. "Son, you're goin' to Syracuse to study law!"

"I know. I can't believe it either." Shannon rocked her. "I'm gonna miss you so much, Vanessa. Girl, I would've never made it out of Langston without you. It's just so sad, man. Everybody's rollin' out. I still haven't heard back from Mel yet. Word, shit is crazy, son."

Hearing Mel's name sent Junior over the edge as the girls talked over his head. Shannon barely acknowledged Junior throughout the visit which enraged him. Eventually, she greeted him.

"Hi, Junior," she said unenthusiastically.

"Sup," Junior replied.

An awkward silence befell the two. Before their silence consumed the visit, Vanessa played peacemaker and switched gears.

"...So, when are you leaving for Syracuse?" she asked. "Yo, that's a long-ass drive."

"Deadass. I'm leavin' tomorrow to move some of my things. I'll still be around, though, here and there. Y'all wanna come in and watch me pack for a few?" Shannon laughed. "I got some Alizé, if y'all want some."

Junior gave Vanessa a baleful stare. He thought to himself that if Vanessa agreed to a drink, she could find her own way back to Casey's where she was parked.

"No, I better not," Vanessa sighed. "I really just wanted to come and see you off. I promised we wouldn't stay long. Maybe another time?"

"Of course, girl." Shannon hugged her. "Anytime you're ever up this way. Son, y'all better not forget about me. I'm gonna hold you to that drink, V."

"You better," Vanessa sniffled. "I'll call you later."

As the girls said their goodbyes, Junior watched, reflecting. There was still a sadness that the crew from Langston High was separating. Caught up in the moment of nostalgia, he decided to make peace with Shannon before her departure to Syracuse.

"Bye, Shannon." He touched her arm. "Sorry that shit got all fucked up the other night at Mel's party. Yo, I think you'll make a great lawyer someday. Take care of yourself."

Junior's selflessness made Shannon's eyes sparkle. She invited him in for a hug.

"I am sorry too, Junior," she sighed. "I got to be honest. I always admired how you took care of my girl, V. Y'all make a great couple. Have you spoken to Mel since the party?" she asked.

"Well, I was… nah," Junior cut it short. "No, I haven't."

After their goodbyes, Junior and Vanessa held hands as they returned to the car. Shannon waved before returning inside to finish packing. Junior placed his hand onto Vanessa's shoulder to comfort her. Her eyes became misty. Vanessa and Shannon had been close since the fourth grade.

"That was so sweet of you, Junior," Vanessa told him. "I know that made her night."

"Well, she's still one of us," he said. "She's still a part of the Langston Gang."

Vanessa smiled at Junior and leaned in to kiss him.

"So, how 'bout some grub?" she offered him. "I know this dope spot around my old way. It's on the way back to Casey's. You hungry?"

"That depends. They got any good carryout spots in Bed-Stuy?"

"Son, are you kiddin' me right now?" Vanessa laughed. "Nigga, it's Brooklyn. We got the best carryout in the world. First, before we eat, I wanna show you where I grew up. After that, I'll take you. You'll love it."

"Yeah, we'll see." Junior fired up his ride. "We'll see."

A Little Girl from Bed-Stuy

"J., not so fast—you're gonna miss it!" Vanessa told him as Junior's car went gliding down 28th Street into the thick of Brooklyn's Bed-Stuy section. Vanessa worked his nerves again, slapping Junior's arm as the two passed some of her favorite childhood landmarks. Her old elementary school, Happy Acres, had since been converted to a halfway house. A Subway shop at the next corner was once a music shop where she rented her first instrument, a saxophone. Her double-jointed arm flung from one side of the car to the other as she pointed out places. It was annoying, but a view into Vanessa's distorted past.

Vanessa told Junior she grew up in a small, three-story apartment building known as Baldwin Homes. It was rumored to be named after African-American novelist, James Baldwin. The building's real namesake, however, belonged to a white man named Willie Baldwin. Willie was a bigot who was once quoted in an article during the 1970s calling his two-block project "a good place for the common, every day under-achieving negro." Despite his racist intent, the building still had a soft spot in Vanessa's heart. It was the last memory she had of her father.

At a red light, Junior saw a car surrounded by a group of young men shooting dice on the sidewalk. They blocked an older woman's path, forcing her into the street. A kid (maybe eight or nine) darted in front of Junior's car on his bicycle as he came to a stop; he barely missed the boy. With his hat cocked to the side, the boy had a pager attached to the rim of his fitted cap. He was dressed better than Junior was. The kid had a wad of cash in one of his hands. He popped a wheelie on his bike and road off into the night. Meanwhile, the cops had a car pulled over on the side of the road. They had a kid's face pressed against the hood of their cruiser. As one cop talked, hovering a flashlight over his shoulder, his partner had the kid placed in a chokehold. They were barking at their detainee as if he was wanted for a triple murder. Across the road, a girl (younger than Vanessa, Junior assumed) pushed a baby in a stroller and talked on the phone as three other smaller children followed behind. Vanessa's old part of town was Brooke's Rowe remixed. "Light's green, J.," said Vanessa, prompting him to push his car deeper into the city's darkness.

At the intersection of 28th and Kirk Street, Junior parked in front of Vanessa's old building number 624. The brakes on his car squealed as he stopped. Vanessa turned to look, admiring her old home. The windows were caged at the terrace level. On the second floor, where her apartment used to be, was a rotting A/C unit. It looked as if a sneeze would knock it down.

"Shit is mad crazy, J.," she paused to reflect. "Just the way life changes so fast."

Sitting near the entrance of the building was a woman and a little girl. The woman was using a rattail comb to remove a row of braided hair as the girl bounced a barbie doll across her lap. When Vanessa waved at the little girl, the mother hoisted her daughter by the hand and took her inside. Vanessa's smile quickly faded.

"I hated our old apartment, but sometimes I do miss it," Vanessa sighed. "It was hell during the summer months, and cold during the winter. The living room window never stayed up, so daddy would use bricks to prop it open when it was hot," she explained. "When it'd rain, we'd take turns holding open the window for each other and tasting the sky's tears. He had a problem," Vanessa sighed. "He tried to get help, but the shit kept kickin' his ass. He and my mother had a fight. She made him choose—but when you got a problem like that and don't know how to fix it, what's the average person gonna choose? Do you ever miss Brooke's Rowe, J.?"

"Not really." Junior sunk. "The hood is fucked up, V."

"Well, it's still home to me. I miss it sometimes."

"Not me. I'm never movin' back to Brooke's Rowe. Fuck that place. C'mon, let's grab somethin' to eat, V. I'm hungry."

"Don't you have any pride for your city, J.?"

"Pride? My city?" He corked his face. "The same city that killed Lawrence? Where cops treat niggas like dogs? And we don't stick together? Where people rob and shoot each other over nothin'? Fuck that place, V.—fuck Brooke's Rowe!"

"You're wrong. What happens in Brooke's Rowe happens everywhere, Junior! It could've been Chicago. It could've been D.C. I swear to God, yo. Brooke's Rowe is still your neighborhood—whether you like it or not. It's your hood."

"Fuck Brook's Rowe. I'll say that to my grave. It's not even..." Junior caught himself mid-flight during his tangent.

He exhaled and shook his head. He placed his hand over Vanessa's. "I'm sorry," Junior apologized. "Look, I just don't feel that same energy for my city, OK?"

"No, I'm sorry. My daddy had a drug problem, he wasn't taken away from me like Lawrence was taken away from your family, Junior." Vanessa squeezed his hand. "So, how 'bout that grub? My treat. My gift to you. It's called Lucky's.

Junior laughed at her. "Why all the good carryouts in the hood be called Lucky's? Man, don't shit be lucky about livin' in the hood. For real."

"Deadass!" Vanessa laughed. "Son, that's hilarious. Aight-aight, but this Lucky's is the real deal. You're gonna love it. Make this left up here at the light."

Six

Inside of a greasy, hole-in-the-wall carryout along Upshur Avenue, Junior and Vanessa shared a box of lo mein with steamed shrimp. The store's owner was so stingy that when Junior asked for a fork, the man pretended he didn't speak English. "Clearly you do when it comes to receiving money," Junior challenged him. Eventually, the man gave up the fork. Occasionally, a fly would wander onto a hanging light bar which flickered from the ceiling as workers packed ticketed orders near the counter. Ironically, its unkempt appearance solidified that the food was good. The carryout's owner used a wooden block to prop open the door, allowing a whiff of the summer air into his establishment. Lost souls trolled the front of the building near the sidewalk sipping forty-ounce malt liquor and debating who was the greatest rapper of all time. At times, their argument made the carryout's owner nervous as he peeped from behind bulletproof glass. It was just after 10:30 p.m. when Junior noticed Vanessa's fork had barely moved throughout dinner. She was oddly quiet despite relishing her favorite carryout. It caught Junior by

109

surprise; he was perplexed by her stillness as he tried to make conversation.

"So, do you think Steny has any spoken word groups like they did at Langston, V.?"

Vanessa lowered her eyes at Junior. "I thought you were done with spoken word?" she asked. "I thought you gave it up back at Luke's the night of Mel's party?"

"Well, I did, but I was thinkin' about maybe trying it out again. I kind of miss it, V.," Junior told her. "It'd be nice if the campus has something for me to join."

Vanessa shook her head at Junior.

"Somethin' wrong?" he asked.

"We'll never have time for each other if you go back on stage, J.," Vanessa told him. "Remember what happened during senior year? We rarely saw each other. You were always on stage, working, or whatever. And if you weren't busy, you were too tired to hang out with me. It's just a big commitment right now. Why not wait until you get a better handle on school?"

"A couple nights a week won't hurt, V."

"What about classes? We both got a full load. Not to mention, you work *and* have to squeeze your parents in on the weekends—and Casey. So, where does that leave me?"

"C'mon, V., I'm not gonna leave you hangin' like that. There'll be time for us. But isn't there shit you wanna do besides be with me all day?"

Vanessa coiled her neck at Junior, ready to bite. "Well, what's that supposed to mean?" She straightened. "I like being around you."

"I like being around you too, Vanessa," Junior tried to explain. "Look, all I'm sayin' is that this college shit is an experience for us both. And I want us to enjoy it together. Yo, we love each other. We'll make it all work out."

"Couples are supposed to be together, in case you're not aware, Junior."

"Why are you tellin' me that as if I don't know? Aren't we always together?"

Vanessa ignored Junior as she began to eat. To keep the peace, Junior swapped chairs and sat next to Vanessa. She turned her head, trying to hide the fact that she was giddy over him. Junior wiggled his finger into Vanessa's rib as she twitched and grabbed his hand.

"Stop, yo!" she squealed. "You tryin' to make me choke or some shit? You get on my nerves. You know that, J.?"

"I know. And you're right. I don't know why I keep goin' back to that shit knowin' how much being on stage took away from us. I'll let it go…for now." He poked her again.

"Ugh! Whatever, Junior. Move, I gotta pee."

Junior slapped her on the backside as she walked by.

While Vanessa was away, two guys and a girl entered Lucky's. One of the boys was tall with army fatigue pants and a black hoodie. The kid had a big, jail scar on the side of his face. When the kid turned to look at Junior, he went back to eating but watched from his side-eye. Believing the carryout was about to get robbed, Junior began wrapping his food to leave before remembering that Vanessa was still in the bathroom. *Shit!* he thought. Suddenly, the water turned on in the bathroom. Junior and the three goons all watched the door as Vanessa exited and gasped.

"Tony?!" Vanessa rushed the kid. The two embraced.

Tony? She knows this clown?

Junior tried not to act jealous as Tony, wrapped up his girlfriend in front of him. He held onto her for an extended period of time. Junior mind-fucked Tony as the two spoke, forgetting he was there.

"It's been a long time, son. How you been?" Vanessa asked him.

"Hey, Beautiful. I'm good," Tony replied. "Goddamn, look at you, girl! All grown-up."

Beautiful? All grown-up?

"Yeah, I'm out in Wilshire, now. Just hangin' out after my first week of college."

"College? For real? Word?"

Yeah! College! What do you do? Not a damn thing, I bet.

Vanessa carried on with Tony and his friends, reminiscing old times in B-K. Junior sucked on a box of lo mein noodles like a lump. He listened as Tony continued to compliment Vanessa before she acknowledged him. Vanessa had yet to introduce Junior as her boyfriend. If not for the hissing noise made from his Sunkist orange soda, Vanessa would've forgotten about him.

"Shit, I'm so rude!" she chuckled. "Junior, uh, this is Tony. We used to date back in elementary school. He was my first boyfriend, ever. What grade was that, Tony? Fifth, wasn't it?"

"Sixth. I can't believe you forgot," he corrected her. "Yo, God. What up?"

"Sup," Junior continued to eat.

Like most attractive girls, Vanessa had fandom. It was nothing for her to run into an admirer. She was an "Around the Way Girl" like the song by LL Cool J. She could kiss and she could hold her own. She spoke Brooklyn but could also speak Wall Street when she needed to. Vanessa was the girl that young boys had wet dreams about growing up. Men gawked at her wherever they went, and Tony was no different. Without Junior's consent, she invited her old flame to join them at the booth. Vanessa's invitation was just as impolite as her leaving Junior hanging.

"Please, we ain't doin' nothin'," Vanessa told him. "C'mon, sit. Let's catch up."

Steam blew from Junior's ears as Tony and his associates piled next to them.

For the next hour, the only time Junior got a word in was when Vanessa brought up his poetry. She didn't want him doing spoken word but praised him for his writing; it was weird. It pissed Junior off because he didn't share that with people he didn't know. Especially not Tony.

"Yo, God, you write lyrics?" Tony asked him. "Son, you ought to come by the studio one day and lay down a track with me. I'm tryin' to get on with this label. My man knows this producer who works with DMX. I got an audition comin' up," he bragged. "Shit, once they hear this mixtape I got comin' out, I'm bound to get signed. I'm all about puttin' other niggas on, you feel me? I ain't grimey like that. How long you been spittin' now?"

"You mean, rap?" Junior asked. "Nah, man. I don't rap. I do spoken word."

"He's not into that kind of stuff, Tony," Vanessa co-signed "Junior ain't the rapper-type. He's a smooth cat. He's sweet."

Tony and his cohorts all nodded their heads in unison. Junior could tell the three dicks wanted to laugh at him. He looked over at Vanessa and shook his head. Humiliated, he went back to picking at his food. He couldn't have been happier when Tony and his crew decided to leave. His plan was to give Vanessa hell and take her back. It got nixed when Tony mentioned a party happening nearby in a section of Brooklyn known as "Lowery". Junior shut down the idea.

"Nah, we really ought to get goin', man," Junior told Tony. "Yeah, it's gettin' kind of late. I probably should get back and check on Casey."

"Check on Casey?" Vanessa repeated. "J., it's after eleven. She's probably asleep, studyin' for her exam or doing something else—you don't have to check in on her. We're not at Langston anymore. We're grown now."

"I know, but she still worries about me when I'm out late. Plus, I should check in on my folks. I haven't seen 'em in a few days."

"Why you buggin'? Just stay out a little longer."

"It's gonna be plenty to drink there," Tony co-signed. "Y'all ought to come."

"Junior, yo!" Vanessa tugged his arm. "Just for a little while. C'mon, let's celebrate our first week of college. We don't have to stay long, I just wanna hang out for a little bit."

With Vanessa's sweet face begging him to go, Junior caved in. "…Well, let me check on Sissy first, I'll be back."

"Check on who?" Tony asked. "Who the fuck is Sissy?"

"It's his sister," Vanessa answered. "He lives with his sister."

Tony didn't say anything, and it was best he didn't. The last kid that talked slick about Casey ended up with a chipped tooth.

With less than three percent battery left on his phone, Junior stepped out in front of Lucky's to call Casey. Usually, when Junior was out late, she'd call to check on him. She didn't that night. When he dialed, she answered and puffed into the line.

"It's after eleven," said Casey. "Do you know where your knucklehead-ass child is, America? Because I sure as hell don't! Where are you, Junior?"

"You still mad at me about earlier, Sissy?" he asked.

"I'm not tryin' to be a bitch, J. But the fact that you didn't do anything I asked you to do today, that's not like you," she explained. "What do you want? So, let me guess: You and Vanessa ran into some old friends and are headed somewhere you ain't got no business being at. So, where's the party gonna be?"

"How'd you know?"

"Because I know my brother," she said. "It's Friday night. Now, tell me about this wack-ass party so I can say 'no' and tell you to come home before something bad happens."

"It's in Lowery. We weren't gonna stay long, though. Just for a little bit."

"Lowery? Do you know *anything* about Lowery, Junior? Anything at all?"

Scratching his head, Junior came up short. "Uh, I know it's near Brownsville, right? Why? What's wrong?"

Casey went dead on him.

"I used to buy my drugs from over there, J." Casey sucked her teeth. "I would highly recommend that you do not go into Lowery tonight. You're gonna give me a fuckin' heart attack one of these days, you know that? I'm not even gonna make it to my exam."

"I'm just gonna go for a little while. I won't be long."

"No, Junior. Look, if you wanna hang out, we'll drive down to Blockbuster. We'll get movies—like we used to. We'll make popcorn. I'll pull out the ice cream machine. We'll have a good time. Besides, I need a break from studying, anyway. Please, Junior," Casey begged him. "Don't go into Lowery. I don't have a good feeling about this."

As Casey went on and on, Junior watched as Vanessa laughed it up at the table with Tony. Casey eventually gave up on trying to convince him to come home.

"Man, you ain't comin'," she blew into the receiver. "I'll just say this and then I have to get back to work. You're 18 now which means you're a legal adult. So, if somethin' happens out there, it's on you."

"Why do you have to say shit like that Casey?" Junior exhaled. "See, now I'm nervous."

"Good, I hope you are nervous!" she shot back. "Because I'm nervous too! You make me nervous. That's why I'm turnin' gray at 34 now and gainin' all this weight. No wonder I'm still single. I look like a fuckin' bowling ball. Besides, aren't you headed down to Brooke's Rowe to see your folks tomorrow?"

"I won't be long, I promise."

"It's not my decision, Junior. It's yours."

"Casey, listen—"

"No, you listen," she interrupted. "I have a very important exam comin' up soon down at my job—I don't have time for this, Junior. I'm hangin' the phone up. You're grown now, right? So then make a grown-up decision because I've made mine. Peace." Click.

Junior returned his phone inside his pocket and went back into Lucky's. He changed his mind about fifty times on his way back to Vanessa. He took a seat next to her.

"Just for a little while, right?" he asked.

"Just for a little while—just like with Shannon. We won't stay long," Vanessa promised. "I won't even drink that much, just a sip."

Junior wanted to say no, but it was hard to with Vanessa rubbing his leg beneath the table.

"OK. Well, I guess we'll go—for a little while."

"Y'all might wanna ride with me. It's not a lot of parkin' over there," Tony encouraged. "I got plenty of room. I'll bring y'all back."

"Nah, we'll drive," said Junior. "We'll find a spot. Even if it's far, we'll walk."

"In Lowery, son?" Tony laughed.

"J., we really ought to ride with Tony. It'll be easier," said Vanessa.

"What about my car? Am I even allowed to leave it here?"

"The car will be fine, J., Will you just come on?"

Outside, Junior left his car in the lot and slogged over to Tony's car as if he was headed to the guillotine. He opened the door to Tony's Chevy SS Impala and turned to look back at his car as if it was his last night alive.

"What are you doing?" Vanessa whispered. "Nobody's gonna steal your car, I promise. Tony's gonna bring us back. I've known him my whole life. He's a good dude."

"You sure this parking lot is safe, V.?" he asked.

"Of course, J. Son, it's just a little dumb carryout. Now, will you please just get in?"

Slow and defeated, Junior got into Tony's car, wondering what he had gotten himself into.

Tony the "Brooklyn Killah"

The hair on the back of Junior's neck raised as Tony's car whipped in and out of lanes. Stopped at a red light, he mashed the brake and feathered the accelerator. His car rocked from side to side as his tires screamed against the pavement sending chalky smoke into the night. His cohorts all egged on his stupidity. "Yo, God, watch this," Tony said before propelling like a cannon down a one-way street. At the end, he repeated his childish act and laughed evilly. Junior kicked himself for not listening to Casey. He looked over at Vanessa and could tell she was unamused. Her expression was full of remorse.

Throughout their death-defying ride, Tony drove with an open casebook full of CDs on his lap. The subwoofers blared from inside of his trunk. He changed out more CDs than a DJ at a wedding reception. From Nas to The Lox. From The Lox to Wu-Tang. From Wu-Tang to Craig Mack. At one point, he lifted a blank CD from his pouch that was labeled in black Sharpie. He held it up high for everyone there to see. The name "Brooklyn Killah" was written on it.

"Yo, Junior," he said. "This is one of the tracks I'm gonna play when I meet with the producer next week. Wanna hear it?"

Already on the verge of nausea, Junior nodded. "Yeah, man," he said unenthusiastically. "Let me hear it."

Tony inserted his CD into the radio and cranked up the volume. The music faded in awkwardly as his vocals emitted through the car's sound system. The beat was elementary, Junior noticed. It reminded him of a Toys R Us commercial or an advertisement to Disneyland. He could feel himself beginning to choke but reserved his laughter for Tony's weak rap game.

I'm the Brooklyn Killah. Ride a four-wheeler.
I am from the zoo 'cause I'm a Gorilla.
I like to chill. My middle-name is Will.
I pop pills that go with Benadryl.
You know how I be. I like to catch Z's.
In the Florida Keys. Chillin' on a Yacht.
Countin' all this cheese...

Junior bit his bottom lip and stayed there. Vanessa did the same. Even the Brooklyn Killah's henchmen followed suit. One of his friends pretended to check his phone. For an avid hip-hop fan like Junior, Tony's song was an insult to the game of rap music. His cadence was weak, and his rhyme scheme was pre-schoolish. It was a joke. "Ugh! I can't believe I used to date him," Vanessa whispered. "What a fuckin' cornball he turned out to be."

Junior couldn't believe Vanessa used to date Tony, either. After hearing the song, he no longer felt threatened by Tony's toxic masculinity. It was the longest three minutes of Junior's life. When Tony's audition ended, he ejected his CD from the radio. He placed it on his finger and blew it. The blow at the end made Junior double-over. His sides split as he laughed in silent agony.

"So, what y'all think?" Tony asked. "Shit was mad hot, right?"

The car went silent. It was so quiet you could hear Tony's turn blinker. Eventually, one of his friends stepped forward to deliver the hard truth.

"Well," the kid said, "if that's your demo, I guess I'll see your ass at work on Monday!"

The car erupted. The only "killah" inside the car that night was Tony's music.

When the group arrived in Lowery, to Junior's surprise, the party was dead. Not a car was in sight. He sighed with relief. Everyone else groaned, including Vanessa. Junior noticed a kid sitting beside a duffel bag on the front steps of the house smoking a cigarette. As Tony whipped into the driveway, the kid flicked his cigarette into the yard and walked over with the heavy bag. It swayed from side to side as he struggled to keep it off the ground. Tony left his car and walked over to help carry it to the trunk. Junior's antenna went up immediately. With Tony gone, everybody went back to clowning his lame demo. Junior lowered his back window to eavesdrop on the suspicious transaction taking place outside of the car. He could barely make it out.

"Yo, God. What happened?"

"Auntie trippin' again. Here's that bag I was tellin' you about. Hold it for me 'til I get out. I got that court case tomorrow. I ain't trippin', though. Them niggas ain't got shit on me, son. Feds took the other bag last week from the other crib. Can't let 'em get this one."

Junior overheard the two struggle to lift the bag into the trunk. It made a loud clunking noise as the car moved.

"How much time you lookin' at?"

"Don't know. Could be six months. My P.O. said he'll try to talk to the D.A. and get it cut down to three. They're tryin' to say that she had a concussion—that bitch ain't have no concussion. It's all good. I ain't worried about it."

"Deadass. Yo, how much is in here? Just so I know."

"I got three burners in there, plus a chopper, and a brick of that white. I would've kept it, but I can't let 'em take this one, too. When the Feds hit the other house, they took the first bag and locked up my bitch and her cousin. They let her go, but they kept him."

"Goddamn. So, what do you want me to do with the bag?"

"Just hold it for now 'til I know what I'm lookin' at. Son, my life is in that bag. I'm gonna need that to get back on my feet, once I get out."

"You know the vibe. I got you."

Their hands came together in solidarity as the two went their separate ways. Tony closed his trunk and climbed back inside his ride as if nothin' had happened.

"No party tonight, y'all," Tony confirmed.

"Why? What happened?" Vanessa asked. "What'd he say?"

"His peeps buggin'. I'll take y'all back."

"Well, do you know anybody else that might have somethin'?"

Junior cut in immediately.

"V., we really ought to get back to the house. I've been out all day. How about another night?" he offered. "Besides, it's gettin' late."

"C'mon, J.," she fussed. "Let's try one more spot. It's barely after midnight."

"Look, it's late enough," Junior complained. "Tony, can you take us back?"

"Yeah, I got you," he said.

"Thank you." Junior gave Vanessa the evil eye.

As Tony backed out the driveway, Vanessa shook her head at Junior.

Seven

Junior was no dummy. He wanted to get the hell away from that black duffel bag. Vanessa could bitch at him later. The night was young with trouble. Five Black kids riding in a car with tinted windows and loud music on a Friday night was a beat cop's wet dream. For Junior, it was a nightmare.

It didn't take long for Junior to decipher the hieroglyphics used between Tony and his associate from earlier. The euphemisms weren't foreign to him. A "burner" was a handgun, and there were three of them. A "chopper" was an AK-47 assault rifle, and "white" was slang for powdered cocaine. From watching the show *Cops* on TV, Junior knew that just being a passenger in a hot car was trouble. Tony's driving only added to Junior's anxiety. He drove erratically, committing every violation in the New York traffic law book. He switched lanes without using his turn signal, sped through yellow lights without yielding and rolled through stop signs without coming to a complete stop. He nearly scraped the side of a construction truck on 21st Street, and had the audacity to give the city worker the finger. Paranoid, Junior leaned forward to ask if he could slow it down.

"Yo, can you take it easy?" Junior asked him.

"Son, we almost there. Chill out," Tony shot back.

Junior returned to his seat. He gave Vanessa another grim look.

"OK, he does drive like maniac. I'll give you that," Vanessa whispered. "But what's the problem? Why don't you wanna stay out?"

"There's some shit in that bag, V.," Junior warned her.

"What bag? What are you talkin' about?"

"Forget it, V. Just forget it."

Vanessa sucked her teeth at him. "Trippin', man." She shook her head.

With Tony's bag sitting just feet away from him, Junior found it difficult to relax. He took mental note of the names of roadways and streets in case of an emergency, the way Sandy had once taught him. Meanwhile, Tony continued to drive like a jackass. It got so bad that even his other friends asked if he could slow it down. When that failed, Vanessa tried to sweet-talk him.

"Tony... for me. Can you slow down?"

Tony pressed on the accelerator. Annoyed, Vanessa returned to her seat.

"I think he's still mad about his demo," she whispered to Junior. "He was always petty. You said there's a bag in the trunk? What does it look like? What's in it?"

"Later," said Junior. "Let's get the fuck out of here first."

124

At a cross between Albany and 23rd Avenue, it suddenly happened. Boom! Tony struck the back of a parked car. The collision sent everybody forward and back. Luckily, no one was seriously hurt, but Tony banged up his car pretty good. His stereo skipped on the point of impact. Before they could check each other for injuries, a police car appeared behind them. Its spotlight shined on the back of Junior's head. His heart raced as he started to sweat. Junior had been stopped by police only once since moving to New York. Two cops, one on each side, approached to check on them.

"Need to see a driver's license, registration and proof of insurance, please," one of the officers requested. His partner played wingman on the passenger side. Tony fished through his wallet but came up short. The two cops eyed each other. According to his nameplate, the officer asking was named Santana.

"License, registration and insurance, please," Santana said again.

"One second." Tony opened his center console and began to look there. He pulled out a stack of old papers and began rummaging through it. Nervous, Vanessa reached for Junior's hand and locked it with hers. The cop on the passenger side shined his flashlight into her face. He placed his hand on the hood of his pistol.

"Don't move!" he barked.

Vanessa let Junior's hand go. Meanwhile, Santana was growing impatient.

"Why is this process taking so long?" he asked. "Don't you have a license?"

125

"Yes, sir," Tony answered.

"So, where is it?"

Tony returned to his wallet to look. Annoyed, Santana turned up the heat.

"Not playin' anymore games," he opened Tony's door. "Out. In fact, everybody out."

Junior's future flashed before his eyes. One by one, the cops searched every passenger there before lining them up on the curb. Junior shook uncontrollably as he thought of what Casey and his parents would say if they saw him. During his search, as ordered, Junior placed his hands on his head and interlocked his fingers. Santana grabbed Junior's hand and cranked it hard, torquing him backward. The cop dug through his pockets and removed his wallet and keys. He tossed Junior's things on the trunk. He slap-checked Junior's chest, legs, and felt around his groin area before making him sit beside his co-defendants. Vanessa was the last to get searched. She was still salty about the flashlight being pointed into her eyes.

"Reach beneath the bottom of your shirt—make sure to leave it down—and shake out your bra. I want to make sure you're not carrying any contraband."

"What? Excuse me?" Vanessa screeched. "Y'all can't do that. It's discrimination."

"Just do it, V.!" Junior hollered.

Sucking her teeth, Vanessa reached beneath her T-shirt and shook out her bra. Afterward, she stood there with a blank look. The cop gave Vanessa another order.

"I need you to lean forward and run your fingers through your hair, go like this," the officer demonstrated. "OK, you do it."

Vanessa ran her fingers through her hair and stood upright. Nothing.

"Good," Santana nodded. "Have a seat and keep your mouth shut."

With her arms crossed, Vanessa splattered beside Junior on the curb. Santana lifted his radio from his duty belt and called into dispatch.

"229 to dispatch, can you send a dog my way?" he requested.

"10-4, 229," dispatch replied. "K-9 is headed to you now."

Santana returned his radio onto his belt. His wingman, Davis, stood beside him.

"Listen, I'm tired of the fuckin' games, alright? Somebody better give me what I asked for real soon or it's all of your asses."

Junior turned to look at Tony. Vanessa's ex looked straight ahead.

"That's fine," said Santana. "Nobody knows anything? We'll see about that once the K-9 gets here. Should be any minute now. I bet there's dope inside of that car, and I'm gonna find it."

As the officers stepped away to converse, Junior looked down at Tony again.

"Yo, aren't you gonna say somethin'?" Junior asked him. Tony didn't move. Neither did his homies. It was every man for himself. The "no snitch" rule was in full effect. With his freedom on the line, Junior took matters into his own hands.

"Excuse me, officer?" He raised his hand. "Santana, is it? Yo, officer?"

"J., what are you doing?" Vanessa pulled at him. "Shut up!"

Junior ignored her.

"Excuse me. Officers? Can I talk to you for a second?"

The cops returned and stood in front of Junior. His co-conspirators all looked on.

"I didn't want it to come to this, but there's a duffel bag inside the trunk," Junior told them. "It's not mine, and it's not my girlfriend's either. I have a New York driver's license, but I didn't offer it to you since I wasn't the driver."

The officers retrieved Junior's wallet, took out his license and looked it over.

"Why doesn't your friend have a license?" Santana asked.

"He's not my friend, sir. I just met him tonight. But after all this, I doubt we'll ever be friends." Junior glared at Tony. "There's a black duffel bag inside the trunk you might wanna look at. Normally, I could care less about helping the police, but my freedom is on the line. Me and my girlfriend here, Vanessa, we're both in college."

Using Tony's keys, the cops unlocked Tony's trunk and went to lift his duffel bag.

"Shit!" Santana grunted. "Th'hell's in here?"

The two cops unzipped the bag and shined their flashlights inside.

"Holy shit, Davis. Get a load of this!"

As the cops looked through Tony's duffel bag, Tony gave Junior a gloomy look. It was the kind of look that said if the two ever crossed paths again, Junior was as good as dead. With the cops there to protect him, Junior gave Tony a piece of his mind. "That's why your demo is shit," Junior taunted him. "You'll never get that rap contract for this pussy-ass move you pulled tonight. Don't drop the soap you fuckin' bitch!" It was uncharacteristic of Junior, but so were the circumstances. He would rather disappoint Tony any day than disappoint his family. It wasn't worth the risk. Vanessa gasped with shock as one of the cops held up a brick of cocaine.

"Son, are you serious?" she shouted. "Tony?! I can't believe you!"

Seconds later, several more cop cars showed up, one of which had a vicious German Shepherd police dog. The dog showed its teeth at Junior from the grated window. The dog clawed and bit at the door, trying to get out. Santana handed Junior back his wallet and sent him and Vanessa on their way.

"Beat it, you two," he nodded. "Next time, be careful who your friends are."

Holding hands, Junior and Vanessa walked off and left Tony and his friends with the bag.

Walk, Don't Run

The trek back to Lucky's through New York City's night life was precarious. Junior and Vanessa hurried through the streets with their senses on overload. They looked over their shoulders at every noise or car that passed. During their trip, they confronted a naked man dressed in a long trench coat. The man appeared to be on drugs. He talked to himself at a nearby bus stop despite no one being around. He sat there unprovoked before springing onto his feet. "Shut the fuck up," he shouted at the glass. The man headbutted the window until it cracked. He butted it even harder, smashing his forehead through the thick glass until it finally gave way. Weary, he crumbled onto his backside. An unfortunate breeze blew open his coat, exposing his hairy privates. His face was bloody and there were bits of glass protruding from his nose, but he didn't appear to be in any pain. He rolled on the ground, continuing to argue with himself. Wisely, Junior and Vanessa crossed to the other side of the roadway. Further up, beneath a crumbling overpass, was a man with a long, salty beard lying beside a stack of wool blankets. He was watching *The Jay Leno Show* on a portable TV and eating a sandwich. It would've been normal except next to him was a pile of excrement. He stunk so badly it made Junior's eyes burn. Insects were flying around his face and head like *Candyman*. As Junior and Vanessa passed him in the roadway, the man eyed them with distrust. Next, a group of young ruffians several blocks up presented a more terrifying challenge. They were huddled around a car parked on a street corner. One of the miscreants made a pass at Vanessa. "What's up, Shawty? Can I get that?" the guy asked her. "For real, you lookin' so good, I'll fuck your man, too." When Vanessa didn't respond, they called her a "stupid bitch" and started following them. For the next several blocks, the group harassed and taunted the two. "Ay?!" One of the kids shouted. "I know y'all heard me. Where the fuck y'all goin'?" Junior and Vanessa took off down Upshur Avenue as the group pursued them. Lucky for them, a cop had just made a traffic stop further up the roadway. It was the first time Junior felt safe seeing blue and red. As the group stopped to turn back, he overheard one of the kids complain. "I swear to God, my nigga, I would've raped that bitch. Son, I would've raped that bitch right in front of her man." The very thought made Junior tremor. Vanessa was hardly flattered by the frightening gesture.

They finally reached the lot at Lucky's—but it was empty. "Th'fuck?" Junior stood in the middle of the lot, spinning in circles. "Man, where the fuck is my car?" He bolted into the carryout to ask the manager if he had seen his car. He could barely make out the man's poor English.

"It's a Buick Skylark with rust on the back panel—it was parked right in front of the door. What do you mean it was towed?"

The owner pointed at a taped sign on the wall.

"See sign?" the man asked him. "Outside? You no park here. Overnight. Walk off. You no good. I tow car for you."

"...HUH?!"

"I tow car! No park here and walk off! You no good. I tow."

"Why the fuck would you tow my car, man? I was in here earlier. Wasn't I?"

"You walk off."

"Fuck you!"

"No, fuck you! Mother-bitch." The man pounded the counter. "I run business. My lot! You walk off. You read sign next time."

Enraged, Junior kicked open the door and went out to the lot as Vanessa followed him. Outside, he walked over to the edge of the lot to look for the sign the owner referred to. *Owner must remain with vehicle at all times. No exceptions. If towed call this number...* Somehow, he had missed it.

Junior turned to confront Vanessa. "I thought you said it'd be safe to park here, V.?"

"They must've added this sign 'cause I've never seen it before." She looked at it, confused. "Listen, whatever it costs to get your car out, I'll help you pay for it."

"It should've never got towed in the first place, Vanessa."

"J., I'm sorry, I didn't know any of this was gonna happen."

"First, you invite Tony and his bank robbers to join us while we're eating. Then, you sweet-talk me to go to some stupid party. We could've been killed coming and going as bad a driver as Tony is," he said. "We could've gone to jail for what was is in that duffel bag, V., and then we nearly get FUCKED tryin' to make it back to my car. And now it's not here!" Junior raised his arms. "Look, V., I'm on thin ice with Casey as it is. I don't need this right now."

"What kind of person do you think I am?" she asked him. "You think I wanted any of this to happen to us tonight? I would never put you in harm's way on purpose. I love you, J."

"I don't know about any of that right now, V."

Gasping, Vanessa walked into the carryout, leaving Junior alone outside.

Junior tossed a fist full of tiny rocks from the ground into the roadway. Occasionally, he'd looked back to check on Vanessa and noticed she was still sitting in the carryout. He chucked more debris into the roadway before returning inside to check on her. He found her sitting at a booth spinning a beaded bracelet on her wrist. She looked up at Junior with foggy eyes and went back to playing with her bracelet. Junior took a seat beside her and placed his arm around her. She laid her head on his chest.

"We'll figure it out, OK?" he sighed. "Don't worry, we'll get home."

"What are you gonna do?" she asked him.

With 1% battery life left on his phone, Junior called the number to the tow and found out that his car had been taken to the Bronx. Using Vanessa's lipstick, he managed to write down the tow lot's address before his phone died.

"Do you have your phone on you?" he asked her.

Vanessa searched through her pocketbook and frowned.

"Shit, I think I left it inside of your car," she told him. "I doubt it'd work anyway. I had about 10% left last I checked. Now, what?"

Out of ideas, Junior played nice at the counter as he tried to persuade the manager at Lucky's to let him use the phone. The man was still sulking from earlier.

"May I please borrow your phone, sir?" Junior asked.

"What for? You need phone?" the owner asked him.

"Yes, sir. I need to call my sister."

"Sitter? You have sitter? Hmph."

"No, sister. My sister," Junior repeated. "I need to call my sister. I have no car."

"Ohhh, sitter. Ah. OK."

"I'm sorry for earlier, OK? May I please use your phone?"

"Yeah, you no good!"

"I know. Please, sir. Just a few minutes."

The owner reached behind the counter and handed Junior the phone. The phone handle was covered in a greasy film. The earpiece was brown with wedges of wax coated near the middle. Junior held it away from his head as he called Casey.

"Please tell me you're on the way home, J.," she answered without greeting him.

"I wish I could," he exhaled. "I'm at Lucky's on Upshur. I need a ride, Sissy. My car got towed from the lot."

"Junior, do you realize it's almost 2 a.m.?"

"Sissy, listen—"

"Junior," Casey raised her voice. "It's late. I need answers. Now, what's going on?"

Junior looked back at Vanessa as she continued to finger her bracelet. He closed his eyes.

"It's a long story, Casey. Here's what happened…"

Casey was on fire when she arrived at Lucky's that night to get Junior and Vanessa. By then, the owner had closed shop but was kind enough to wait around. "I wait for you," the owner told Junior. "Sitter come. I go."

Casey showed up cussing with a bonnet covering her head as she whipped her Toyota into the lot. "Motherfuckers!" She cranked her parking brake and kicked open her car door. The car shifted as she climbed out. The owner of the carryout sped off. He wanted no part of Casey's wrath. She shot out of her car wearing rain boots, a jacket, and pajama pants. She'd obviously been worried and rushed into the quickest outfit she could find. It would've been funny if not for the circumstances. She marched over to Junior like a drill sergeant and bopped him on his bonehead. Vanessa wisely backed away.

"I should hit your ass, too!" Casey crossed her arms. "Th'hell is wrong with y'all? It's after 2 a.m., and y'all are out here in the middle of the night with no car, no money—or brains, obviously! Y'all are college students," Casey berated them. "Do y'all have any idea how close you could've been to going to jail tonight—or hurt?"

"We're sorry, Casey," Vanessa spoke up.

"You shut up!" Casey snarled. "I'm fuckin' steamin' at you, Vanessa—and I want a new hairdryer—and a new towel. You don't come up in my house and wipe your little nasty body on my stuff without my permission. You don't live there, and you don't pay bills there. You want to shower? You take your ass to Motel 6 or someplace else. You got that?"

"Yes, ma'am."

Casey marched to the edge of the lot to read the tow sign.

"How did two graduates from one of the most prestigious high schools in the area not see this sign? Two college students?" she asked them. "Stevie Wonder could see this fuckin' sign." She got back into Junior's face. "Do you realize how expensive it is to get a car towed from Brooklyn to the Bronx? You got money like that just chillin', lyin' around, J.? I don't. I barely got my half of your tuition paid this month."

Right there, Casey began massaging her temples to keep from killing them both. Junior knew she'd been under the gun lately with her studies. The last thing she needed was any trouble. He reached inside of his pocket for the tow information he'd written down earlier.

"What's that? Lemme see. Give it to me," she ordered.

As Junior went to hand it over, she snatched it from his hand. Casey looked down at her watch and went back to massaging her temples. The paper went sailing down onto the pavement. Junior picked it up and put it back into his pocket.

"We'll go early tomorrow," she sighed. "I'll have to put it on my credit card for now."

Casey swatted at Junior as if he was a fly.

"Get in the car. Go," she shoved him. "Hurry up before I put my rainboot up your ass! Go!"

Vanessa didn't move. She wanted no part of Casey.

"Th'fuck are you lookin' at me for?" Casey invaded

Vanessa's space. "You want me to kick your ass too? Huh? Is that it?!"

"No, ma'am."

"GET IN!" Casey screamed. Quickly, Vanessa slipped into the backseat. Casey climbed into the driver's seat right after. She slammed the door so hard, her leafy air fresheners swayed. Junior looked straight ahead. Casey bopped Junior again and drove off.

Casey didn't even bother to turn the radio on during the drive back. Junior wondered how much more of him she was willing to take. Had he finally gone too far? He wondered. He knew Casey had gone to great lengths to care for him, and also knew it hurt her to see him gambling with his future in such a way. He slouched throughout the ride, angry at himself. Occasionally, he'd glance over at Casey's angry face. He could tell she was disappointed. Junior was too. How could he be so stupid? he thought. He'd done a lot of foolish things since moving to New York, but nothing this bad. By the time they made it back to the house, without a word, Casey turned off her car and went inside, leaving Junior and Vanessa alone in her car. Her abandonment made Junior feel nauseous.

"I've never seen her so upset," Vanessa choked. "She's so sweet. I did that to her…"

The two climbed out of Casey's car and stood in front of the house. As the night wore on Vanessa's soul, she teared up in front of Junior. Junior gave her a blank stare. He'd had enough of Vanessa to last him a lifetime. He wanted to break it off right then but couldn't find the strength to do it. The night was her fault—all of it. From Tony and his black duffel bag to nearly getting devoured by the city's darkness. Vanessa knew it too. She leaned her head onto the roof of Casey's car and wept as Junior consoled her.

"Fuck, I feel like the worst girlfriend in the world, man—and I don't wanna be!" she shrieked. "Junior, you have to believe me, I didn't mean for any of this to happen."

Junior wiped Vanessa's tears. He held her soft face but didn't kiss it.

"It's been a long day, V. Why don't you go home and get some rest, OK?"

Vanessa sniffled, nodding her head.

"Yeah. Maybe I should. Are you gonna call me later?"

Junior shook his head.

"OK then. I guess I'll go. Can I have a kiss, J.?"

Junior looked on at Vanessa, unable to hide his disappointment. He looked down at his feet and back up at her, shoved his hands into his pockets and exhaled.

"I understand, J. I get it." Vanessa shrugged.

Junior stood on the step and watched as Vanessa dragged herself to her car and left. Normally, he'd walk Vanessa over to her car, open her door, kiss her, close her door, and watch her from the roadway as she drove off. Not that night.

Junior entered the house and went looking for Casey. He found her sitting on her bed inside of her room. She stared lifelessly into her TV set. She didn't move. Tears were rolling down her puffy cheeks. He stood at her doorframe.

"Can I come in?"

Casey rose from her bed and wiped her eyes. She didn't give an answer but moved throughout her room to fold a batch of clean laundry that had been there the past week. Junior looked over at her clock; it was close to 3 a.m. He stood near the door and watched as Casey folded her clothes and cleaned up her bedroom, anything to keep from crying. It hurt Junior to know he had done that to his sissy, one of his biggest fans.

"I'll pay you back, Casey. I'll give you my whole check if you want it."

Casey shook her head at him with pity. Her cold silence made Junior realize that it wasn't the money that got to Casey. It was everything altogether. He had broken her heart and was on the verge of breaking his promise. She curled her lips inward to keep from losing it, ignoring him.

"Casey, please, I'm really sorry about tonight." Junior felt his voice hoarsening.

Casey walked over to her closet, opened her door and stood there. Junior walked over and placed a hand on her shoulder. She turned and began swinging wildly at him. He ducked and blocked as many of Casey's free shots as he could before grabbing his sissy and holding her. She broke down in his arms before pushing him away.

"Do you know what you did to me tonight out there, J.—to us?" Her voice wavered. "You could've lost your freedom or worse. You were about to throw it all away. I'm tired of playin' cleanup to your shit, man. I got a fuckin' life to live too, Junior," Casey reminded him. "If you still want this like you claim you do, you need to rearrange your priorities. I won't let you break my heart like this ever again. The next time, it's gonna be very different—I can promise you that. I really hope you think about your priorities over the weekend at your parents. Now, get the *hell* out of my face. I don't even wanna look at you right now. Go away."

"Casey, please… just hear me out."

"No, J.— go away! Leave!" she hollered, crying. "Get out!"

Junior lowered his head and headed toward the door as Casey followed behind him. He stopped to plead his case, but Casey moved him along. She closed the door in his face. *Thoom!*

Seconds later, Junior overheard the spring in Casey's bed creak as she began to sob. Not only had Junior broken her heart, he had broken her spirit too. He knocked on her door, hoping to make peace with Casey. She walked over to the door.

"What do you want from me, J.? You've broken my heart one time tonight already—please, just go away!"

Junior gave up and returned to his room for the night. He sat on the floor next to his bed with the lights off and covered his head with his shirt.

Eight

"Tell your folks I said 'hello,'" was all Junior managed to get out of Casey the morning after on their way into the Bronx to the tow lot. Casey left him at the gate. It was cold compared to their normal banter. As he tried to make friends with her again, she pulled off. His car didn't start when he first got in. Luckily, the tow yard guy gave him a jump.

The drive down to Brooke's Rowe afterward was as reflective a ride as Junior had ever had. Usually, he'd talk either to Casey or Vanessa during his long ride. Mostly, it was Vanessa. He placed his girlfriend's bag with her extra clothes along with her cell phone on the steps of her house and left without speaking to her. She called him crying a half hour later.

"Wow! Really, J.?" she sniffled. "Really, son? Yo, I know I messed up, but you couldn't even face me? That's fucked up!" Vanessa hung up on him. Junior drooped along Interstate 95. In less than a day, he'd managed to break both Casey's and Vanessa's hearts. He hoped to make a peaceful visit down to see his family without any incident. It was a daunting way to start his weekend.

Junior thought about Vanessa until he crossed into South Philadelphia's Brooke's Rowe. Returning to his old neighborhood distracted him from his troubles. He parked and stood on the sidewalk looking up at his old house. The numbers "1401" were faded and crooked, weathered by time and the fierce northeastern winters. To Junior's left, a couple houses down, young kids took turns playing hopscotch on a makeshift board along a row of cracked asphalt. They hopped on one foot, gliding along the fractured pavement, blissfully ignorant to their environment. To Junior's right, a kid sold crack to an elderly customer who was desperate for a high. "C'mon, baby!" the man said, clawing at his neck, unable to stand still. "The last one ain't did nothin' for me. I need somethin' stronger!" The seller blessed the old man with a fist full of white, powdery rocks. The old man clasped his hands together in worship and left. The young dealer peeled through a stack of hundred-dollar bills. He looked about Junior's age when he'd left back in '95. Junior stared at the boy. "Th'fuck you lookin' at, nigga?" the kid scoffed at him. "I gotta get mine." The boy shook his head and pedaled away. The harsh realities of life in Brooke's Rowe were degrading for any young boy. After not visiting his family in nearly a month, the sights and sounds of his old hood were a stark reminder that Junior had come a long way.

As Junior pushed through the rusty wire gate to his front yard, he peered over at the dried, patchy dirt where, for years, his daddy had tried to grow grass. He grinned as he thought of old times, reminiscing the days Senior would slam his big, black fist onto a broken lawnmower. The days Senior would spend hours detailing his truck just for a bird to fly by and shit on it. One time, his daddy got so upset he lobbed the bucket over the house. Junior and Lawrence laughed for days.

Sometimes, in July, despite the gunshots, kids set off bottle rockets in the streets, blocking traffic after dark. They scattered like roaches when the cops showed up. Down on the north side one summer, a cop, with his gun drawn, cornered a kid and ordered him not to move. Terrified, the kid tried to run, and the officer shot him in the back, killing him instantly. The boy was eleven years old, about Lawrence's age before he died. The shooting made the news for two days before it quickly washed away. A week later, a white girl from Penn State went missing off the coast of Florida from a yacht party. It aired all summer and into the fall.

As memories of his beloved city flickered throughout his mind, Junior stood at the door of his old house. Before raising his fist to knock, he realized he still owned a door key. That's how long it had been since he'd visited. Before he could place his key inside the lock, suddenly, the door opened. His brooding, angry daddy, Senior, stood on the otherside. Gray hair rising from his head, at 51 years old, he was even more menacing than Junior had last remembered. With cobra-like eyes, Senior's glare was enough to make an onion cry. Where the Robinsons lived, on Kennedy Street, *everybody* was afraid of Junior's daddy. At 6'5 and with long, wide arms, Senior was too much man for one person to handle. Nobody fucked with Leonard Gerard Robinson Sr.

Not even the dickhead cops who patrolled Brooke's Rowe. They called for backup when dealing with him. Three squad cars—maybe four. He barely laughed, smiled, or joked, Junior's daddy. One Halloween, Sandy dressed him up in overalls, a plaid shirt and stood him in front of the house with his axe and no decorations. That year, the city awarded the Robinsons $500 as the second most terrifying house on their block. For two hours, all he did was stare at visitors. The man was terrifying, period.

As Senior stood in the doorway, Junior dropped his head. He reminded Junior of the comic book villains he used to read about as a child. His daddy unbolted the screen door and scowled at him.

"Sup, Daddy?" Junior slowly raised his eyes. "I know it's been a while and everything, and uh… *how you been,* man?" his voice suddenly gave up on him.

"Where you been?" Senior asked him. His voice penetrated through Junior's shoes.

"I been a little busy."

"Yeah, you been busy sho' nuff. Busy chasin' Vanessa's pussy all over New York City. You been using them condoms like you supposed to?"

"Of course, Daddy," Junior lied.

Senior looked over his son's head at Sandy's old car.

"How's the car runnin'? No more tickets, I hope?"

"Just that one," Junior lied again. He had accrued six total. Casey paid them all to keep Senior from killing him. The first one, a parking ticket for $200, nearly got Junior beheaded.

"How's the writin' comin' along? You still doin' it?"

"Not as much as I should," Junior admitted. "I just been so busy."

"Well, don't be too busy. You see where that got you." Senior shook his head. He then moved to the side. "Go'on inside. Your momma's been waitin' on ya. It's been a long time, son. Don't leave us like that again."

"I won't, Daddy," Junior agreed.

Something about returning home to Sandy's meatloaf with cornbread and collard greens was reviving to Junior. Above the sink on the kitchen windowsill was a janky-ass, hand-held radio Sandy had had since she was a teenager. All it took was four double-A batteries from the drugstore, and it'd play all night long. Right in the middle of the dining room table was a container of cherry Kool-Aid, just like Junior remembered it. One glass of Sandy's sweet beverage could turn a healthy man into a diabetic. Back when Junior was little, he'd drink a full glass and eat a handful of chocolate chip cookies. "Junior!" his momma would say to him. "Don't you eat all of those cookies and drink that Kool-Aid like that. You're gonna get the sugars!" That night, Junior drank so much of Sandy's Kool-Aid that his mouth turned red. He also ate two full meals. Casey, bless her heart, couldn't cook worth a damn. After dinner, Sandy cleared Junior's plate for him.

Since Junior had left for New York, Sandy Robinson had retired from the post office after twenty-three years of service. At the time of her illness, she had enough time to go but chose to stay on. Against management's wishes, she limped into work every day and went to physical therapy in the evenings. When asked why she continued to work, Sandy's goal was clear. "Is y'all crazy?" she looked at her supervisors as if they were nuts. "I got Junior's tuition comin' up!"

Up until the Robinsons' final payment to Langston High, with one arm cupped into a half-fist, and the other one holding a cane, Sandy worked her faithful mail route in North Philly. On her last day on the job, Junior, Vanessa, Casey, Senior, and Sandy's co-workers all threw her a surprise party as she arrived back at the post office. She sat inside of her mail truck, 0808, for nearly twenty minutes before climbing out. Her family and curious co-workers all watched with worry, waiting for Sandy. Senior offered an ageless explanation. "Sometimes, you just wanna talk to the good Lord for a little bit," he said. The room conceded in awe of his insight. When Sandy finally made her way inside, her supporters leapt from behind the counter with balloons and cake. She placed her hand over her heart.

"What y'all doin'? Tryin' to give me a heart attack or somethin'?" she whined.

Senior walked over to his wife and kissed her. "Well done, Boobie," he said.

The room offered Sandy a standing ovation, a plaque, and named her Postal Worker of the Year. When Junior presented his momma with the plaque, she cried right there. The sugary gesture made Casey cry which of course made Junior cry. Vanessa cried next. Senior didn't cry. He

146

never did. He looked on but with a slight smile of awe in celebration of his wife.

After clearing Junior's plate, Sandy returned to the dinner table next to Senior who was just finishing his meal. He pushed his empty dish to the side and grunted before removing a pack of Newports from his breast pocket. He tore off the seal and slapped the pack against his big palm as a single cigarette fell out. He placed it in his grim mouth and walked over to the stove to light it. It drove Sandy crazy whenever Junior's daddy would do that.

"Dammit, Leonard!" Sandy fussed. "Why can't you use a lighter like everybody else?"

Senior took a puff of his favorite snack and exhaled a cloud of smoke into the kitchen air. Afterward, he shared his snack with Sandy. Since Lawrence had died, Sandy had started smoking again, despite her stroke. Junior looked at his momma with dissatisfaction. As the nicotine hit her system, she melted in her chair like an addict. She trimmed her eyes at Junior.

"Don't be lookin' at me like that." She blew from the side of her cheek. "I need this." Her eyebrows raised. "I been under a lot of stress lately."

"That's just an excuse," Junior said, rolling his eyes. "The doctor said you shouldn't be smokin'."

Sandy dipped her cigarette into a porcelain ashtray and gave it back to Senior.

"Well, maybe if you ain't get my car towed last night, I wouldn't need to smoke. Would I?"

Junior's mouth popped open.

"Don't you make that face!" She glared at him. "The car is still registered to me, knucklehead. What'd you think—I wasn't gonna find out? The tow yard called us this mornin' to tell us about the car. I figured you done got into somethin'. So, I called Casey, and she told me what happened. She tried to cover for you, but I got it out of her. I know 'bout all those damn tickets, too."

Junior shifted his eyes over at his daddy. Senior stared back at him with an undertaker's glare.

"Don't nobody got no money for no tow, Junior. Things are tight as it is."

"I know, Ma," he said. "Look, it was an accident."

"Accident, my ass!" Senior tagged himself in. "Hear me? Accident-my-ass."

"I didn't see the sign. It was dark. I didn't even know it was there."

"Casey said Stevie Wonder could've saw that goddamn sign, Junior," Senior fussed. "You got to be more careful with what you're doin'. And what you doin' ridin' 'round in some car with some people you don't know nothin' 'bout? I taught you better than that."

"Those were Vanessa's friends from back in the day."

"I told you a long time ago *ain't* no real friends out here in the world. Hear me? Half the people walkin' 'round in the world ain't worth a jack shit! You'd be better off gettin' you a *dog* or somethin'," Senior told him. "You goin' fuck 'round and end up like your damn uncle—and you gonna pay Casey

148

back." He pointed with his cigarette wedged between his fingers. "Every goddamn nickel, Junior. If you ain't gonna do right, then leave that car here and walk to school—I don't give a goddamn. Hear me? And the next time you lie to me, I'm gonna put my foot up your ass."

"I got it, Daddy," Junior flattened.

"Also," Sandy returned, "the weekends are supposed to be our time, Junior. You ain't been here in almost a month. We know things get busy from time to time, but check on us once in a while. You barely call unless we call you. We're your family. Leonard and I are gettin' old, son. We could use your good presence once in a while."

"I'll do better, Ma. Promise."

Junior's parents finally backed off. Before leaving the dinner table, Senior leaned over to kiss his wife goodnight. He glowered at Junior as he bypassed his son. His big feet went thumping up the steps. When the door closed, Sandy reached inside of her shirt and handed Junior two hundred dollars in cash. She placed the money in Junior's hand and held it close.

"What's this for?"

"SHHHHH," she shushed Junior, chopping at the air. "Don't tell 'em I gave it to you. Lord knows that man will raise *hell* if he finds out about that two hundred dollars. Put it in your pocket."

Junior tucked the money inside of his pants. He smiled at his momma.

"Thanks, Ma," he said. "Sorry for all the trouble this weekend."

Sandy held onto Junior's hand.

"Now, you listen to me," she whispered. "What happened last night can't happen again. You're all I got, Junior. I talked to Casey this mornin'. She's really worried about you, and I am too," she said. "I need you to focus, Junior. Now, I don't know what's goin' on up there, but you better fix it…before it fixes you."

As Sandy got up from the table to wash the dishes, Junior met her at the sink.

"I'll finish these," he said.

"I got it, Junior, let me—"

"I got it, Ma!" he raised his tone, respectfully. "I got it. You go relax."

Sandy placed her hand on Junior's shoulder and walked off, leaving him at the sink to wash. Behind him, Junior could feel his momma watching him at the door. She eventually hobbled upstairs for the night. Overwhelmed, Junior leaned over the sink and exhaled. With one week of college down, he had four more years to go, he thought.

When the dishes were clean, Junior retired to his old bedroom for the night and closed his door. He turned on his light and laughed to himself as he reminisced on the precious memories of his not-so-distant childhood. On the back of his bedroom door was a poster for the movie, *House Party* starring Kid-N-Play. It was Junior's favorite movie as a kid. Across the room was a huge Michael Jackson poster and another of Whitney Houston performing "The Star-Spangled Banner" at Superbowl XXV. Time had aged his prized belongings. Beneath his bed was a container full of poetry books he had written not long after Lawrence passed. Atop his dresser was a picture of Junior and his baby brother at a football game some years back. Junior picked up the photo, kissed it, and returned it to his nightstand. He turned off the light and climbed into bed. As he lay there, thinking, his cell phone began to ring. It was Vanessa, likely calling to talk about the other night. Junior silenced his phone. *Not tonight*, he thought.

Roses Are for Sissies

Junior snailed throughout his shift down at the Mart that Sunday after returning from his weekend break in Brooke's Rowe. He was on time but missing the zeal and charisma he was known for. Concerned, Mr. Wilkinson pulled him to the side. "I'm good, Boss," Junior told the man. "Can I get back to work?" Junior figured the boss knew something was off. Thankfully, he didn't press it.

At the registers, Junior rung up customers but seldom smiled. He even volunteered to sweep the lot that evening. It was weird to everybody there but him. With his broom and dustpan, he dragged his feet along and swept up debris where he could. He slugged to the dumpster to empty it.

For his dinner break, Junior preferred to work instead of eating. The only break he took was to use the bathroom. "Junior," Mr. Wilkinson stopped him. "You got to take a break, man. I don't need another EEOC complaint on my ass, please." Junior sat in the breakroom that evening, but he didn't eat. Instead, he played Snake on his phone with his head propped against his fist. At the end of his shift, the boss called Junior into his office. *Great, now I'm gettin' fired*? he wondered.

"I never seen this side of you before," said Mr. Wilkinson. "Now, if there's somethin' wrong, I can't help you if I don't know about it. You need some money or somethin'?"

"No, sir, but thank you," said Junior. "Just havin' a rough day, man."

As Junior turned to leave, the boss met him at the door.

"You know somethin'," Mr. Wilkinson said. "I think I know what's been botherin' you. I can only guess at my age."

The boss tapped Junior's heart.

"It's somethin' in there, ain't it?"

"Damn, you're pretty good," Junior laughed. "How'd you know?"

"What'd you think I'm old for?" Mr. Wilkinson grinned. "I've been there. Whatever it is, it'll get better, OK? Just hold your head up."

"Yes, sir." Junior smiled. He hadn't smiled all day.

The boss walked from the warehouse over to the florist section and gave Junior a set of beautiful calla lilies.

"Why don't you give her some of these bad boys, Junior? Take 'em. It's on the house."

Junior took the flowers and cheesed.

"Thanks, Mr. Wilkinson," he said. "I know exactly who could use these right now."

Junior left and returned home to Casey.

When Junior got in, he arrived to find Casey asleep on the couch. Her reading glasses were hanging from her face. On the floor beside her was her workbook. She had fallen asleep studying for her placement exam once again. Playing on the TV was *Living Single*, one of her favorite shows of all-time. Like the typical young student, she preferred to study with the TV on, or some kind of noise. She was immature but mature at the same time.

Quietly, Junior removed the vase from the coffee table and placed Casey's lilies inside of the dish. He removed her glasses and placed them inside of the case which was on the floor next to the book. Junior then wrapped Casey in her New York Jets blanket. He tucked it beneath her chin the way she liked it. Casey moaned as her eyes slowly opened. "Shhhh!" he patted his sissy on the arm. "Go back to sleep." Casey closed her eyes and turned over. The couch squeaked under her weight. Junior opened his wallet and placed the money his momma gave him next to the lilies. He gently stroked Casey's hair. "Take it easy, Sissy," he whispered.

Before heading up for the night, he surveyed their living room full of artifacts from their years together. On a table in the foyer was a portrait of him and Casey on the day he graduated from Langston High. It was Casey's favorite picture in the whole house. Junior lifted the oak frame and stared at it. It made him laugh. Her eyes were closed in the photo. The photo next to it was a picture of him, Casey, Courtney, Brother Gay, and his parents. Brother Gay, his old teacher, had since moved back to Cleveland to care for his ill mother. Meanwhile Courtney, Casey's sister, had got deployed to the Middle East where she had been stationed not long after Junior moved there.

Junior's favorite photo was in a picture book which sat atop the entertainment cabinet. The photo was of he and Casey at dinner celebrating her remission. He could remember the day Casey had been diagnosed with cancer like it was yesterday. He came home from school one afternoon and found his sissy on the kitchen floor. The news was devastating. "I have breast cancer!" she said, shattered, barely able to get it out. "Fuck, man! What am I gonna do?" For the next week, Casey cried herself to sleep on the sofa. Junior slept beside her on the floor, not leaving her side. When Junior returned home from Langston that Friday, he found her sitting outside on the steps.

"I need a favor, J." She held his hands. "It's big. Whatever you do, please don't tell your family about the diagnosis—not yet. I don't want them to worry. You got it, man?"

Junior placed Casey's hand against his heart.

"I got you, Sissy," Junior told her. "Not a word."

Somehow, the two managed to keep her cancer a secret from Junior's parents. Casey worried that if the Robinsons found out, it could ruin his opportunity at Langston. Even on her worst day, she was still looking out for her brother. Junior made it to every single one of her chemotherapy trips, and on the days he visited his family, he didn't utter a word of their secret. Eventually, Casey's cancer went into remission, and so did their secret. With little money to spare, the two celebrated at an IHOP in Queens. Junior pulled out an old polaroid camera and asked a stranger to snap their photo. As Casey covered her face, Junior pecked her on the cheek. She broke down in tears.

"God, I hate you!" she sniffled. "You always make me cry!"

The words echoed inside of Junior's soul as he held the photo with tears in his eyes. He walked over to Casey and stood behind her as she slept peacefully. He spoke to her as if she was still awake. "I won't let you down," he whispered.

Junior went upstairs and sat at his work desk. He turned on his computer and started his homework. He opened his anatomy book and began to read but couldn't find a chapter on the feeling in his heart. He flipped through his book, acknowledging the artsy photos inside of it. Suddenly, Casey appeared at Junior's door. In her hand were the lilies and the money Junior left her.

"Hey," she said.

"Hey." Junior turned in his chair to face her. "Didn't expect you to be up. I know you've been studyin' like crazy. Are you OK?"

"Better now." Casey shrugged. "Thanks for the money— and the lilies. They're beautiful."

"You're welcome, Sissy. Anytime."

Casey grinned at Junior. "Can I come in?"

"Of course."

Casey entered Junior's room and took a seat on his bed behind him. Casey looked at Junior. Junior looked back at her. In a show of silent forgiveness, the two of them laughed. They couldn't be serious if their lives depended on it.

"Can I sit next to you, Casey?" Junior asked her.

"Of course, J.," she chuckled. "I'm not an alligator, man. Get over here."

Junior sat next to Casey on the bed. She placed her arms around the boy and held him. She leaned her head onto his.

"I forgive you," she said. "OK? We straight?"

"Yeah, we straight. Thanks, Casey. I needed that," he sighed. "Yo, I was buggin' the whole weekend at my parents. I can't have you mad at me. You know that."

Casey released Junior and held him by his hands.

"Listen, you're gonna make mistakes up here, I know that. You're still a kid. Things are gonna be fucked up some-times, but you gotta learn from your mistakes and move on. I'm not gonna keep bailing you out of trouble, J. I meant what I said the other night about having my own life to live. You gotta do better, man. You and Vanessa. C'mon, don't make me go crazy on you!" she placed her brother into a headlock. "I'm still your big sissy. I run this! All good?"

"Yeah, it's all good," Junior surrendered. "Thanks, Sissy."

As Casey went to leave, she stopped at his door.

"Don't forget what I said, J."

"About you runnin' this?" he asked.

"Before that," she said. "You've got to be the one to make the improvements in your life, Junior—you. No one can make those decisions for you. Only you can," she told him.

Casey pulled Junior's door shut, leaving him to mettle over her wisdom. For Junior, the writing was on the wall, literally. He looked over at the pictures of he and Vanessa on his wall and groaned with displeasure. Indeed, Junior had a lot of improvements to make.

Nine

Our love is a deck of cards I can't fathom.
I will never understand this hand. What is our plan?
Are you my ace? Am I your mighty king? Are you my queen?
Let the voices in the choir all sing something melodramatic.
With you its automatic. I can't separate
from all of our mistakes.
It's hard to say no to your beautiful face.
It's hell to incorporate those boundaries needed
when I'm constantly thinking about needing you.
What to do?
When all that I want in this world is you.

—LEONARD G. ROBINSON JR.

Junior couldn't stand the sight of Professor Freemont. He stopped midway through his lecture and cheered upon realizing Junior finally had the correct book. The lemmings followed suit, all but one.

"Hooray for Junior!" Mr. Freemont raised his arms. "The book gives you about a fifty-fifty chance of actually passing the course at this point." Freemont was a son-of-a-bitch of a teacher: arrogant and condescending. He called one girl a loser for spelling "ventricle" incorrectly on a quiz, and called another guy a dork for wanting to be a veterinarian. Despite his fuckery, the students found his crudeness humorous. Junior didn't and neither did his creepy neighbor from the other day, Rachel. She showed her braces to him for much of the afternoon.

When Junior's classes ended for the day, he returned to the concourse level and recognized an old friend performing spoken word out in front of the building. It was the Trolling Poet he'd seen on his first day the week prior. A crowd of students and faculty was formed around him. Junior pushed his way outside to get a glimpse of his most favorite artist to date. The kid wowed his audience with his words. He was dressed in a pair of rundown sneakers, jeans, a dirty sweatshirt and a heavy coat with gloves. It was eccentric fashion for September in the big city. He looked as if he was homeless. Beside him was a big, ugly suitcase. In his hand was a jar with a pickle inside and a newspaper. Junior squeezed his way through the crowd to get a closer look. He nudged a girl beside him, asking for the kid's name.

"Don't know, but he's incredible!" the girl said. "Why do you think he's dressed like that? Everybody thinks somethin' might be wrong with 'em."

Junior disagreed. The troll's lyrics were magnetic, a far improvement from Tony's demo tape Friday night.

Public drunkenness. Disorderly conduct.
Failure to obey a lawful order.
Th'hell with this new world order.
He must be a crazy old fool, a tool,
who breaks every rule at this school.
He failed in life. He fucked up.
That's why he is where he is with nowhere to live.
I'll never understand, the food that the fortunate
toss into the garbage can.
Half-eaten meat that I struggle to find
while living out on these streets.
If we're the most powerful nation
why are resources so discreet?
Why are the elite so cheap?
Why do they perpetuate such hate
for the mistakes that they make every single day?
Why are the corrupt so stuck on not giving a fuck?

Without a word or as much as a "thank you", the Troll picked up his belongings and left. Some laughed at his eeriness, and few awed over his complexity and sick rhyme scheme. Junior chose the latter.

Determined to meet him, Junior pursued the enigmatic artist. He tailed him throughout the building down to the men's bathroom. Junior waited for him like an obsessed groupie. Minutes later, the kid left the bathroom dressed like a normal college student: sneakers, T-shirt, jeans, a cap on his head. Junior barely recognized him. If not for his ugly suitcase, Junior could've easily missed him. Suddenly, it made sense. The clothes. The poem about homelessness. The jar with the pickle—a tribute to Damon Wayans playing the homeless character from *In Living Color*. The newspaper. The kid didn't have a problem; he was a genius. Junior chased him down to the lunchroom.

"Yo! Wait up!" he called to him, shuffling through his peers. "Hey! Hey, you!"

Junior caught up to the cagey poet, cornering him near the lunchroom. The kid looked on at Junior with an inert expression, unimpressed.

"*Damn*, you walk fast," Junior breathed heavily. "Anyway, my name's Junior. Yo, how'd you get so good? Where does that come from?" he asked.

"Practice," the nameless poet told him, his face barely changing.

"That's it? Man, you did all that and you're tellin' me it's just practice?!"

"What else would it be?" the kid said. "Nice to meet you, Junior, but I have to—"

"Wait-wait-wait," Junior stopped him. "What's your name? At least tell me your name. It can't just be practice. I listened to every lyric out there, and the ones from last week. You can't fool a fellow artist, OK?" Junior patted his chest. "The heavy clothes in the summer. The newspaper. The jar with the pickle. The lyrics about feeling rejected by America. People think you're crazy—but you ain't crazy. Nah, not at all."

The kid looked at Junior, impressed. He nodded his head.

161

"This is my fourth time doing that poem this year, and no one ever got it," he said. "I'm Parris, but my poet name is Prophet. That was a good catch, Junior."

"Uh, thanks." Junior smiled. "I used to do spoken word at Langston High, but I got distracted and fell off. I wanna get back to it. So, what's up? Are you from New York? Where you from, man? Look, I ain't weird or no shit like that," he told him. "I just wanna get to know you and learn how it is you do your thing. Can you teach me?"

"Did you say you went to Langston?" Parris asked.

"Yeah, why?"

"Great school," he said. "I can't help you though, Junior."

"Why not?"

"You just said that you were distracted, which means you're not serious," Parris told him. "How can you be any good if you don't practice?" Parris asked him. "Sorry, Junior. Take care of yourself, man."

Just like that, Parris disappeared from Junior's life again. He took a seat inside the lunchroom at a table by himself. Junior thought of chasing after him again but decided against it. As he turned to leave, his gummy neighbor from anatomy, Rachel, appeared beside him. She had little teeth which made her braces appear huge. The thought of kissing her was almost as nauseating as the gooey diaper Junior had swept up in the lot outside of the Mart.

"Hi, neighbor!" She smiled warmly at him. Rachel fingered through her blonde hair. "I was just about to catch up with a friend if you're interested. You busy?"

"Hey, neighbor," Junior sighed. "Maybe another time?"

"Hmph. Well, suit yourself."

Junior shuddered as Rachel passed by him. He turned to leave and was shocked to find Vanessa standing there behind him. Her arms were crossed with discontentment as she gave Junior a piercing look. The two hadn't spoken since Saturday morning. Junior had ducked her all weekend.

"Vanessa, hey!" Junior waved awkwardly.

"Don't 'hey' me, Junior." She looked at him glaringly. "Where were you on Saturday night because I called you. I even left a message, where have you been? Didn't you get my message? You weren't even on the Messenger last night. We normally talk on Instant Messenger on Sunday nights. So, you're just gonna avoid me now?"

"I told you I was gonna see my folks, and that I had to work, V."

"Yeah, whatever. So, who's the white girl? The one I just saw you talkin' to—who's she?"

"Who? Rachel?" Junior grabbed her hand. "Just a girl in my anatomy class. C'mon, V. I've been with family just trying to chill out since Friday night. I worked 'til late on Sunday. Why are you buggin'? It's not even like that."

Vanessa let off the gas. "Well, I hope not." She moved into hug him. "Yo, I been a mess all weekend thinkin' about what happened. You could've called me, J. It would've been nice to hear from you. You just dropped my stuff off and left."

Junior kissed her hand. He hid his contempt for Vanessa well.

"I didn't mean to leave you hangin' all weekend. I just needed a little time to clear my head. I'm sorry, V., OK? Can we just let this whole thing go and move on?"

"Son, how can I when I feel like you've been avoiding me?"

Junior gazed into Vanessa's eyes. He lowered his voice to a murmur. "Will you stop fuckin' worryin' about losin' me, V.? Just for once?"

Vanessa's eyes dampened. "There I go, again," she sighed. "I'm sorry, Junior. I still wanna make it up to you for Friday. Oh, I got some money for you to give to Casey. You know, for the car? Here, let me get it for you."

"Don't worry about it. Keep it."

"Well, can I at least treat you to lunch somewhere?"

"Actually, I was thinkin' about surprising Casey down at her job. She's taking her placement exam today. You know if she passes, the government is supposed to pay for her to go back to school. I thought it'd be a nice way to say sorry for dragging her out of the house late. Plus, I gotta work later."

"That's a great idea, J. In fact, yo, we can grab a bite to eat downtown and then you can go meet up with Casey. That's perfect."

Junior didn't plan on meeting up with Casey that afternoon. It had seemed like a good excuse to get Vanessa off his back. His heart was still in limbo over the relationship.

"How about tomorrow, or Wednesday?" Junior offered.

"I'm busy those days," she laughed. "Why don't you let

me treat you? Just a quick bite."

"What about Thursday?"

"Wow! Really, J.? Why can't we just go today? We could kill two birds with one stone. Don't you trust me anymore?" she laughed at him. "Son, I know I messed up on Friday, but I'm tryin' to fix it. C'mon, J. Work with me."

Junior finally conceded.

"You're right. What am I even trippin' for?" he asked himself. "Friday is gone. We can't get it back. Even Casey said that things won't always be perfect, you know? We both messed up last Friday, but we acknowledged that shit. Now, it's time to move on."

"Deadass," Vanessa grinned. "Yo, I know a nice place downtown we can go chill at. You'll love it. We'll catch the train down. Afterward, you can head over to see Casey."

"You know the vibe," Junior adopted one of her slang lines, winking at her.

Fight 4 Love

I'm a hopeless love-addict.
My world is forever fascinated with love.
Even though love doesn't love me back,
I still love love as if love was another person.
The thought of being alone is devastating.
So, I'm in love with love.
Love saves me from me.

So, repeat after me.
I'm a hopeless love-addict.

—LEONARD G. ROBINSON JR.

Junior tried to put out of his mind the anguish Vanessa had put him through last Friday night. Together on the train, he stared through the glass at the flicker of New York City commuters, reflecting on their relationship. He propped his head against the glass as Vanessa packed tightly beside Junior, leaning on him. She looped his arm around her. She was clearly beyond their latest debacle. Vanessa rubbed him throughout the ride, indifferent to the other riders wedged tightly on the train beside them. Touch was Vanessa's love language, and she required it often regardless of where they were, or if Junior was in the mood. While in public, she'd lay across his lap sometimes or want to snuggle. She'd feel on Junior's thigh, tracing her finger across his tool. It was cute somedays. Other times, it bothered him. Once, at the movies, Vanessa's touchiness led to her head in Junior's lap with his jacket being draped over her. Junior spilled half of his popcorn that day. Like most of the concerns in their relationship, he took a passive approach to addressing their problems. Thus, Vanessa never truly got the memo. Riding into Midtown Manhattan that afternoon was no different. She slipped her hand beneath Junior's shirt and began feeling his chest. Junior grabbed her wrist to stop her.

"Yo, we're on the subway, V., chill out," he laughed.

166

Vanessa removed her hand from beneath Junior's shirt and placed it on his leg. She moaned succulently, rubbing against his thigh.

"Oooh," she fingered his girth through his jeans. "I'm sooo wet right now. C'mon, let's find somewhere!"

"In this nasty-ass subway? Shiiiit."

"But I haven't had my meds in a few days. I'm goin' through withdrawal, Doctor," she giggled. "Son, remember when we did it under the tarp inside of my mother's car? Remember that? My parents came in the garage, and I was scared as hell. That shit was so much fun."

"Yeah, you always like to do that white people shit," Junior chuckled. "Aight, we'll hop off and see what's around. It's gotta be quick though. Don't be makin' a lot of noise and shit either, V. You know how you get."

"Son, whatever!" Vanessa roared.

When the train stopped, the two blended through the crowded tunnel hoping to find a decent spot to satisfy their desires. New York's filthy transit system didn't offer much. A bathroom further up the subway's platform seemed promising. Attached to the door was an "Out of order" sign. Junior removed the cone in front of the door and went in to check it out. The floor was wet and covered in old newspaper clippings and soiled toilet paper. A large rat swam across before disap-pearing through a crack in the wall beneath an overflowing urinal. Junior returned to Vanessa immediately. His face was green with doubt.

"Let's do this another time," Junior suggested.

"Nooo, let's keep looking, J. There's gotta be someplace down here."

The two struck gold when they found an open janitor's closet further up the platform. They sidestepped the bustling crowd, slipped inside and closed the door behind them. The only light was the subtle glow from inside the subway.

"Yo, this is so dope! I love doin' shit like this, J. Where are you?" she asked.

The two went in for a kiss and bumped heads.

"Right here—ow!" he laughed. "Damn, V. You and that big-ass dome of yours."

"Fuck you. C'mere," Vanessa grabbed Junior by his face and kissed him.

Junior tasted Vanessa's citrus-flavored lip-gloss as he backed her against the door. She loosened Junior's belt buckle and grasped him through the slit of his boxers. She lowered her panties and braced herself against the wall. Junior rubbed his veiny will against Vanessa's vagina, teasing and smacking her as she arched and moaned with contempt. She grabbed his steel rod and jammed it inside of her. "Ah—oh, my God—Junior!" Vanessa panted as she palmed the wall. Suddenly, the two were interrupted by the sound of a masculine cough. Junior shriveled instantly.

"Th'fuck was that?" Junior whispered.

"I thought that was you!" said Vanessa. "That wasn't you?"

Quickly, the two got dressed. Vanessa reached for a lighted keychain inside of her purse and shined it throughout the room. The light hit upon a row of metal shelves stacked with disinfectants and other cleaning supplies. A slumbering snore startled the two again. Vanessa handed Junior her keychain. "Fuck that—you look!" she told him. With Vanessa on his arm, Junior traced the noise to the back of the room and found a napping city worker knocked out in a metal folding chair. The guy looked like Bookman from the 1970s show, *Goodtimes*. He rested with his arms folded and his head slumped forward. Bookman was dressed in a navy-blue uniform with black boots. He snored terribly. Unable to contain themselves, Junior and Vanessa covered their hoots. Vanessa's light went wagging throughout the room.

"V., watch this!" Junior told her.

"Junior, no!" Vanessa wheezed. "That man has been workin' hard all day—leave 'em alone!"

Junior knocked down a row of cleansing cans onto the floor and shut off Vanessa's light. The cans rolled throughout the darkened room as the two snickered like elves. Bookman grunted and woke up.

"Ay? Who that? Ay?!" Bookman said. "Willy, that you? Willy?"

Junior's stomach twisted in knots. Vanessa's legs were so weak, he had to hold her up. Unable to contain themselves, their laughs escaped them. Suddenly, Bookman turned on the light.

"You goddamn little kids!" Bookman barked. "Why don't y'all get the hell outta here!"

Junior and Vanessa darted out into the city's subway system, breathless.

Déjà vu

Déjà vu. Déjà vu. Déjà vu.
All I wanna do is be with you.

—LEONARD G. ROBINSON JR.

With their laughs behind them, Junior and Vanessa lolly-gagged throughout Midtown Manhattan like old times. Junior stood at the base of a street post and wheeled himself in a full circle. "Wheeee!" he snickered. "Get a shot of this, V." Vanessa looked inside of her bag and shrugged; she hadn't carried her polaroid in months. Junior hopped off onto the asphalt. Their short walk ended at a Footlocker shoe store instead of lunch as Vanessa had proposed earlier. They stopped to kiss in front of customers and staff at the door, unapologetic about their love for one another. Afterward, Junior veered to the men's section.

On the wall behind the register, was a pair of silver-and-black Nike Bo Jackson sneakers. Junior had once owned a pair but returned them after kids teased him. He lifted the gorgeous shoe from the rack and checked out the price. The shoes went for $160. Junior opened his wallet to take a look. Inside was eleven dollars, a backup key to his car, lint, and an outdated condom. He returned the shoe back to its rack as Vanessa appeared beside him.

"Those are dope; you'd look hot in these, J. You gettin' 'em?" she asked.

"Nah," said Junior, staring up at the shoes. "I used to have a pair, though."

"Why'd you get rid of 'em?"

"I don't know," he shrugged. He looked down at his watch. "I guess I should probably get over to Casey soon before I have to be in at work."

"OK, I wanna look around a little more. Can you wait for me outside?"

Outside, Junior leaned against the brick wall with his hands shoved inside of his pockets. As much as he wanted those damn shoes, he was somewhat happy he didn't have the cash to get them. The pair he used to own got him bullied so badly he returned them. Minutes later, Vanessa exited the store with a Footlocker bag. She handed it to Junior. Stunned, he reached out to take it.

"What's this?" He peeked inside.

"It's a gift, duh!" Vanessa laughed. "Well, aren't you gonna open it?"

Eyeing her, Junior removed the bag and opened the box. Inside were the Bo Jackson sneakers. His heart swelled at the thoughtful gesture. Junior stared at Vanessa with renewed faith. She touched his face.

"Just a little token of my appreciation for you. Sorry about Friday, J."

Junior placed the box back inside the bag.

"I don't know what to say, V.," he told her. "Are you sure about this?"

"I'm always sure when it comes to you, Leonard Robinson. You're a such a good dude, man. Real and authentic. If more guys were like you—and puttin' it down the way you do, girls would be happier and there would be world peace!"

Junior blushed as he leaned in to kiss her. There heavenly moment was soon interrupted by a group of youths who came thugging up the sidewalk. The kids quickly surrounded the two, cussing and threatening bodily harm. Confused, Junior removed his arm from around Vanessa. He stood in front of her. Before long, one of the miscreants stepped forward. Junior recognized the kid as one of Tony's passengers from Friday night.

"Word is bond, these the motherfuckas that snitched on us the other night, son," the boy said. "Small world, you bitch-ass nigga. Knew I was gonna catch up with you eventually. Son was talkin' mad shit the other night. Now what, nigga?"

The kid pulled out a knife and slashed Junior across the hand. Junior dropped his bag in agony, clutching his bloody hand. Vanessa picked up the bag and flung it at the kid, striking him in the face.

"J., run!" She pushed him along.

The two raced towards the subway as the summer air cut through Junior's wound. It bled and throbbed during their escape. The pain was intense. Junior inadvertently plowed through an old man, knocking him to the ground. The poor guy fell backward, striking his head on the pavement. "You're a fuckin' scumbag for that, you muddafucka," a pedestrian barked at Junior. A cyclist suffered a similar fate when their accosters pushed him off his bicycle into the roadway. Bystanders were hollering and screaming as many careened out of their path. Their pursuers chased Junior and Vanessa into an alley. At the end was a tall, chain link fence. Junior and Vanessa sprinted toward the gate to climb it. A dicing pain ripped through Junior's nervous system as his wound touched the wiry steel. It seared as if on fire. Near the top, Junior's shirt got caught on an exposed wire; it hooked right through the fabric. Behind them, the group was closing in on the two. The kid holding the knife was leading the pack.

"V., I'm stuck!" Junior panicked. "Shit, I can't move!"

Quickly, Vanessa scrambled back to the top to help free him. Meanwhile, the group went after Junior's flailing legs, trying to pull him down. He kicked one of the kids square in the jaw and booted a second in the face. His attacker flailed the knife at his leg and missed. The second swing nicked Junior on the ankle. Lucky for him, he was wearing jeans that day. The blade was so sharp it sliced through the bottom leg of his pants.

"Shit, it won't come loose!" Vanessa cried.

As Vanessa struggled to free him, lucky for Junior, the wire tore through his shirt setting him free. Junior delivered a swift and final kick to his tormenter. With Vanessa's help, he overtook the gate and landed hard onto the pavement. During the fall, he scraped his injured hand across a row of gravel. He screamed so loud that his momma could've heard him. Vanessa grabbed him by his holey shirt, lifting him up. The two zipped across the roadway and into the subway tunnel before blending in with commuters.

Exhausted and in pain, Junior's hand dripped on the floor of the train as germaphobe riders scurried out of his way. He rocked back and forth, holding his hand. It throbbed to all hell. He breathed through his clenched teeth, it hurt him so badly.

"Let me see it, J." Vanessa pulled at his arm. "C'mere. Let me see."

Junior placed his bloody hand onto her lap. The gash extended from Junior's ring finger inside his left palm and across his hand. He fanned and blew into the wound hoping to cool down its sizzling sensation. Still, it continued to burn.

"Take your shirt off," Vanessa told him, digging through her purse frantically. "C'mon, Junior. Hurry! I don't want it to get infected."

With his arm outstretched, Junior removed his T-shirt and handed it to Vanessa. She left him in a tank top. She tore the shirt in half as curious passengers looked on. She cleaned out the captured debris from Junior's fall as he winced in pain. Vanessa then pulled out an alcohol swab as Junior scooted away.

"I'll wait 'til I get home," he told her.

"J., I *have* to." Vanessa reached for it. "It could get infected."

Reluctant at first, Junior returned his hand back to Vanessa's lap. She gave him the other half of his ripped shirt. He placed it inside of his mouth and bit down as hard as he could. Vanessa removed an alcohol swab from her pack. "I'll make this quick," she told him. She placed the swab onto Junior's gash and began to blot it. He yelped, twisting and turning in distress "I know—I know, I'm almost done," she told him. "Just hold on, J." Junior's eyes welled with tears, it burned so badly. Vanessa removed the half of Junior's shirt from his mouth and wrapped it around his hand like a torniquet and double-knotted it. Junior flexed his fingers, impressed by her combat dressing.

"That should hold 'til you get home," Vanessa sighed. "You OK, Junior?"

Junior stared at the torn gray shirt wrapped around his hand. His wound burned almost as badly as his searing thoughts. There he was again, he thought to himself: caught in Vanessa's shit. He used his pinky to gently prod at his hand, checking his pain tolerance. Each touch made it ache.

"Stop, don't mess with it!" Vanessa held him. "It should hold for a while. An Advil or Ibuprofen should help with the pain, J."

Junior lowered his hand down to his side and looked over at Vanessa.

"Th'fuck was that?" he raised his voice. "What the fuck was that, V.? Huh?"

"What are you talkin' about?"

"You know what I'm talkin' bout—this!" Junior held up his hand. "Damn, it's like every time we're together somethin' happens. Look at this shit, man. I gotta go home and my sister's gonna be asking me about ten thousand fuckin' questions."

"But we weren't doing anything wrong. They started with *us*, J. Look, I know you're upset, but you really ought to take it easy." Vanessa touched him. "You're just gonna make the pain worse."

Junior pulled away from her. He leapt to his feet. "Man, I should've gone to see Casey. I should've known better than to be fuckin' around with you!"

"What?" Vanessa's lips began to curl. "J., I didn't have anything to do with that—honest. Why would you say that to me?" She began to cry. "I didn't know that was gonna happen. Shit, they were after me too. We both were running for our lives back there. You got stuck; I came back. I helped you. I was just as scared as you—just like Friday night. I'm your girl, J.," she ugly cried. "You know me better than that. Son, I *always* held you down. Haven't I?!"

Junior shook his head at Vanessa. "Not anymore—not after today."

With her eyes glittery, Vanessa got off at the next stop. Junior watched as she hurried up the escalator. She wailed with her hand covering her face. They'd argue. They'd fuss. They'd even hang up on each another occasionally. As often as they'd fight, however, they'd make up for it. Not on that day. It was all over. Junior pounded the empty seat beside him. Fuck!

Ten

T'hell with falling in love.
Every time I fall, I break something and it hurts.

—LEONARD G. ROBINSON JR.

"Look, Ma, I can't talk right now. I'm already late for work," Junior told Sandy over his cell phone as he pulled up back at Casey's. Junior drove with one hand on the wheel and his phone wedged between his head and shoulder during the drive. He barely got a word in. If not for his momma yawning, she'd still be talking. Junior used the short break to escape. "I'll call you tonight when I—"

"I enjoyed you over the weekend. Did you make it to work on time?" she asked him.

"Yeah, Ma. Look, I really have to—"

"Didn't Casey take her exam today? Do you know if she passed?"

"Not yet. I haven't seen her."

"I am glad this New York thing is workin' out for y'all. By the way, I was talkin' to your auntie the other day. She sends her love, Junior. Her and her new husband," Sandy laughed. "She says that her foot's still botherin' her. You remember that fall she had last year?"

"Uh-huh."

"Uh-oh, hold on, I'm gettin' another call. Hang on one second, OK?

"Sure, Ma," Junior told her. "I'll hold."

Junior hung up as soon as his momma clicked over.

He eased up the staircase to the door and gently unbolted the lock, careful to avoid Casey. Her choir voice illuminated from the kitchen. She was cooking what smelled like burnt spaghetti, dancing and rapping to Lil' Kim. She appeared to be in a good mood. Quietly, Junior closed the door behind him and headed upstairs to deal with his hand before work. He made it to the third step before the wood creaked underneath him.

"Junior? That you?" Casey called to him.

He shot up the stairs into the bathroom and closed the door.

"Sorry, Sissy! I had tacos for lunch again!" Junior yelled.

He grabbed a can of Febreze and sprayed it throughout the bathroom. He flushed the toilet to sell his alibi to Casey. Junior turned on the sink and removed the dressing Vanessa applied earlier. If nothing else, she'd make a fine medic if college didn't work out. Junior tossed the wrapping on the sink beside him and placed his spent hand beneath the water. The soothing warmth provided immediate relief. Casey tapped on the door seconds later to check on him. Junior turned off the sink and stood next to the door.

"Yeah, Sissy?"

"Damn, I didn't even get a 'hello'. You wanna talk about it?"

"I can't right now, Sissy. Gotta get dressed for work."

Casey jiggled at the door handle.

"So, we're playin' this game again, I see," she said. "Open the door, J."

Junior leaned against the sink. He knew that if Casey saw his hand, she'd lose all of her mind at him *and* wanna slaughter Vanessa. Casey knocked on the door again.

"Don't make me be the bitch I was on Friday night. Let's not do that."

Junior hung his head, wishing for a secret tunnel to escape into without Casey seeing the hand. There was none. Before long, Casey pounded the bathroom door hard. BOOM-BOOM-BOOM. It startled Junior as he leapt from the sink. She was all business.

"Open my door, Junior!" she barked. "I'm not playin'. Open this motherfucker right now, or else I'm gonna kick it in."

Out of options, Junior unlocked the door and opened it. Casey was standing there on the other side waiting for him. Her hands were on her meaty hips. Her eyebrows slanted in anger.

"Th'hell is wrong with you today?" she asked him. "Why are you being stupid?"

Junior looked down at his injured hand and back up. Casey's eyes did the same.

"How'd you get that?"

Junior looked down at his hand again and back up at her. Casey crossed her arms and stood in the doorway, blocking

Junior from leaving the bathroom.

"I could give a shit if you gotta work. How'd you get that? Did Vanessa do that to you? I bet she was involved in some kind of way—wasn't she?"

Junior lowered his head. Casey threw up her hands and walked off.

"I'm done. I'm done!"

"Wait a minute, Casey, Vanessa didn't do this." Junior went after her. "This happened because of Friday. Those cats we were ridin' with saw us and they followed us into town. I had a little time to think about it on the way here, but it wasn't Vanessa's fault."

"Junior, don't you see what's happening here? Vanessa is the reason your hand got cut. She's the reason you almost went to jail. Almost got mugged. She's at the head of this whole thing. This is all her bullshit," Casey told him. "You know what, J.? If you're gonna go down in flames next to Vanessa, you go right on down to hell beside her because I won't be joining you. Fuck, Junior. I was having a good day until you showed up."

As Casey turned to walk off, Junior stood at the top of the stairs.

"I just need a little time to get it all figured out."

"Get what all figured out, Junior?" she asked him "What's it gonna take, man? A bullet? Because that's the direction you're headed in if you don't take back your life. Right now, Vanessa is in control of it."

Junior hung his head pitifully as Casey turned to leave. She turned around at the bottom of the steps to look back at him.

180

"You know, I never thought I'd say this to you, Junior," she told him, "but I'm starting to wonder if this whole New York thing is even a good idea anymore."

"What's that supposed to mean?" Junior gasped.

"I let you stay here under the condition that you do somethin' positive with your life. If you're gonna run yourself into the ground for Vanessa, then fuckin' go live with her!"

Casey walked off into the kitchen to finish cooking. Junior stood there, stunned. He looked down at his hand and shook his head. The notion of leaving Casey's rocked his foundation. He stormed into his bedroom and ripped through his closet for his uniform and work apron. He re-wrapped his cut hand and headed down the staircase, bypassing Casey as she was coming up. The two passed one another like strangers on a subway train. When Junior got to the bottom, he turned to watch as Casey went off into her bedroom. She closed her door. He had finally pushed her over the edge, Junior thought. He exhaled with defeat and left for work.

Let Me Give You a Hand

Junior's hand still ached when he arrived for work three minutes past his start time. He sprinted through the warehouse entrance in the back with his hand glued to his chest. He slipped through the loading dock, signed himself in and began sifting through a pile of old boxes as if he was a model employee. As expected, Mr. Wilkinson came back there looking for him. Junior hid his hand behind him as the boss walked over to him. "You been back here the whole time?" the boss asked him. "Get those fast hands on the registers, Junior. C'mon, we're busy!" For once, Junior had outsmarted his boss.

On the floor, Junior avoided the registers at all costs. He pushed around an iron hand cart loaded with meats and re-supplied goods all with one hand. He yelped when a piece of plastic on a chicken bag found its way beneath his wrapped hand. "Argh!" he dropped the bag onto the floor. The contact sent a jolt throughout his entire arm. He looked up to see Mr. Wilkinson watching him. Quickly, he went back to work.

On the registers, Junior typed with one hand and ignored his colleagues' inquiries about his injury. Nosy customers asked too. "You alright there, Sonny?" an older gentleman asked him. Junior placed his hand down at his side and gave a fake smile. Later, when Mr. Wilkinson walked over to add change to Junior's drawer, he placed his hand inside his apron pocket. He screamed as the blade of his box cutter pricked him. "ARGH!" he hollered, ripping his hand from his apron and holding it. Mr. Wilkinson called over a colleague to cover for Junior and walked him to the back.

"So, what's up with the hand?" the boss asked him.

Junior placed it behind him.

"It's just a little sore, that's all," said Junior. "I can work."

"Not with you screamin' in my ear like that. So, what happened? Let me see it."

As Mr. Wilkinson reached for it, Junior backed up. The boss became irritated.

"Either let me see that hand, or else I'm gonna let you see that door!"

Junior gave the boss his hand. The boss removed his glasses from his breast pocket and placed them over his face. His beady eyes looked like a goldfish as he removed Junior's wrapping.

"Uh, shouldn't you use gloves while you're doing that, sir?" Junior asked him. The boss eyeballed Junior, ignoring him. He flipped and rotated Junior's hand. He returned his glasses to his breast pocket and sighed.

"Go'on down to aisle four and get you some of that witch hazel, some swabs and those double-strength bandages. Go to the bathroom and take care of that hand—and don't come out until you do. How'd you get this by the way?" the boss asked him.

"I had an accident at home."

"Accident at home, eh?" the boss nodded. "Is that why you came in late today? Don't look at me like that, son—I saw you run across that lot. You think old, Mr. Wilkinson is stupid? You're supposed to be in at 4:30 on the dot, not 4:36 p.m., Junior. You know that's gonna cost you, right?"

"C'mon, Mr. Wilkinson," he begged. "Look, you can see my hand is all jacked up, man; do you have to write me up? I'm in a lot of pain here, sir. C'mon, that's not fair!"

"Columbine wasn't fair. Taxes aren't fair. Kendra Webdale, the young girl who got pushed in front of a train back in January of this year—that's not fair. Don't talk to me about fair, Junior. The way you disrespect me and every co-worker here by showing up late all the time is not fair. Now, go do what I asked."

Fuming, Junior marched to aisle four and grabbed the stuff the boss requested. He pushed through the plastic curtain, bypassing Mr. Wilkinson and went into the bathroom. He kicked open the door, pissed off. He walked into the bathroom, threw the stuff down into the sink beside him and turned on the water. Mr. Wilkinson showed up behind Junior, ready to snatch the life out of him.

"Th'hell is your problem?!" he threw his clipboard down onto the floor, hollering at him. "Don't you ever disrespect me like that again, Junior. Don't take it out on me that you can't get here on time. That's your responsibility. Don't nobody give a damn about your hand."

"Why you keep fuckin' with me all the time, man?" Junior teared.

"You wanna know what my problem is with you, Junior?" the boss raised his voice. "You got a lot of potential—a lot more than most of these folks here got, but you bullshit too much. That's OK, though. Because one of these days you're gonna bullshit your way out of my store. I'm tired of gettin' half from you. The next time, I'm gonna throw you out of here."

"I told you I cut my hand. Can't you just give me a break?"

"You didn't tell me nothin'!" Mr. Wilkinson said. "You parked your car and snuck into my warehouse. I saw you with my own two eyes. What'd I look like givin' you credit

184

for showin' up, you crazy? That's what's wrong with you damn kids now. Always want a freebie from somewhere—don't wanna work for nothin'. If you don't like me as your boss, then quit!" he told him. "Otherwise, I'm gonna ride your ass like a bull every shift. Now, finish up that wound and get back on my floor—and the next time you swell up on me like that, I'm gonna flush your ass down that toilet over there! You want the world to feel sorry for you Junior, and it *don't*. The world don't feel sorry for no-damn-body. Not even old, Mr. Wilkinson."

Clipboard in hand, Mr. Wilkinson ripped open the bathroom door and left. Enraged, Junior hurled the bottle of alcohol at the wall and leaned over the sink.

When Junior got home from work that night, he walked in to find Casey curled on the sofa watching TV. Next to her was a big bucket of Edy's ice cream, donuts, and a slice of pound cake. The sight was familiar to him; whenever Casey was stressed, she ate. She eyeballed Junior, looked down at his hand and shook her head at him with pity. Junior placed his keys onto the rack and headed up to his room. Neither said a word to each other.

With his door shut, Junior tossed his stained apron onto the floor, kicked off his sneakers and plopped down at his work desk. He took a deep breath. He looked down at his hand and sighed again as he thought about his dreadful day. He reached over to turn on his computer, and signed into his AOL account where Vanessa was waiting for him. She messaged him within seconds. Her instant message blocked his screen, interrupting his surfing. He wrote back with one hand.

[10:07 PM EST] NyCShawty81: ☹

[10:09 PM EST] BRowePhilly: ☹

[10:10 PM EST] NyCShawty81: You hurt my feelings 2day.

[10:14 PM EST] BRowePhilly: Im sorry.

[10:15 PM EST] NyCShawty81: ☹

[10:15 PM EST] NyCShawty81: I still luv u. Can I bring u anything at all?

[10:19 PM EST] BRowePhilly: I'm good.

[10:20 PM EST] NyCShawty81: ☹☹☹☹

[10:21 PM EST] NyCShawty81: What u doin?

[10:27 PM EST] BRowePhilly: Just got home. Long day. Brb.

[10:30 PM EST] BRowePhilly: Back.

[10:32 PM EST] NyCShawty81: K. I miss you, J. I'm sorry for what happened.

[10:36 PM EST] NyCShawty81: R u still there????

[10:37 PM EST] BRowePhilly: Yeah, V. Miss u 2.

[10:39 PM EST] NyCShawty81: ☺

[10:39 PM EST] NyCShawty81: What did Casey say about your hand?

[10:41 PM EST] BRowePhilly: ☹

[10:41 PM EST] NyCShawty81: ☹

[10:43 PM EST] BRowePhilly: I think she's comin upstairs to my room, hold on.

[10:44 PM EST] BRowePhilly: Never mind. She went into her room.

[10:45 PM EST] BRowePhilly: ☹

[10:46 PM EST] NyCShawty81: I feel so bad…

[10:51 PM EST] BRowePhilly: Me too…I'm gonna go. Nite.

[10:51 PM EST] NyCShawty81: ok…I guess.

[10:52 PM EST] BRowePhilly has left your chat invitation.

By the middle of his second week of classes, Junior was floating through life on autopilot. He spoke to Vanessa sparingly and stayed out of Casey's way. For two whole days, Junior and Casey seldom spoke. At work, Mr. Wilkinson rode Junior. By Wednesday, the boss lightened up on the boy. At the end of Junior's shift that night, he passed by his boss in the warehouse and Mr. Wilkinson bopped his head with his clipboard. Junior tried to not smile, but failed.

"Damn knucklehead," the boss said. "You know, when you're on your game, you're one of my best workers. I don't know what all that was Monday night, but I hope we never go back there, Junior. I'd hate to lose you. I really would." The boss walked off, leaving Junior to marinate.

Meanwhile, Junior kept his troubles from his family. He was getting it from everywhere: school, work, Casey, life, his hand, poetry. By Thursday night, Junior had had it. While sitting at his desk, he tried to medicate through writing but failed miserably. Unable to tap into his artistry, he swiped his journal off his desk. It sailed across the room and struck the wall. He hit up his momma, hoping she could shine some light into his dark world. Their impromptu webcam appointment was much needed. Junior smiled as his momma's big face appeared on screen.

"Move back, Ma!" Junior chuckled. "You're too close again."

Sandy put her eye up to the lens.

"You mean like this?" she laughed before backing away. "So, what do I owe the pleasure to this visit tonight, Junior?" she asked him. "It's Thursday. *New York Undercover* is on. What is it?"

"I'll try to be quick," he said. "I don't know, Ma, just been feelin' kind of down with things lately. Nothin' seems to be goin' right. It's just got me feelin' all fucked—"

Sandy's eyes widened.

"I-I-I mean, you know, like, messed up," Junior straightened. "Bad. Awful. Like that," he sighed. "I'm tryin' to do right, but I just feel like I keep comin' up short. These last two weeks of college have been so overwhelming. I never thought it'd be this way. I just never imagined life would be so hard outside of Langston, you know?"

"Now, you know why your daddy was so hard on you all these years," she said. "It wasn't just to be mean, Junior. But to prepare you for these times," she explained to him. "If you think it's hard now, wait 'til you get to be our age. It only gets harder as you get older."

"That's what I keep hearing," Junior sighed.

"Yeah," said Sandy. "But you're in good hands up there with Casey, I think. I know it's a little tough adjusting with some things, but it'll all come together soon. I believe the good Lord will show you which way to go."

"You keep sayin' that, but I feel like when I try to talk to him, Ma, he doesn't listen."

"Yes, he is. He's listenin'. Maybe you the one that ain't listenin', Junior." Sandy nodded. "The good Lord always talks. You got to learn to listen, Junior." Sandy grabbed her ear. "That's why you got two of these."

Junior didn't blink. "Yes, ma'am."

"OK, then." She smiled. "I'm still workin' on tryin' to get Leonard to chat with you on here. He still won't come into the room. He can't get past the computer talkin' back to him. He thinks the government is spyin' us—you know your daddy. 'You talkin' to them goddamn gubment peoples again, ain't ya?!'" Sandy mocked her husband. "Don't worry though, I'll get him."

Junior smiled at her.

"Just know that I love you very much," she told him. "I can't wait 'til you get me another certificate to hang up 'round here. My walls are gettin' pretty bare. I need another plaque!"

"I'll do my best. First, I gotta get out of this semester. Anatomy is killin' me."

"You will. Talk to you soon, my love."

After Sandy signed off for the night, Junior tried to sleep off his warding thoughts about his relationship with Vanessa but couldn't do it. His momma's wisdom played inside of his

189

head on repeat. He reached over for his cell phone to leave Vanessa a message. It was just after 1 a.m.

"Hey, V. Sorry, it's so late. I know you're asleep," he said. "Can you meet me in front of the building tomorrow. I need to talk to you about somethin'. Peace."

Eleven

"What up, J.? Everything straight?" Vanessa asked as she embraced Junior the next morning in front of the building before the start of their classes. Her pretty face made it hard for him to end things. She was dolled in her favorite shade of lipstick with her hair pulled back into a cute bun. She pecked Junior on the mouth, and held him by his hands. Junior breathed in her sweet aroma and exhaled. Saying goodbye was harder than thinking it. "I got a few minutes if you need to talk. What's on your mind?" Junior always liked a long hug, but not quite as much as he needed one that day. He held onto her as he cycled through a mixture of painful emotions. Overwhelmed, he crashed onto her shoulder. He couldn't stand to do it; he couldn't say goodbye.

"Yo?" Vanessa's eyes glistened. "J., what's wrong?! Son, stop. You're makin' *me* cry, and I don't even know what's goin' on. What happened? Did somethin' happen to Casey? Something's wrong, isn't it? Talk to me, J. Please."

Each time he opened his mouth to speak, Junior felt himself crack. It was the first time Vanessa had truly seen him collapse. Junior knew that Vanessa may have been screwed up, but she truly loved him. The thought of letting her go cut him deeply. He backed off from his initial plan to end the relationship. Somewhere in the back of his mind, he was hopeful things would get better.

"Just been a fucked up week, that's all. Sorry for exploding like that on you, V. Yo, I don't even know where that shit came from. I didn't mean to—"

"J.," Vanessa held him by his face. "Stop. Just *stop*. You know you can cry in front of me. I'm not like that. You wanna talk about it? Is it about Monday? I feel bad, too."

Junior stared back into Vanessa's beautiful eyes. He could only lie.

"It's just a lot of shit, V. Like I said—just a rough week. That's all. I'm good."

Vanessa interlocked her hand with his.

"You know I don't believe you." She smiled at him.

Junior lowered his head. He couldn't help but laugh. "Yeah, I know. You're like Dionne Warwick with all that psychic shit."

The two laughed. Vanessa raised Junior's hand and kissed it.

"Let's talk later," she told him. "I been thinkin' of some things, too."

"You have?" he asked. "But, yeah, let's do that. Let's just talk later, V."

As Vanessa disappeared through the crowd of college-goers, Junior headed to class.

192

Junior stared lifelessly at the board watching Mr. Freemont make an ass of himself. He spent much of the morning thinking about Vanessa and mulling over how (or if) he should end things. With his face smushed against his fist, he daydreamed their breakup. Junior looked so pitiful that even Mr. Freemont felt sorry for him, or so he thought. During first break, his teacher asked Junior to stay behind. "You OK, kid?" he asked him. "I would've picked on you like normal, but I figured I'd ask first."

Junior walked away.

"Is that a yes?"

After break, Junior returned to his dead-to-the-world posture. He wished he had a rock to throw at his teacher. Some days, he even wished he was as thoughtless as his daddy was. He envisioned his daddy strutting to the front of the room at the first improper joke; Senior wasn't the joking type. "C'mere, you little golf-playin' motherfucka!" *Slap.* It made Junior grin.

At one point in the morning, Rachel leaned over to check on him. "Hey, neighbor!" Rachel whispered. "You OK today? You don't seem like yourself. Not tryin' to be nosy, but you might wanna jot these notes down. Once you fail the first exam, it's like a domino effect in Freemont's class. Fuckin' everything starts fallin' down, dude."

Junior was used to shit falling down around him. Unphased, he shrugged and removed his journal from his bookbag. He flipped until he found an empty page, bypassing a collection of weak poems he'd written over the past several weeks. He looked over to notice Rachel staring at him.

"I got a booger on my face or something? What is it?" he asked her.

"I knew it!" she whispered. "I knew there was somethin' special about you when you walked in here the first day without your book—I fuckin' knew it!"

"Knew what? What are you even talkin' about right now? Look, I got a girlfriend, OK?"

"Girlfriend?" she snickered. "I don't want you, you damn fool. I'm lesbian. I want the book." She pointed, reaching for it. "The journal. Give it to me!"

"No." Junior moved it. "Yo, what the hell is wrong you, man?"

"If you don't give me that journal and let me look, I'm totally gonna bite you!" She showed him her braces. "I'll do it, Junior. As God as my witness, I'm gonna bite you."

Junior used his finger to slide his journal over to Rachel. He looked on as she turned through his journal, looking at his work. She passed his journal back to him. She reached into her bag and removed her own journal and handed it to Junior.

"You write too?" he asked her.

Rachel removed an inhaler from her bag and doped herself up.

"Since I was eleven." She winked. "I've got terrible asthma, forgive me. This is such a startling revelation. I can't believe I'm sitting next to an actual poet such as yourself. It's an honor to meet you. There aren't too many of us scholarly gems around these days. We're the last of a dying breed, aren't we? Let's meet after class. I have a proposition for you."

For the rest of class, Junior stared ahead as if he'd seen a ghost. He wished he'd never taken out his journal for her to see.

Junior didn't know what to think of Rachel or why she wanted to talk to him after class. She was a creepy-ass, white girl with baby-blue eyes and lenses that fogged with trapped condensation. He waited outside for her after class. He was too scared to leave, knowing he had to sit next to her for the rest of the semester. He looked down at his scabby hand and imagined her teeth marks on his flesh. He closed his hand and shuddered. Meanwhile, inside, he overheard Rachel giving Mr. Freemont a piece of her mind. He lingered near the doorway to listen. "You're a pig," Rachel blasted him. "Fail me a third time, I don't give a shit if it takes me forty years to graduate. One of these days someone is gonna kick your fucking ass!" Rachel combed her blonde hair through her fingers and walked out. Junior couldn't believe it. As she came out into the hallway, he called his new friend over to celebrate her courage.

"Over here, Rach." Junior waved as she walked over; her face was red with anger. "Yo, you *took* it to that fool," Junior laughed. "I wish I had the balls to say some shit like that."

"What else was I supposed to do? Let him continue his condescending bullshit?"

"Well, thank you. That made my day. So, what's up? You wanted to talk?"

Rachel went into her purse, fishing out a stack of cards. She thumbed through them and handed one to Junior. He looked down at the card to read it.

"Rachel Kirkpatrick, City Peace Corp Alliance," Junior read her name and affiliation aloud. "So, you work for 'em?" he asked. "Is the pay any good? Man, I could definitely use a new job."

"Actually, it's volunteer," she told him. "Really neat stuff. I'm looking for poets to do spoken word for a couple of projects I'm workin' on. I'm trying to put together a group of talented spoken word artists to showcase. Are you interested?"

Junior looked down at the card again. "I wish I could, Rach, but I just don't have the time these days. I'm just so busy. I'd have to get paid if I was to do that. I really could use the cash."

"Well, everything isn't always about money. The fucking government is about money," she said. "Those greedy sons-of-bitches down on Capitol Hill could give a shit about the future for us youngsters, or their parents who are struggling to make ends meet. That's what my division of the Peace Corp Alliance does, Junior. I've got a few schools I'm reaching out to. I wanna spread hope to young writers. I've got hundreds of journals with writing utensils ready to donate. These folks are so gracious despite their unfortunate backgrounds. Can you help me?"

"Spoken word?" Junior scratched his head. "I don't know, Rachel. It's just been so long for me, and my girlfriend is—"

"So, bring her. She can come too," Rachel offered. "Look, why don't you just come to the meeting this

196

afternoon. You can get a feel for if it's your thing. I'd really love for you to just come and meet some of the other poets there."

"Yeah? Hey, do you know Prophet? The Trolling Poet here on campus? I forgot his real name—but do you know him?" Junior asked her.

"Oh, Parris? He's one of my roommates, dude."

"Wait a minute. *You* know Parris?"

"Yeah, he's part of the Peace Corps Alliance," she told him. "A few of us are gonna meet in the multi-purpose room later this afternoon. We'll be in Room 317. Come check us out. If you don't like it, you can leave. I gotta get going. Hope to see you there!"

Junior placed Rachel's card in his wallet and headed to his next class.

Junior couldn't wait for sociology to let out. He fired down to the concourse level to wait for Vanessa. He was going to do it—get back in the spoken word game. The past two weeks of his college experience had been daunting. He hoped that working alongside new company would help rejuvenate his passion for spoken word. It was also an opportunity to get to know Parris. Rachel's project with the Peace Corp Alliance could be huge, and Junior decided he didn't want to miss out. As soon as Vanessa appeared in the distance, he bumrushed her.

"What up, V.?" Junior kissed her. He showed Vanessa the card inside of his wallet. "Yo, remember the white girl you saw me with the other day? Her name's Rachel—but anyway—listen, she just gave me this card. She volunteers with the Peace Corps Alliance here on campus. She's got this writer's project happening later this month. She saw my journal and invited me to this meeting later this afternoon. She said you can come, too. You down?"

Vanessa raised her eyebrow at Junior.

"Peace Corps Alliance? You mean like, volunteer work?"

"Yeah. She said she's lookin' for writers to work with for this project throughout the city. I think it's a great way for me to get back on stage. I still miss it sometimes, you know."

Vanessa looked down at the card and turned it over. She was hardly impressed.

"You know they aren't gonna pay you, right?"

"Fuck the money, V. Man, that would be so dope to work with other writers. Who knows where that could lead, you know?"

"What about earlier?" Vanessa asked. "You were cryin' on my shoulder just a few hours ago sayin' you wanted to talk. Now, all of sudden, you wanna go to this meeting? I thought we were supposed get together and talk? Make up your mind, J."

"Well, we are gonna talk, but can we do it afterward?" Junior asked her. "C'mon, V. Work with me. I just wanna check it out. Maybe ten, fifteen minutes? Afterward we'll talk."

Vanessa rolled her eyes. "There you go again, puttin' other things ahead of our relationship." She shook her head. "If you wanna talk, then let's talk. So, what's on your mind?"

"Well, I just wanted to rap about us, nothin' bad. Just how we can better, that's all."

"OK, so let's rap. What's up?"

Junior stared at Vanessa with discontent. "Why do you have to make this shit so difficult, V.?" he asked.

"Yo, if you wanna rap about our relationship, then let's rap," Vanessa straightened. "I don't care about the Peace Corps Alliance's mission, J. I care about our mission and where we're headed. You just been bouncin' all over on this stage stuff, and it's frustrating."

"Frustrating? No, V. *This* is frustrating." Junior lifted his sore hand. "I get stabbed for tryin' to save my future from a bunch of low-lifes. Gettin' searched by the cops for shit I ain't have nothin' to do with and almost losing my freedom. Don't get me started."

"See, that's fucked up, you didn't have to go there—you know I feel bad about that shit happenin' to you, J." Vanessa's voice cracked. "Fine, Junior. If you wanna go to your meeting, go. I'll just wait around here somewhere, I guess."

Vanessa walked over to a lone bench and took a seat. Junior splashed beside her. Her eyes teared up, and he knew she was recalling their frightening ordeal from the other day. Junior sat beside her, consoling her.

"Son, I haven't slept well in fuckin' days since that shit happened, yo." She wiped her eyes. "I've been tryin' to hold it together, but it's really hard, J. I just can't forgive myself for any of this stuff. I'm a wreck. I really am. I wish it was me that got stabbed. I deserve it."

Junior rubbed up and down Vanessa's spine as she recounted the terrifying day.

"That's it." He shrugged. "I'm not going to the meeting. I'm gonna stay here with you. Why didn't you tell me you were goin' through this?"

"I didn't wanna upset you. It's just been hard holdin' all this in. I feel terrible, J."

"Well, we should really talk then, V."

"Word." She shook her head. "Let's just go someplace where we can feel comfortable. Anyplace but here, you know. My parents aren't home if you wanna go there?"

"Wherever you want." Junior put his arm around her. "I'll follow you."

Junior stood to his feet and helped Vanessa onto hers. The two kissed. Vanessa left Junior briefly to freshen up her face in the bathroom. As soon as he was alone again, Junior found himself struggling to concede with the reality that Vanessa was getting over on him. Why did he always get sucked in to her needs? What about what he wanted? *What's fifteen minutes after all you've put me through lately,* Junior wondered. He launched to his feet, ready to tell Vanessa off as soon as she left the bathroom. No, I won't leave campus. I'm gonna go to that damn meeting (whether you like it or not), he coached himself to say. Junior's plans changed when Vanessa exited the washroom.

"All set." She dried her hands on a paper towel. "You ready, J.?"

Junior opened his mouth to answer, but his rebuttal suddenly left him.

"Yup. Ready."

Opposites Attract

I think too much. You drink too much.
We are the perfect concoction of poisonous toxins.
Two lost souls.

—LEONARD G. ROBINSON JR.

Vanessa's parents did well for themselves. Their single-family neighborhood in Wilshire, New Jersey was the perfect depiction of the "American Dream" house. Trees. Lawns. Picket fences. Dogs who stood on their hind legs, wagging their bushy tails at passersby. A community golf course. A kid on a bicycle slinging the city's paper rather than dope. It was the ultimate contrast to Junior's former neighborhood, and a far cry from Vanessa's days in Bed-Stuy. It was the typical *Leave It to Beaver*-esque, white, middle-class neighborhood. Vanessa's family was one of six Black families that lived on her street, Summers Lane. As eye-appealing as it was, Vanessa hated it there. Junior couldn't understand it. "It's just too white for me, J.," she once told him. But the white folks there treated Junior better than the Black folks treated him in Brooke's Rowe. Upon learning that he had got accepted into Langston High out of state, Junior's neighbors called him a "sell-out". They mocked and ridiculed him. Sandy could only laugh. "I bet half of them niggas don't even know who Langston Hughes is," she chuckled. "The ones that call you all those names—they the real sell-outs."

That afternoon, Junior followed Vanessa to her house

and parked his car several houses down from Vanessa's crib, then walked to her door. Her neighbors greeted him along the way which made him feel bad since he could never remember their names. She was already inside, so he pressed the bell to Vanessa's house. It chimed beautifully as she answered the door and stood at the entrance, blocking Junior from entering.

"Yes? Can I help you?" she asked him.

Junior joined in on the fun.

"Yeah, I'm lost," he said. "My car just died. Do you happen to have a phone that I can borrow?"

"If I let you use the phone, what's in it for me?"

Junior forced his way into the house and pinned her to the wall. She shrieked as if she was being robbed. The two kissed and laughed as Vanessa closed the door behind them. Holding hands, Junior trailed behind Vanessa's plump backside into the kitchen. On the wall, above the kitchen countertop, was a cute clock and a sign which read "Home Sweet Home". To the left was the fridge. Junior could tell by the magnets that Vanessa's family had been everywhere: Greece, Japan, Siberia, Thailand, Johannesburg, and many more places. Sometimes it made him wonder why a girl so well-traveled as Vanessa could even miss her old life in the inner city. Growing up, the furthest Junior had gone was his city limits.

Connected to the family's kitchen was the living room area. Unlike his parents' house, there was no plastic liner on their furniture. There were pictures of Vanessa on every wall but at different stages of her life. Above the fireplace was a photo of her with her stepdaddy and momma. She looked 12 or 13. In the photo, she wore a fake smile as Steve posed behind them. His hands were cupped around Vanessa's shoulders. "I hate that picture of us," she sulked at it. "C'mon, let me show you somethin' in the basement."

By the hand, Vanessa led Junior down the stairs and over to the bar area. She flipped on the light switch before showing off Steve's beloved bar. Junior sat on a stool, admiring its lit shelves, and TV attached to the wall. It looked like a typical meet-up bar in Manhattan. The collection of domestic and imported alcohol offered the perfect escape for a salty spouse, Junior thought. Vanessa poured their first drink, a shot of German scotch. Junior couldn't pronounce the name, but it seared his throat.

"Th'fuck is that?" he coughed.

"It came from Berlin." She showed him the bottle. "Supposedly they came up with the recipe during the Hitler regime around the time of the war. They rarely make it for consumers. It has to be special-ordered. Dope, right?"

"Well, I don't want that shit if they made it for his punk-ass. Hitler was probably drinkin' this and tryin' to figure out how to take over the world or some shit."

"That was a long time ago, Junior."

"So, what. Fuck Hitler." Junior slid his cup back. "What else y'all got?"

Vanessa laced her stepdaddy's apron over her proud body and poured them both a shot of brandy. Together, the two toasted their glasses.

"To this college bullshit," she chuckled. "Wait, I got one better—I got one better. How about, to us? Above and beyond?"

"Is that the best you can come up with?"

"Oh, shut up and have a drink with me!"

Junior held his breath as he took it down the pipes. It charred his chest as Vanessa laughed at him. She shook her head and chugged hers. She wiped her mouth like a wino.

"Whew!" she shuddered. "So, what's on your mind? You said you wanted to talk? Or, did you just come for the drinks and live entertainment?"

"You go first," said Junior.

Vanessa poured the two of them a rum and Coke. She stirred her drink, took a sip, and placed it down onto the table before fixing her ponytail. It had come loose during their forged home invasion when Junior got there.

"Aight, this is gonna sound silly, but I'm just gonna say it anyway. I get scared sometimes. Sometimes I'm scared this whole thing is gonna blow up in my face and that I'm gonna lose you, too. Like, for real, most girls don't know how to act when they got somebody good. We're not used to that shit. We're used to gettin' dogged. Deadass, I met a lot of cats but you're the first guy I ever truly felt a genuine connection with," she told him. "You inspire me, J.," she teared up, laughing. "You really do. You make me wanna go the right way. But I just got so much of this pain in my heart. I gotta get that out of my system. Just be patient with me, that's all."

Junior sipped, listening with a nonjudgmental ear. The

two had been together since halfway through eleventh grade. Yet, Junior was still ponying to Vanessa's unresolved issues from her childhood. He wondered how much more patient he needed to be. He took in a mouthful of his drink and placed his cup in front of him. He picked at the scab on his left hand.

"I got some shit to tell you, V.," Junior told her.

Vanessa grabbed his hand to stop him. She held it. "What is it?"

Junior looked down at Vanessa's hand. The nails on her delicate fingers were the same shade as her lipstick. He interlaced his hand with hers. He couldn't bring himself to end things. Not now, not after everything they've been through.

"Word, you gotta chill out with some of that bullshit, V.," Junior told her. "When you get all into your headspace about things, you only make it harder for us both. And I feel like I don't have a say in our relationship—at all. I know your daddy leavin' hurts, but I feel like you take that shit out on me. Why take it out on me when I'm the one that's been here, you know?"

"Very true." She nodded her head. "Is there anything else? You don't have to spare me, Junior. If I'm a fucked up girlfriend, tell me. I might cry, but I can take it."

"You're not, V.," Junior spared her. "I just wish you'd think through shit a little more before you pressed the button on stuff."

"I'm impulsive," she concurred. "That's what impulsive people do. Tell you what, let's make a pact right here, right now. No matter what happens between us, we gotta squash that shit and move on. We gotta fix it," she said. "I wanna grow beside you, Junior. Let's agree to that."

Junior tapped his glass into Vanessa's as the two sipped their drinks together. Afterward, Vanessa reached into her pocket and pulled out a bag of marijuana and pack of Backwoods. Junior rolled his eyes at her. He hated that Vanessa was a recreational user, let alone a smoker.

"If I light this up, will you hit it with me, J.?"

"Veeee. C'mon," Junior complained.

"I'm walkin' a straight line after this. I'm serious—I don't even wanna drink anymore, J. I wanna do right 'cause I don't want to lose you." She touched his hand. "I know you don't like this kind of shit, so I'm gonna stop. You deserve a better girlfriend than who I've been. Just hit this with me, and then we'll start new."

Junior's silence was convincing enough to Vanessa. He watched as she used the teeth on her house keys to split open a Backwood cigar down the middle and emptied its guts into an ashtray. She then used her skilled hands to stretch out the cigar paper. She placed it in her mouth and licked it before emptying her bag onto it. She neatly aligned her kush, rolled it, licked it again and fired it up. She took two puffs of her joint, turned it sideways and blew out the excess flame. She puffed again before handing it over to Junior.

"Go like this." She gestured, offering him a crash-course on smoking bud.

"Man, I know how to smoke!" Junior shot back, offended.

Junior took a hit of Vanessa's blunt and passed it back. He

206

talked as if his throat had been run over by a car.

"See, you be thinkin' I'm a fuckin' square, man," he exhaled.

"But you're *my* square!" Vanessa puffed. "That's what I love about you, J. You got your own style about you. I fuck with that, word up. That's why I fell so easily for you. You're not a dime-a-dozen kind of cat. You're a rarity," she said. "Guys like you only come around every thirty years! I'm curious, were you always like that growin' up?"

"Not always."

"Shit... I'm sorry, I didn't mean to—"

"No-no-no, it's fine, V. I can talk about it," Junior stopped her. "Man, when I lost Lawrence, it just...it wrecked me. It took everything out of me. I didn't care about nothin', man. Then all of a sudden, I met Casey and then..." Junior paused to keep from crying. Vanessa finished his sentence for him. By then, the alcohol was starting to take its effect on them.

"She's your sister. Period." Vanessa touched him. "Yo, deadass, I'm so jealous of y'all. I wish I had a Casey in my life, too. And I'm so glad that your parents let you out of Brooke's Rowe. How else would we have met? But even if we didn't, Junior, you're so deserving. Word is bond. Sometimes, I just think about you, and I get so fucking emotional, J., that I actually cry. Shit, I'm about to cry right now," she laughed. "You're just such a glowing soul. Like I said, I'm so scared sometimes that I'm gonna lose you."

"There you go again... I thought we made a pact, V.?"

"I'm just sayin'—I don't know, you might wanna spread

your wings one of these days. You said it earlier. I'm diffi-cult," she giggled. "See, I'm honest. I own my shit."

Junior gazed into Vanessa's eyes through the weed fog.

"I don't want a season, V.," he said. "My love is year-round."

"Wowwww. Really, though? You just got mad deep on me. Let me hear somethin' else."

Caught in the moment, Junior recited a poem from memory.

"Some have streams that are filled with running dreams," he said, looking Vanessa in the eye. *"Some have lakes with waters that can anticipate. Some have rivers too shallow to enter. Some have oceans like the Pacific with depth elegant and prolific."*

Vanessa did a double-take. "Son, how do you do that? How do you come up with shit like that? I wanna hear more!"

"Well, I ain't that good," Junior laughed.

"Yes, you are!" She bopped him. "Now, stop. Tell me another. I want to hear more."

"OK, well, you should remember this one.

"Fall in love. Fall out of love. Fall for love. Some just enjoy the fall of love because it gives them something new to think of. Some fall in love. Some love to fall, but few ever give their all."

"That was the first poem I ever heard you recite," Vanessa cheesed.

The two lovers gazed at one another, infatuated by their endless chemistry. Their entrenched souls spoke with blissful togetherness before heading off upstairs to Vanessa's bedroom.

On Vanessa's nightstand was a lamp that projected orbital shapes throughout her room. She had a queen-sized mattress that was encased in silk. It was soft and toned just like her. She turned on her five-disc player which opened with a mixture of her favorite R&B jams. The first song on her playlist was "Nothing Even Matters" by singers Lauryn Hill and DeAngelo. The bass filled the speakers atop her dresser, as the two kissed and unpackaged one another. Vanessa scooted backward across her silk bed, trapping herself against her headboard as Junior pursued her. She reached behind her for the wooden bed posts and panted with urgency; she loved to be chastised. Her drizzly canal pulsated rhythmically as she waited to be taken. Junior obliged her request. He placed his hand over her inflamed vagina and fondled Vanessa's seeping love-button with his middle-finger. Vanessa twisted violently against his will. She was so sensitive, her pedicured toes curled inward. "Juniorrrr," she whined agreeably, convulsing with delight. Vanessa's legs closed and opened on repeat as she lifted from the bed. Junior blew his hot breath onto Vanessa's sex, kissed it, and mounted her. They both whimpered in accord as Junior inserted his engorged limb. The skin on his shaft shed as he pushed his raw flesh through Vanessa's orifice. Her back arched under his authority as she moaned devilishly. Vanessa wrapped her legs around Junior, bracing him as he invaded all of her. "Oh, my God," she breathed heavily. "Please, fuck me."

Junior drove through Vanessa, pounding her insides with malice afterthought as she wept in ecstasy. Vanessa dug her burgundy nails into his back as he kicked into high gear with young energy. Junior put so much dick into Vanessa that afternoon her hands did sign language. She scraped her claws down his back as Junior seized and exploded inside of her. Vanessa's eyes rolled back as she joined him with collective enjoyment. Her leg trembled violently beneath him. Junior pressed his body against hers, allowing her to speak to his soul. "*Ungh*, I love it!" she whispered into his ear. "I need it all, J.—all of it." Junior gave it all to Vanessa. Depleted, Junior crumbled into Vanessa's arms as she kissed the side of his head, tracing her finger along his back. Before long, the two were out.

Twelve

You're perfectly imperfect. You're one of a kind.
You're an earthly treasure. You will forever be mine.

—VANESSA A. BAILEY

Junior held Vanessa for hours. He kissed the tattooed spot of her name along her back shoulder as she grinded her backside against his flesh. Her five-disc changer had since stopped, but her starry lamp continued to revolve outer space throughout her bedroom. Its mellow glow offered the perfect ambience as terrestrial shapes circulated the room. On Vanessa's dresser was a large, scented candle Junior had got her for her birthday. The sweet, raspberry wax had since melted to a small wick.

"J.," Vanessa turned to face him. She fingered his lips. "Can I tell you something?"

"You can tell me anything."

Junior noticed Vanessa's grin fade as she continued playing with his lips. Junior allowed her finger to slip inside of his mouth as he began to suck it. Her expression suddenly changed.

"You're the *only* guy I've ever truly given my heart to, Junior. I talk about my daddy a lot and how much I miss him, but I always knew things were gonna go left with the drugs—I could tell then. I never thought I'd—son, I can't even believe I'm cryin' right now," Vanessa laughed as a single tear rolled down the bridge of her nose and onto her bed. "You can't break my heart, J. I just… I can't take that shit. I don't wanna be alone in this."

"Can I say something now?" he asked her.

Vanessa shook her head. She removed her finger from his mouth and placed it on his lips.

"No," she told him. "Whatever you need to say, think about it first. I'm gonna take a shower. When I come back, you can tell me then."

Vanessa slid out of her bed and sat along the edge as Junior looked on. He crawled close to her, and placed his head onto Vanessa's lap. Junior looked up to admire her beautiful face as Vanessa ran her fingers through his hair.

"I already thought about what I wanted to say," he said. "You're everything to me."

Vanessa stroked Junior's features before patting his cheek.

"C'mon, let me up," she said. "I'm gonna take a quick shower and then we're gonna get you the hell out of here so you can get to work."

Junior moved back as Vanessa rose to her feet and stretched. She grabbed a towel from atop her dresser and headed for her parents' bathroom. Junior crawled back into Vanessa's bed

212

and placed his hands behind his head. He could never leave her, Junior thought. He loved her too much. Whatever bridge needed to be crossed, they'd cross it together. Simple. She was the love of his life, Vanessa Bailey. Someday, he'd give her the world. Swept away in his youthful ignorance, Junior's peace was disturbed by the garage door. He sprinted down the hallway to get Vanessa. Naked, he ran into her parents' bathroom and pulled back the shower curtain.

"Someone's home! I just heard the garage open!"

"WHAT?!"

Vanessa wrapped herself in a towel and ran out into the hallway to investigate. She retreated back into the bathroom and closed the door, leaving wet foot tracks during her travels. She turned on the bathroom fan to drown out their voices as the two talked.

"Quick, get in the tub!"

"What? Man, fuck that tub. I'm out of here!"

"Junior!" She clapped her hands. "Steve is on his way up. Yo, will you please just get in the fuckin' shower before he kills us both?"

"What the fu—what am I supposed to do if he walks in here, V.? What is he doin' home? He's not supposed to be here."

"Don't you think I know that? C'mon, get in—get in!"

Junior climbed inside of Steve's tub as Vanessa pulled the shower curtain closed. She began drying her hair as if nothing was wrong. She played off her deceit well. It made Junior wonder how often she'd snuck other boys into the house before he came along.

"Yo, how long am I gonna be in here?" he asked her. "I gotta work today, V."

"Hopefully not long. Will you shut up?"

When Steve tapped on the bathroom door, Junior could hear his heart pulse inside of his head. He was at Vanessa's mercy once again.

"One second!" she told her stepdaddy. Vanessa pulled back the curtain. She placed her finger against her juicy lips, signaling for Junior not to breathe. As he nodded his head, Vanessa pulled back the shower curtain. She carefully adjusted it, ensuring there were no peek-spaces along the edge. Junior could barely make out her shapely silhouette, but could still see her. Vanessa opened her parents' door and stood there. Steve crossed his arms.

"You're in our bathroom again." Steve looked on. "What excuse do you have this time?"

"I don't like the shower in the hallway. I've been saying that for months," Vanessa shrugged. "The pressure's too weak. You said you were gonna get it changed. Besides, I thought you and Mom were gone for the day?"

"You've been smoking again, haven't you?" he laughed. "That's not until next week. C'mon, get out, I need to use the bathroom."

Junior's heart pounded.

"Why can't you just use the one in the hallway?"

"Because it's my bathroom, Vanessa. Now, get out."

Vanessa ignored Steve and went back to drying her hair.

Irritated, Steve grabbed her by the arm and spun her out the door.

"Ow! Th'fuck did you do that for?"

"Keep it up, next time I'm gonna cut off your tuition," Steve threatened.

"Cut it off then—I don't give a fuck. Don't be grabbin' me like that. You ain't my father, and you ain't my boyfriend, either."

"Thank God, I'm not," he said. "I feel sorry for Junior. He's got a trainwreck of a girlfriend. You just hide it so well. Don't worry, he'll catch on eventually, and then he's gonna leave you like the last kid did."

"Fuck you, Steve!" Vanessa growled as her stepdaddy closed the door in her face, trapping Junior inside. She cussed and clawed at the door.

For the next half hour, Junior was forced to smell Steve's waste as he turned through a *Sports Illustrated* magazine. His runny stomach cut up throughout. The sound of rapid-fire diarrhea was nauseating to Junior. He prayed for a miracle as he tried not to move, cough or gag under Steve's abhorrent guts. Afterward, Steve turned off the light and left, leaving Junior in the dark. Junior thought he was in the clear until he overheard the TV in the next room. He peeped through the edge of the curtain and saw Steve stretched out on the bed. Trapped against his will, Junior sat on the cold, tub floor. Where else was he to go?

Do You Have the Time?

The musk from Steve's ass still percolated throughout the bathroom when Junior overheard footsteps. His heart raced with worry as he tried to make out the shadowy image in the dark. Wisely, he kept quiet as the bath light turned on suddenly, blinding him. He shielded his eyes as he waited for his peepers to adjust as the bathroom curtain ripped open. "C'mon, let's get you out of here!" Vanessa handed Junior his clothes. Junior scrambled inside of his threads, careful to avoid the cut on his bad hand.

"Yo, where's Steve?" Junior asked. "How long have I been in here?"

"Barely an hour. He went to pick up my mother. You're not late for work, are you?"

Junior looked down at his watch. It was just after 3 p.m.

"Nah, I'm straight," he sighed. "I don't have to be at the Mart for another hour or so. Damn, V. I thought you'd never come back for me," he laughed.

"Fuck that, J.," Vanessa helped him to get dressed. "If I had to, I was gonna find a way to get you out of here for work. It's a miracle we didn't get caught. But J., can you please do me a favor the next time? Stay the hell inside of my room! Hide in the closet," she laughed at him.

Junior was so happy to get out, he wasn't even mad at Vanessa's botched plans from earlier. Once he was fully dressed, she walked him down to the door. She straightened Junior's T-shirt for him and placed her wrists around his neck. Junior held Vanessa by her waist.

"Thanks for puttin' up with me today, J.," she kissed him. "Yo, call me later."

Junior kissed her and left.

To Junior's surprise, he arrived for work with minutes still to spare. He bypassed Mr. Wilkinson near the entrance. The boss looked down at his watch, back up at Junior and kept going. Junior carried on to the back, signed in and began his shift.

He hummed and whistled throughout his shift to what was a record-breaking night for him down at the Mart. That evening, he received two pinches on his handsome cheeks from old ladies; a $5 tip from one, and $20 from another. It was the best shift he'd had in months. All was right with the world as he helped to push out the evening rush. On the register, he impressed with blistering speed and was so good that a customer called the boss over. "You ought to give this young man a promotion," the guy told Mr. Wilkinson. The boss made a face and walked off.

Near the end of his shift, Mr. Wilkinson came walking down Junior's aisle as he restacked his section. The boss tapped the boy on the shoulder.

"Hey there, Junior. Got a second?"

"Sure thing," Junior responded.

Junior followed behind Mr. Wilkinson's wrinkly, bald head toward the back. At a phone near the plastic curtain, the boss paged one of Junior's colleagues to take over in his section. His voice echoed throughout the Mart: "Judy, you're needed in dairy. Judy in dairy." The boss and Junior continued toward his office in the back.

During their walk, behind the plastic curtain, Junior stared at the glare spot on the back of his boss's head. He figured there was some sort of clerical error on his paycheck, or that the boss wanted to show him an invoice from a previous shipment. At his worst, he thought, Mr. Wilkinson would make him sweep up the lot again before he left for the night. As the two entered the office, Mr. Wilkinson motioned for Junior to take a seat. The boss sat at the corner of his desk.

"Everything good, sir?" Junior asked him. "Quite a night we had."

Unamused, Mr. Wilkinson thumbed his eyes.

"What time were you supposed to come in today, Junior? Do you remember?"

"4:30," Junior said assuredly. "I punched in early, actually."

The boss sighed with disappointment. "Let's try this again. What time were you supposed to come in *today*, young man?"

"…At 4:30, right? That's what time I normally come in."

"I know what time you normally come in," the boss snapped. "But I asked you what time were you supposed to come in today, Junior. Not last Thursday. Not the Thursday before. This Thursday, son. What time were you supposed to be in?"

Trembling, Junior's heart rate elevated. The boss shook his head at him and walked over to the wall clock to retrieve a recent copy of his employee work schedule. He removed his glasses from his breast pocket and placed them over his bulldog face. As he began to read, the words sounded familiar to Junior.

"Attention *all* employees." He looked back at Junior. "Please be sure to check your schedule daily. Hours are subject to change—do you remember that, Junior? That conversation we had a few weeks ago? The one when you decided to show up a half-century late for work?"

The boss walked over to Junior and placed the schedule into the kid's hands. Junior's eyes scanned the schedule looking for his name and the time he was due to work. His eyes did a double-take when he saw that he was due in by 3 p.m. His eyes became misty. Junior read his name again, hoping for some sort of discrepancy to save him from his third write-up in less than six months. Instead, he came up short. The boss snatched the schedule from his hands and returned it to the wall.

"'Oh, shit'—remember that? That's what you said," the boss reminded Junior. "Dammit, Junior. Why can't you do right? Why does it have to come down to this?"

"C'mon, Mr. Wilkinson," he begged. "Please, sir. I need this job."

"Please-my-ass, Junior." The boss looked dead at him. "Not this time and not no other time. Not only do you show up to my store late, but you show up in here smellin' like reefer? You don't think I can smell that stuff on you? I had a customer complain about it over in dairy. I thought you were a smart boy? Didn't you go to Langston? Ain't you in college?" he asked him. "Lately, you've been givin' me your ass to kiss, and I'm tired of it."

Junior drooped his head. "I know I was wrong, but you gotta forgive me, man! It's been a tough week and—"

"I ain't got to do nothin'," the boss interrupted. "You got a lot of shit with you boy, OK? You got every excuse in the book, but no excuse is going to be good enough this time. I believe I'm at the end of this book, Junior."

"C'mon, Mr. Wilkinson. Please, sir. I swear on my brother, I'm gonna—"

"It's over, Junior." Mr. Wilkinson held out his hand. "Let me have that apron."

Junior tried not to cry as he placed his apron into the boss's hand.

"Afraid I'm gonna need your ID badge too…"

Junior reached onto his shirt and handed the boss his work badge. A teardrop splashed onto his smiling photograph. Mr. Wilkinson thumbed it away. He wrapped up Junior's apron with his badge and tossed it behind him on his desk. He then placed his hands around Junior's pencil neck and squeezed the kid. Junior's eyes sprung a leak as his nightmare became a reality.

"Junior, look at me," the boss said. "Look at me, I said."

Slowly, Junior raised his head.

"I think you're a good kid, I really do." Mr. Wilkinson told him. "But I can't stand for anymore bullshit, son. I've got a business to run. You'll understand as you get older. You'll be alright. You'll bounce back. Look, why don't you try us again next summer. We'll see where you are by then. If I'm still around, hell, I'd love to give you another shot."

"I need that shot now, man!" Junior cried. "If I could just have another chance, Mr. Wilkinson. I swear to God, I'll—"

220

"Junior." The boss shook his head at him. "Nope."

Junior cried right there as the boss hoisted him onto his feet. He then hugged him.

"C'mere." He patted him across the back. "You're fired, son. OK? No hard feelings."

Junior's shoulders bounced in despair. He sobbed miserably onto the boss's shoulder.

"Stop all that cryin'," Mr. Wilkinson said. "In life you gotta learn to take your lumps. Don't nobody out there give a damn about no grown man cryin'. No one ever does. OK? You stop it."

"Yes, sir." Junior's voice hoarsened.

Afterward, Junior exited through the warehouse bay so no one could see him lose it. The boss followed him to the garage and let him out. When Junior got outside, Mr. Wilkinson lowered the bay door on him, forever banishing his employment at the Mart on 32nd Street. When the door sealed tightly against the asphalt, Junior felt a part of his soul stay behind. For the past year and a half (about as long as he had been dating Vanessa), he had worked there at the Mart. Memories of his first day on the job entered his head, followed by his tragic end. With his pride shattered, he took the long walk back to his car, allowing himself enough time to weep.

Junior's eyes were so foggy he could barely see the road on the way back home that evening. At an intersection, he stared off into the distance, washed out. An angry cabbie laid on the horn, urging him to go as he plodded through the intersection. He replayed his final conversation with the boss inside of his head. The more he thought of the firing, the less valuable he felt.

Junior pulled up at the house and shut off the motor. The firing weighed heavy on his mind as he slumped down into the driver's seat. Slowly, he felt his world around him unraveling. Although he was grateful for college, he was barely keeping up. Junior blamed himself for everything: his problems with Casey, troubles with Vanessa, and not seeing his family. No matter how hard he tried to stay out of trouble, he couldn't. Above him, the sky opened as showers poured over New York. He sat there for nearly an hour in the car, afraid to tell Casey that he fucked up once again. Over and over, he replayed the dismissal inside of his head as he prepped himself to deliver the bad news to Casey.

Just as he was about to get out, he spotted his sissy running up the street with her jacket covering over her head. In her hand was a soggy envelope. Junior scooted to the passenger window and winded it down. "Casey!" Junior called to her. Turning, looking, she rushed over to Junior's car as he opened the door. She splashed onto the seat beside him. The two had barely spoken since Casey had found out about his hand.

"Stupid fuckers!" She slammed the door, shaking out her hair. "Someone took my space, J. I had to park all the way up by the Mitchells' house. Look at my envelope. It's all wet—look." She showed him. "Anyway, what are you doin' sittin' out here all by yourself in the rain?"

"I'll get to that in a minute," said Junior. "Where you comin' from?"

"Just got my exam results. I wanted to open it with you. Figured it'd be a great ice breaker for us since the past few days haven't been so great. You OK?"

"Hell nah," Junior sighed. "I got fired today. Guess I can't blame nobody but myself."

Casey invited Junior in for a hug as the two warmly embraced.

"You know it's been days since I've had a decent hug from you." She held him. "I got to admit though, I saw this shit comin' from a mile away. That's what I've been tryin' to tell you all this time, J. You gotta slow down sometimes."

Junior held onto Casey tightly, allowing his head to fall onto her shoulder.

That night, as heavy rains covered the city, Junior and Casey conversed. They began at 1995 and ended at the present day. They dissected their once-glorious friendship and where the two had gone wrong. It was authentic and honest with real tears raining from both sides of the car. Exhausted, Junior contemplated giving up. New York was too big, college too difficult and loving Vanessa was even harder; he opted out. As always, Casey was there to encourage him.

"I gotta be honest J.," she said. "Some days, I just wanna grab a big hockey stick and beat the livin' shit out of you 'cause you're so hardheaded. I want this for you, J., this New York thing. But I can't want it more than you do. I'd just hate to see our story end so abruptly after everything we've been through. That's not the way, man."

"I know, Sissy." Junior cleared his lungs. "I don't know why I can't just put this shit together. I got a great opportunity here in New York. I get to be with you, go to college, have a job—had a job. I got to figure this all out."

Casey turned to face him. "Well, I think we both know what the problem is," said Casey. "You moreso than me."

Junior opened his mouth to speak but nothing came out. He'd run out of excuses.

"Exactly," Casey said. "You know exactly where I'm goin' with this, don't you? Here's your problem, Junior." She placed her hand on his heart. "It's right in there. You're puttin' Vanessa over your future and you can't do that. You're doin' what a lot of young people do—what I did—put love ahead of life. It's the other way around. Life first, then love. Because when life is love everything else falls into place. I ain't judgin' you for fallin' in love, but I will judge you for *how* you love. That matters too. Am I makin' any sense?"

"You make it all sound so easy, Sissy, and it's not."

"Junior, do you even know why I brought you to New York in the first place?"

"Yeah, I'm supposed to go to school and—"

"—It's got nothin' to do with school," she stopped him.

224

"No, I brought you here for the experience. Don't you see? The experience, J. That's what this is all about. It's supposed to be an experience for you. Not a nightmare," she explained. "You've got the whole world in front of you up here, Junior. Right now, Vanessa, in my opinion, plays too much of a role in your world, and it's killin' you. You're starting to lose yourself, Junior. Think about what happened today. I wasn't even there, but yo, I'd *bet* my life Vanessa was somehow involved in you losing your job. Just like your hand, Mel, and everything else that's happened. It's just a tip of the iceberg, and we both know what happened in *Titanic*. Don't you remember? With Leonardo DiCaprio?"

"...The ship went down."

"Exactly." Casey held his chin. "The ship went down. So, just try not to hit anymore fuckin' icebergs and we'll be good," she laughed.

Junior grinned back.

"Man, you always give such good advice. How'd you get so smart?"

"I wasn't *born* yesterday, you dummy." Casey plucked his ear. "I made mistakes too. I don't want to send your body back to Brooke's Rowe chopped into pieces, but I will. But you wanna know somethin'?" She held Junior by his cut hand. "I'd be really sad if I had to do that, Leonard Robinson Jr. That would be a fucked up day for me. I love you, little brother." Casey's lips shook as her voice changed. "Now, let's get out of this rain and go inside, OK? You with that, J.?"

"Love you too, Sissy." Junior fought back tears. "Yeah, let's go in. Count us down."

"Three... two... one!"

With their jackets covering their heads, Junior and Casey braved the city's downpour and hurried inside for the night.

Thirteen

You made me believe.
You steered me from my wicked existence and gave me love.
My soul became bright and my conscience inflated.
My sense of self became elevated.
I couldn't've anticipated it. Casey, when I was lost,
you stayed and you waited.
Your love, I could never repay it.

—LEONARD G. ROBINSON JR.

"Whew, shit!" Casey stripped off her jacket inside the foyer as Junior closed the door behind them. Her crinkly orange hair made her look like Sideshow Bob from *The Simpsons*. Their jackets were so wet that Casey had to put them in the dryer. Inside her coat pocket was her sodden test results from her exam. She passed it over to Junior.

"Here, you open it. I'm too nervous," Casey told him. "No, wait! Uh, let me change first."

Junior waited as Casey rushed off to her bedroom to change. In his hand was Casey's future; the results of three

227

months' worth of intensive studying. Casey's back-to-school journey had started back in May just before he graduated from Langston. It was a big step toward furthering her education and life. It was Casey's dream to practice family law.

"Will you hurry up?" Junior yelled from the bottom steps. "What are you doin' up there?"

"Just a few more minutes!" she yelled back. "Don't look at it without me."

"Man, I ain't gonna look at it, but hurry up."

Junior moved from view and peeked inside at Casey's results. He looked through a small slit in the envelope and closed it. He stopped reading at "We regret to inform you." Heartbroken for her, he plunged near the bottom of the staircase and wore his best mask for Casey. She ran down the steps minutes later and sat beside him.

"Alright, I'm ready," she said. "Yo, I think I passed—you think I passed?"

"Yeah, Sissy," Junior deflated. "I think you passed."

"Well, open it up. C'mon, let's have a look."

Slowly, Junior handed Casey the letter. She snatched it from his hands.

"Oh, just give me the damn letter, boy!" She bopped him on his head and opened it.

As she started to read, Junior placed his head on her shoulder and hugged her. Casey's grin collapsed the moment she saw her failing score of 54% stamped near the top. She needed at least a 70% to pass. She'd spent months eating, sleeping, and shitting next to books. Her mouth hung open in shock as the letter fell from her hands and floated down the steps into the foyer. She couldn't believe it.

"I'm sorry, Casey." Junior squeezed her. "I know how hard you worked."

Disappointed, Casey looked down at her hand to play with a spot inside of her palm.

"Well, it is what it is." She sprang to her feet. "I didn't think I'd pass it anyway. So, I guess I didn't really lose anything, you know. I mean, it's just a stupid little test. It doesn't mean nothin'. I'm good. You hungry? You want a snack or somethin'?"

"No, thank you. You sure you OK, Casey?"

"Yeah, of course." Her eyes reddened. "Why wouldn't I be? Like I said, it's just a test. You know, I learned a long time ago that if you don't expect much, you won't be disappointed. So, I'm not disappointed. I'm really not."

Casey *was* disappointed. She headed into the kitchen to medicate. Her face was red with broken dreams. At the icebox, she unpacked a gallon of Häagen-Dazs double-chocolate-chip ice cream along with a slice of pound cake, oatmeal raisin cookies, and two twinkies. Casey's destructive eating habits had started during her teen years after learning she wasn't any good at suicide. Her eyes were filled with fury as Junior looked on. "What? Th'fuck are you lookin' at?!" she yapped at him before slamming the refrigerator door. She placed her snacks on the counter top and walked over to the sink to wash the dishes. Casey got so upset that she busted a plate. She then leaned over the sink and began to wail as

Junior walked over to comfort her. "Fuck!" She pounded the sink. "Why can't I just get my life together, man? I'm always at the back of the *goddamn* line! I'm such a loser, J."

"Stop, you're not a loser, Sissy." Junior petted her back. "Why not just take it again?"

"What for? Man, I worked my ass off on that test, J., and I still came up short."

"Casey, you got a 54%."

"Yeah, no shit. I failed."

"No, it means that you're close," he explained. "Shit, all you need is a 70% or better. That's only a few questions. You can pass it. Just don't give up."

"Man, th'hell with that stupid-ass test. Should've never taken it!"

"Casey, NO," Junior ordered. "I'm not accepting that. You have to take it again. Because if you don't… I'll call Mom. Yeah!" he threatened. "She'll lecture you for three hours about the importance of diversifying our justice system. I *know* you don't want that shit. Nobody wants that!"

Casey sobered up quickly.

"You would do that, wouldn't you?" She half-smiled.

"In a heartbeat." Junior smiled back. "Yo, how *dare* you call yourself a loser when you beat so many things already, Casey? You beat cancer. You overcame your childhood. You beat the staff at Medgar High. You even overcame yourself all those times you tried to end it. You beat everybody. You're undefeated, Casey—and you know what? You're gonna defeat that exam too."

Casey looked at her brother in awe.

"Damn, how'd you get so strong?" She sniffled. "What are you, Dr. Phil now or some shit?"

"Man, my team is strong," Junior told her. "You're part of that team, Casey."

Casey lowered her eyes and exhaled.

"Well, can I at least have the weekend to think it over? Maybe we can talk about it Sunday after you get back from Brooke's Rowe.

"Of course," said Junior. "Yo, that test ain't gonna know what it hit it once we put our heads together, Casey. We got this!"

"Yeah, right." Casey shrugged. She loaded her arms full of snacks and headed over to the couch. As she turned on the TV, Junior headed upstairs to prepare for a long weekend.

"Lawrence's Things – 1994"

"So, how is this all my fault?" Vanessa asked Junior over the phone the next morning during his drive into Brooke's Rowe. The busy weekend traffic along the interstate slowed his commute. Being trapped behind a smelly waste truck without A/C only added to Junior's fervor as the two dissected their treacherous relationship. Junior's logic sailed over Vanessa's head throughout their discussion.

"I never said that, V.," said Junior. "Stop puttin' words in my mouth. Just hear me out."

"Son, you're the one that called me all pissed off that Mr. Wilkinson fired you. You make it sound like it's my fault. You read the schedule wrong, J.—you said it yourself."

"Me losing my job *was* my fault. But I'm talkin' about the other shit, V. All I wanted to do was go to the Peace Corps meeting, but you wanted to go back to your crib and look what happened. I ended up trapped inside of your parents' bathtub, butt-ass naked, when you said they were gonna be out of town. Yo, I'm tired of fuckin' gettin' in trouble everywhere I turn."

"Wowww! Really? Really, Junior? That's what we're doin'? OK."

"C'mon, Vanessa. The way we've been actin' these past few weeks? Shit's been fucked up. We can do better than this. You keep sayin' you wanna grow with me, but I don't be seein' that shit. Straight up. If we're gonna talk about it—we should be about it, too."

"Hmph. Did Casey tell you to say all that?"

"Man, Casey didn't tell me shit!" Junior raised his voice. "I'll tell you what, V. How about I just see you at school next week? I can't do this right now."

"Next week?" she laughed. "Wowww. So, you're not hangin' out with me over the weekend because I don't agree with you? Is that how I'm takin' it?"

"You can take the motherfucka any kind of way you want to, Vanessa."

She gasped and hung up on him. Junior tossed his phone in the seat beside him and pounded the wheel with his fist.

For the rest of Junior's ride, he called Vanessa things he wouldn't normally say.

From the moment Junior arrived home, his parents went at it. He pulled up to find Senior and Sandy trading barbs near the mailbox. In Senior's hand was an envelope which he tried to keep Sandy from seeing. He moved it from side to side as Sandy cussed and flapped at him. Junior leapt from his car and bounced between the two.

"Dammit, woman!" Senior fussed. "Ain't no love note in here. It's a check."

"What check? From who?" Sandy questioned.

"Do y'all have to argue out in public like this?" Junior interrupted.

"Shut up, Junior!" his parents said in unison. Junior shut right up.

A weekend from the big city was well-needed after a tough week, but returning home proved to be anything but peaceful as the Robinsons shouted at one another. At times, Junior had to play parent to two bad-ass kids who couldn't get along. Embarrassed, Junior took the check from his daddy's hand. It silenced their tirade.

"Told you I ain't been nowhere," Senior whispered to Sandy.

"Shhhh!" Junior silenced him as he read. "Wait a minute, y'all. This ain't no check. It's a bill from the electric company for $150."

Sandy went off on her husband again.

"How in the hell did you miss that?" she asked him.

"Dammit, Leonard. Those eyes are bad. You can't see worth a damn. You ought to get 'em checked."

"Ain't nothin' wrong with my eyes, woman. Shit, I can see!"

Junior gave up and went inside.

An hour after his parents' first tiff, Junior helped Senior clean the gutters of their rotting house. His daddy used the time to vent to him about Sandy's erratic behavior.

"Goddamn woman is crazy, man," Senior told him. "I don't know what her problem is. Ever since our neighbor Mickey left his old lady, she thinks I been messin' 'round on her."

Junior didn't speak, hoping not to egg Senior on.

"Somethin' is wrong with her. Woman ain't been right since you left. All she does is walk 'round and look for shit to fuss 'bout. Talkin' bout my eyes is bad and all that ol' shit. I'm tellin' you right now. It ain't *nothin'* wrong with my eyes."

As Senior set the ladder up against the house, he mistimed its landing and struck the gutter so hard that it detached. It dangled like a crane tower over his parents' window. Sandy slid back the glass within seconds. When she saw the section of hanging gutter, she went off.

"Dammit, Leonard. Why you got to be so rough with everything? Ain't nobody tell you to slam that damn ladder up against the house like that. You're too rough."

"I ain't slam shit—I tapped it. That's all."

"You ain't tap shit. Somebody ought to *tap* you. Sounded like a damn bomb went off!"

"Junior," Senior turned to him for validation. "Now, tell

the truth, son. Didn't I tap it?" Caught in the middle, Junior didn't know whose side to take as his parents both waited for his response. He took the politician's route.

"I wasn't paying attention," said Junior. "I didn't see it."

Sandy threw up her hands and closed the window. Senior went in after her. Seconds later the sound of explosive language emitted from inside the Robinson castle. Junior sat on the back steps and waited for them to finish. They yelled so loud that neighbors could hear them bickering from the roadway. In Junior's mind, both of his parents were rough. His daddy "tapped" things, and so did his momma. Some days he wondered why they were even married for so long. In their 27 years together, all they did was shout and cuss. Their heavyweight prizefight carried on throughout the evening.

After Junior and Senior finished working outside, they entered through the kitchen to notice a patch of fog emanating from the stove. On the back burner was a pot of grits Sandy had forgot to turn off. Lucky for her, they caught it just in time. It was an honest mistake but ammunition for Senior who had been in Sandy's crosshairs all day. He shut off the stove and picked up the pot full of charred grits and showed it to Junior. "Look-a-there. Look-look-look!" He shoved the pot into Junior's face. "Wait 'til I show her this shit."

Pot in hand, Senior went charging up the stairs to confront her.

"Goddammit, woman," his voice bounced throughout the house. "What you tryin' to do? Burn this motherfucka down? Why you ain't turn this shit off?"

"Don't act like I'm the only one who leave shit on 'round here," Sandy fought back. "I came back from bingo the other night and you got lights on in every room."

"Woman, I ain't leave no lights on. What you talkin' 'bout now, Sandy?"

"You'se a damn lie! Go'on somewhere. I ain't in the mood!"

"Well, I ain't in the mood neither!" Senior growled. "Next time, turn this shit off!"

Senior came stomping back down the steps into the kitchen. He bypassed Junior and threw the pot into the sink. *Thung!* He grabbed his keys and walked out, slamming the door behind him. Junior headed upstairs right after to check on his momma. She'd been fussy all day. He sat at the top of the staircase next to her bedroom, careful not to irritate her. On her bed was a box labeled "Lawrence's Things – 1994." Sandy's foul mood suddenly made sense. She came out into the hallway looking for another round at Senior.

"Where's that crazy, old fool at? Is he gone?" Sandy asked.

"Yeah, he's gone," said Junior. "I didn't know you were plannin' on goin' through Lawrence's old things, Ma. Would you like some help?"

Sandy looked back at her deceased son's belongings on the bed.

"I got it," she sighed. "It's still hard, you know. His box has been sittin' here in the attic since we moved from Crawford. I kept pushin' it off."

"Well, I'm here if you need you me."

As Sandy hobbled back into her bedroom to finish, Junior changed the subject.

"So, Ma. How come you and Daddy fight so much? Are y'all ever happy with each other?"

"Well, we have our good times just like any other couple," Sandy explained. "But people get on your damn nerves after a while. Take you and Vanessa, for example. Y'all are young. Y'all got y'all whole lives ahead of you. Everything's fun now. But havin' fun with somebody ain't the same as marryin' a person."

"How so?" Junior asked.

"Well, there's bills and budgets, lifestyles, family, responsibility, kids—if y'all want any. All those things matter when you're with a person for a long time. Y'all have to mesh. As much as I hate to admit it, your daddy and I mesh. He's sweet in his own street-corner kind of way."

Just as Sandy said that, Senior hollered at her from outside the window like *Romeo and Juliet.* Sandy opened the window to listen.

"Stop leavin' French fry boxes in my damn truck!"

"You go to hell!" Sandy closed the window back. "So, anyway. Like I was sayin'—"

Before she could finish her thought, the house phone rang. Sandy walked across the room to peep at the caller ID.

"Lemme get this, it's your aunt. We'll talk more later, Junior."

Junior gave Sandy her privacy and went to look for Senior. He found his daddy out front working on his truck and went to keep him company. Junior walked over to Senior and touched him on the arm, startling him so badly that Senior busted his head onto his hood. He yelped and rubbed the back of his head. He gave Junior a dirty look.

"Didn't mean to scare you, Daddy," said Junior. "Maybe I should come back later."

"You're here now." Senior returned to fixing his truck. "What do you want?"

"...How'd you know Ma was right for you?"

Senior looked over at him.

"That a love question?" he chuckled. "I ain't too good with them kind of questions."

"Well, just do your best. How does one know if a person is right for them?"

"Hell, I don't know. Finding the right woman is like that damn lottery: all them numbers, you just hope to match 'em up right."

As Senior moved around his truck, Junior followed him. "That's it?"

"Yup. Can you pass me that wrench over there, son?"

Junior reached for a rusty, metal wrench inside Senior's toolbox and handed it to him.

"So, how do you know which numbers to play?" Junior asked him.

"You don't, I just said," Senior replied. "You just keep matchin' 'em up 'til somethin' hits."

"But what if nothin' ever hits? Then what?"

Senior looked at him.

"What's all these funny questions 'bout? What are you tryin' to ask me?"

238

"Well, I was just curious because... forget it. Forget I even asked."

As Junior turned to leave, Senior called Junior back over. He placed his oily palm onto Junior's shoulder, forever ruining his T-shirt. Lucky for him, it was an old shirt.

"I ain't no love doctor, Junior. I don't even know what love is. I married your momma at the time because it felt right. And even though we get on each other's nerves, it still feels right. It's got to feel right, Junior. That's the best I can tell you."

"What if I don't know what's right for me yet?" Junior asked. "Is it wrong to be unsure?"

"You can't give love to somebody else if you ain't got it for yourself, Junior. How in the hell you gonna give somethin' you ain't got?"

Senior removed his hands from his son's T-shirt and left behind a greasy print not only on Junior's shirt but inside his thoughts. He stared at the gleam inside of his daddy's eye, lost in his wisdom. Senior shook his head at the boy and went back to working on his truck.

By Saturday night, the war between Junior's parents was still ongoing. He nodded in and out of consciousness, disturbed by their constant bickering. The latest saga was elementary. Sandy wanted the TV on. Senior wanted it off. Unable to sleep, Junior tried to write, but his thoughts were drowned under his parents' squabbling. He tried to play his Walkman, but that didn't help, either.

"Woman, why you got the TV up so loud?" Senior fussed. "I'm tryin' to rest. Can you turn it down some, Sandy?"

"Can you go to hell some?" Sandy fired back. "As many damn lights and TVs and shit you leave on 'round here, don't you start with me about no TV tonight."

As the noise eventually leveled off, Junior began to nod. They started up for round two.

"Ow, Leonard! I told you 'bout those sharp-ass toenails of yours!"

"Well, why you got your leg all the way on my damn side?" Senior shot back.

Round three was much of the same with Sandy pinning Senior on the ropes. By then, Junior had had it. He threw off his blanket and marched into his parents' bedroom to confront them. He cut on their room light, unplugged the TV from the wall, and stood before them. Junior's parents both rolled their eyes at one another like siblings fighting over a ball.

"I come all the way down here to spend the weekend with y'all, and this is what y'all do?" Junior complained. "Ma, the TV is loud as hell; Casey can hear it all the way from New York. Daddy, you really ought to consider trimming your nails, and it's true, you do have trouble seeing things. There, I said it." Junior crossed his arms. "Do y'all need a timeout? Knock it off!"

Junior returned across the hall to his room. He tried to write again, but the fury of his parents' warpath humbled his works. Before long, Sandy entered behind him to apologize.

"Hey, Son." She smiled. "I'm sorry about all of that. Just been a rough day. You know, dealing with Lawrence's old things."

Junior sighed.

"I know, Ma. It's been a rough week for me, too. Still can't believe I got fired. You haven't told Daddy yet, have you?"

"Not yet," said Sandy. "When should I tell 'em?"

"How about after I leave?"

Junior and Sandy both laughed.

"Well, anyway, I put some of your brother's old things out on the curb for Goodwill pickup in the mornin'. Just thought you'd like to know. You be safe gettin' on the road. Again, sorry about the noise. We'll keep it down, I promise."

As Sandy went to pull the door close, Junior stopped her.

"Ma, hold up." Junior met her at the door. "Why'd you let me go to New York in the first place? Why'd you even do it? How'd you know it was the right move to make?"

Sandy pushed Junior's door shut. She guided Junior over to his bed and sat next to him.

"Well, I didn't know at the time," Sandy told him. "But what I did know was that any place was better than this old rut 'round here. Don't get me wrong. I was not thrilled about sending my teenage son away from here. Now, that I know Casey can't cook, I'm even more worried!" She nudged him, jokingly. "But sometimes in life, you got to do things you don't want to but are necessary to get ahead, Junior. And look what I got out of that decision. My son graduated from one of the top high schools in the area. He's in college… I even got a daughter out of it."

Junior looked over at his momma and smiled. Sandy patted his face, stood up and walked over to his bedroom door.

"You'll figure things out, Junior. Just don't ever be afraid to explore your options in life—never be afraid to do that. And no matter what," she said, eyeballing him, "don't let nobody tell you what you can or can't do. Not even your momma…goodnight, son."

Junior looked on as Sandy pulled his door close for the night. He stared at the door after she left, processing her advice. He processed it all night.

Early the next morning, Junior packed his bags and headed back to New York. His soul departed when he opened the door and noticed Lawrence's old belongings strewn wastefully along Kennedy Street. It broke his heart. From the huge box he'd seen on Sandy's bed the other day, his momma kept two items: Lawrence's baby shoes, and a Batman action figure she got him on his birthday just before he died. Lawrence loved Batman. On the side of his brother's box was a sign that read "Goodwill pickup". Next to her chicken-scratch writing, Sandy had drawn a set of Black, praying hands. Someone had removed her artsy sign and left a shoe print on the paper. Quickly, before she awoke, Junior walked up and down his street and collected what was left of Lawrence's things. He tossed his brother's stuff inside of his trunk and closed it. He returned inside afterward to say goodbye to his parents. Sandy groggily rolled over.

"Did Goodwill pick up Lawrence's stuff?" she asked him.

"Yeah, Ma," Junior told her. "They got it all."

Satisfied, Sandy turned over and went back to sleep.

On his way back to New York, Junior stopped at a nearby church and donated what was left of Lawrence's things.

Fourteen

When Junior returned to Casey's later that Sunday morning, he entered to find his sissy plastered to the couch. She looked as if she hadn't moved since he left. The table was covered with junk food and empty wine bottles, and Casey was still wearing the same clothes. Her hair was atrocious, and the house was a mess. She slugged with one of her feet dangling from the sofa and the other tucked beneath her. She greeted Junior with a faint "Hey" as he walked through the door and went back to lifelessly flipping through channels. Junior stood in front of the TV, blocking her view.

"I bet you ain't moved since I left." Junior shook his head. "Scoot over."

Casey moved an inch, offering Junior the corner. "Can't you see I'm busy, J.?"

"Doin' what? Tryin' to get diabetes? Look at all this shit, man. Triple-chocolate-chip Pop-Tarts, cinnamon rolls, *and* honey buns?" Junior tossed the box to the floor. "You know how much sugar is in all this stuff, Casey?"

"I don't know, and I don't care."

"Well, you ought to care. Like, what about the exam?"

"What about it? I've decided not to take it—fuck that test."

"Yeah, but you were so—" Junior ripped the remote from her hands and cut off the TV, "—you were so close the last time. C'mon, get up. Where's your book? Let's study."

Casey childishly pulled the blanket over her head. Junior threw it down onto the floor.

"Will you stop?" She reached for it. "Leave me alone."

"No," Junior told her. "Get on up, Casey! If you need a study-buddy, you got one."

As Junior went to pull Casey from the sofa, she held on. Junior turned on the TV and flipped to a live Sunday service. He cranked up the volume and placed the remote inside of his pocket. Casey hated church on TV.

"You're an asshole, you know that?" Casey fought with him. "Gimmie that remote, J."

"Nope." Junior swatted at her. "Get up, first."

Casey sucked her teeth and turned over on the couch. Junior's first attempt to remove her from the couch failed. He tried pulling at Casey's arm as she went deadweight on him. Her big body was immovable. He grabbed the couch cushions and whacked her across the back. She didn't move. Junior even threatened to throw her food away: nothing. He went back to wailing away at Casey with pillows and tried prying her from the sofa again but wasn't strong enough. Junior shoved her in frustration.

"Man, you're actin' like a big-ass baby, you know that? Get your ass up from there."

Casey gave Junior the finger with her back turned. She covered herself with the blanket.

Winded, Junior collapsed to the floor to recoup. He lacked the muscle to move Casey's stubborn mass before recalling her dreaded weakness: her feet. Junior grabbed one of Casey's socked feet, locked it beneath his arm and gave her a quick jolt. She came to life, thrashing wildly before going airborne onto the floor. Junior peeled off Casey's sock and threw it at her.

"Look motherfucker, I'm not playin' with you—I ain't Vanessa!" She flailed desperately, trying to kick him with her other foot. "I will beat the *brakes* off you, boy! I swear to God, Junior, if you tickle me, I'm gonna fuck—"

"You're gonna do what?" Junior began raking at her meaty sole. "You're gonna do *what?!*"

Casey levitated from the floor under Junior's assault. Her big, angry body flopped like a dying fish as she cackled with goofy laughter. Casey hated being tickled, especially on her feet. It drove her insane. Each time she tried to speak, Junior tickled the words right out of her mouth. She could barely put together a complete thought.

"That's it! You're outta here... I'm gonna call the cops... wait-*waaaaiit*... Staa-aa-aaa-ap!"

Junior paused to give Casey a break. "So, when is the next test?"

"CUT IT OUT, JUNIOR!" She growled like a linebacker. "You will go back to Philly today! Let me go!"

"Either give me a date, or we're gonna keep going. So, when are you going back?"

"How the FUCK should I know?"

Casey howled once again as Junior revved up his attack. Her foot flexed and pawed the air as she struggled desperately to break free.

"You're taking that exam again, Casey—as soon as possible. No more junk food for the rest of the day. You're gonna clean up this mess you made—oh, and I need some gas money. We straight? I can't hear you, Casey!"

"Yesssss!" she screamed and writhed. "Goddammit, yes!"

Junior finally let her go. Casey laid on the floor, dead. Her hair was even worse than it had been before he arrived. She used her hand to fan herself. Her shirt was covered in pig sweat. She kicked at Junior's leg.

"Fuckin' asshole, why would you do that?"

"It worked, didn't it? Now, I want you off this floor, changed, and back inside of that book when I get back from the Mart, Casey. I'm not playin'."

"Damn, what's got into you? Where you goin'?"

Junior headed up to his bedroom to change as Casey came limping after him with one sock on. She followed Junior over to his closet as he fished for something dapper to wear.

"Did you just say you were headed down to the Mart?" she asked. "I thought you got fired?"

"I did," Junior agreed. "I'm going to get my job back."

Casey took a seat down at Junior's desk. She scratched her head.

"J., hold up," she stopped him. "All jokes aside, look, I know you're feelin' good and ready to redeem yourself, but the real world doesn't work like that," she explained. "You can't just walk into your old job after getting fired and expect for the boss to take you back. That shit doesn't happen. Look, getting fired isn't the same as leaving on good terms."

"Oh yeah? Watch me."

Second Chances

Junior entered the Grocery Mart wearing the gray suit and French blue tie Senior got him for graduation. He walked into his old job with a look of resolve as he detoured his ex-colleagues in search of his old boss. He stopped one of his former co-workers near the deli section, Deborah, to ask about the boss's whereabouts. "Wilkinson should be floatin' around here somewhere," Deborah told him. Junior checked both the cereal and condiment aisles; nothing. "Try the office," another employee said. In Junior's hand was a crisp manila folder with his resumé. His dress shoes were polished and shined. He searched up and down every aisle, eventually spotting Mr. Wilkinson doing inventory in the pastry section. Mr. Wilkinson did a double-take when he saw him standing there. Junior had been gone a total of three days.

"Junior?!" the boss walked over to him, surprised to see him. "What brings you out this way, man? That's a bad-ass suit you got!"

"Thanks, Mr. Wilkinson. You got a minute, sir?" Junior asked.

Mr. Wilkinson called over an associate to take over his inventory and then led Junior back to his office. During their walk, Junior recalled all the times he'd walked behind Mr. Wilkinson and gave him the finger. The days he'd call him a motherfucker beneath his breath. He regretted those moments. The boss wasn't a motherfucker like Junior once believed. When they reached his office, Mr. Wilkinson gestured for Junior to take a seat. He closed the door behind them.

"So, what can I do for you today, Mr. Junior?" he asked. "Want a soda or somethin'?"

"No, thank you, sir." Junior cut to the chase: "I came to ask for my old job back. I know I let you down, Mr. Wilkinson, but I'd be grateful for a second chance. I did a lot of thinkin' about what happened over the weekend. I took things for granted. I got carried away," Junior admitted. "I would love to have another shot to prove to you that I can be reliable, sir."

The boss sat with his arms crossed. He looked Junior up and down.

"Why would you wanna work for me again?" the boss asked. "I thought you said I was too hard on you? Didn't you tell me that one time?"

"You were just tryin' to make me a better person. I didn't understand that before," Junior explained. "C'mon, Mr. Wilkinson. Can't none of these cats in here work the registers like me. You said it yourself. You said that I had the fastest hands you'd ever seen. You said my hands were faster than Muhammad Ali's," Junior reminded him. "Let me prove it to you again."

Mr. Wilkinson scratched at his face. He thumbed his eyes and exhaled.

"I wish I could help you, Junior, but I can't. I love the suit, and the new attitude, but there's nothin' I can do for you. It's too late, and I just—"

"Boss, I need that job, man," Junior interrupted. "It's not just the money. I need it for my own personal stake. I know I can do better. I can't go back to my sister's house without that job."

"Well, you should've thought about that before you showed up late, smellin' like reefer. Ain't no way in the world you comin' back in here. You don't deserve it, Junior. Now, I gotta get back on the floor. Is there anything else?"

"Well, what if I volunteer?" he offered. "We'll start from scratch. If you like what you see, you can bring me back. If not, I'm gone. I'll never bother you again. Would that work?"

"Junior, Junior." The boss placed his hand onto the boy's shoulder. "Did you hear what I just said, son?" he told him. "You'll get a crack at another job, but it won't be here. Let it go."

Junior sagged his head. He wanted to cry, but he sucked it up.

"I understand, sir. The way I messed up, there's no comin' back from that. It's just a part of life. Right? I mean, I do wish you would've said yes—but I realize I did that to myself. But hey, thank you, anyway, sir. Thanks for everything. I'm just gonna keep on keepin' on, you know? I'm sure I'll find some-thin' somewhere. Yeah…"

Junior's eyes filled with regret.

"Take care of yourself, young man," Mr. Wilkinson told him. "It'll be alright, OK?"

A tear left Junior's eye as he smiled. "Yup."

Junior shook his old boss's hand and exited through the warehouse again. At the bay, Junior turned back to wave at Mr. Wilkinson. The boss tilted his head at Junior and lowered the garage door on him. Junior walked to the edge of the loading dock area, turned over an old milk crate and took a seat. He felt a good cry coming on, but was able to ward it off. Before long, he stood with his head held high and returned to his car at the end of the lot.

When Junior returned home after his botched trip down to the Mart, he arrived to find Casey hard at work. Her glasses were stuffed over her face as she bit on the back of a mechanical pencil, in deep thought. He removed his suitcoat and whipped it onto the back of a chair. He placed his phone down onto the table and headed to the icebox for a soda. Casey looked on, waiting for a verdict on his job status.

"So, you were right." Junior loosened his tie. "I didn't get my job back, but I feel pretty good about myself, Casey. It's a learning experience."

As Junior took a sip from his ice-cold can, his phone began to ring. It was none other than Vanessa. Junior and Casey both looked down at her flashing picture on the screen. Once upon a time, a call from Vanessa was enough to stop Junior's world from turning on its axis. Junior lifted the device to get a closer look and returned it to the table.

"Aren't you gonna get that?" Casey asked him. "What if it's important?"

Junior cleared his lungs. He picked up his phone and turned off its ringer. Awe was painted on Casey's face.

"What could be more important than helping you prepare for your exam, Casey?" Junior asked. "Vanessa can wait. I said I was gonna help you, and that's what I'm here to do."

Casey's face softened. She left her chair and went over to squeeze his handsome face.

"C'mere, little brother." She hugged him. "I'm sorry you didn't get your job back. You might've messed up, but I see the changes already. Keep going, OK?"

"Thanks, Sissy," Junior sighed. "Have you ever been fired before?"

Casey laughed.

"*Shiiiit*, have I? Let me tell you!"

Casey walked over to the icebox and grabbed herself a beer. She twisted the cap and took a sip of her frosty beverage before passing it over to Junior.

"Just a sip."

Junior took a short sip of Casey's beer and gave it back to her. She took a satisfying gulp and belched like a city truck driver.

"Not everybody gets fired, but most people do. It happens," she said. "I've been fired a few times. But the last time I got fired was from McDonald's."

"What'd you get fired for?"

Casey laughed. "You'll never guess! Snortin' coke in the bathroom."

Junior nearly choked.

"*Dayumm*, Casey!" he laughed.

"See, J.? Nobody's perfect," she chuckled. "I also got fired from IHOP for stealing food—but that didn't count. I'll tell you about it later. I even got fired from Circuit City for stealing electronics. Shit, if you were to open up a dictionary and look up 'fired', my fat-ass picture will be right next to it. My middle-name is 'Fired'. It's on my birth certificate."

The two shared a hardy laugh together.

"Adulting is hard, J.," she told him. "I'm twice your age, and I'm still tryin' to figure this bullshit out. Don't beat yourself up, OK? The main trick is not to repeat the same mistakes. That's where I fucked up. Learn and move on. You got it?"

"I got it." He smiled.

"Cool." She smiled back. "By the way, thank you."

"For what?"

"For getting me straight earlier. I was being stupid—I deserved that." Casey handed Junior a stack of three-by-five-inch flashcards. "OK, now quiz me."

Junior thumbed through her heap, looking for the perfect flashcard to kick-off their study session. He looked up at Casey as she stared back at Junior waiting for him to begin. It felt good for him to be on the right track. He grinned as he thought of Casey's story about the cocaine.

"What?" she asked him. "What's so funny?"

"I ain't say nothin'," Junior chuckled. It felt good to be his old self again.

Fifteen

I talk, but you don't listen.
You don't speak into my soul the way you used to.
You've grown cold and you speak into that dark hole.
You're reckless with my heart.
You don't speak my love language—
I don't know what you speak.
I just know it's not what I need,
or what I can pretend for it to be.
I'm tired of not being me.

—LEONARD G. ROBINSON JR.

Junior's soggy, cornflake cereal was more entertaining than Vanessa criticizing him for asking for his old job back. The Mart was still a touchy subject to him. He had barely survived the weekend thinking about the firing. The two rendezvoused for a quick breakfast before the start of their classes.

"I don't know why you went back there in the first place," she told him. "That couldn't have been me. I would've never gone back." Vanessa bitched through much of breakfast.

Junior sat at the table unamused, watching as she compressed a lemon into a cup of hot tea. Even the way she stirred her drink annoyed him. She continued her fierce rant on a myriad of shit Junior could care less about. He looked down at his watch to check the time and stood up from his chair.

"I gotta bounce, V. I got anatomy in a few minutes."

"Why can't you just wait for me?" she asked him. "I'm almost finished. We're not at Langston anymore, J. Nobody's gonna mark you down for being late. Besides, we haven't seen each other all weekend. C'mon, sit."

Junior sighed and returned to his seat. Vanessa took her sweet time finishing her styrofoam cup of tea. She even got back in line to buy a grapefruit. Junior waited for her like a moron, watching the minutes pass by on his sports watch. It was the same irresponsibility that cost him his job at the Mart. Before Junior knew it, he was five minutes late to class. He sprung to his feet and pushed in his chair.

"I gotta go, V. Let's get together this afternoon."

"Yo, relax. It's only the third week, J. You ain't missin' nothin'."

"You don't know that. What if he's having us dissect an owl or some crazy shit?"

"Son, an owl, though?" Vanessa giggled. "Aight-aight. Just hit me up later. An owl!"

Junior raced up the nearest stairwell and down the second-floor hallway. He made it to the door of Mr. Freemont's class and saw his classmates with their heads all buried down at their desks. The students weren't dissecting an owl; they

254

were in the middle of taking an exam. His asshole teacher was nowhere to be found. Quickly, Junior grabbed a blank test from Mr. Freemont's desk and sat next to Rachel.

"You better hurry!" she whispered. "You only have a few minutes left."

Vanessa had fucked Junior yet again. He flipped over his test and noticed it was six questions. All were fill-in the blank. He nudged Rachel on the arm.

"C'mon, man. Help a brotha out. I don't know this shit."

"That's cheating! You could get kicked out for that, and so could I if I helped."

"You're right. I'm sorry for even asking. I should've got here on time, man. *Damn!*"

Rachel looked over at Junior and exhaled, feeling sorry for him. Quickly, she exchanged papers with him. Junior couldn't believe it. He looked down at Rachel's old test and back up at her.

"Put your name on top of the paper," she told him. "Hurry up!"

Junior scribbled his name at the top.

"Thank you. I appreciate it. I wasn't expecting to walk in and all of a sudden—"

"Will you shut up?" she interrupted him. "I'm trying to concentrate, Junior."

Junior left Rachel alone to finish. Seconds later, Mr. Freemont walked in the door with a cup of coffee in his hand. He stood behind his desk, sipping and staring down at his watch. He looked over at Junior. Shock was painted on his face. Junior could tell Mr. Freemont couldn't believe that he had finished on time after arriving late. Junior played it off by pretending to read over his test answers. Before long, the teacher ordered his tests to the front of the room. Mr. Freemont eyed Junior with suspicion as he turned in his exam. He offered Rachel the same precarious glare. During first break, he called the two over to the back of his classroom. In his hand were their test papers. Junior shook with trepidation.

"I can't prove it, but if I find out that either of you were screwin' around on my exam, I'm gonna have you both thrown out of here," the teacher threatened, focusing his attention on Junior. "How in the world did you finish so fast? You weren't even here when I put those tests down."

Before Junior could own up to his blunder, Rachel threw herself into the fire.

"What are you talking about?" Rachel fussed. "I'm the one that copied off him!"

"What?!" Mr. Freemont's mouth hung open.

"*Whaaat?!*" Rachel mocked him. "What's the matter? You're not used to seeing a Black student finish before a blonde-haired white girl? Hmm?" she questioned. "Junior's been busting his ass to survive in your course—maybe you ought to back off and find some other poor sap to pick on for a change. Leave the kid alone."

"Yeah, man!" Junior adlibbed. "What's up with that bullshit?"

Mr. Freemont scowled at Rachel with a look of disdain.

"Stay behind after class, young lady. I know exactly how we can settle this."

Junior waited for his new best friend out in the hallway after anatomy ended. Mr. Freemont ordered Rachel to re-take his examination. If she failed, he threatened to turn over to the dean. Instead, Rachel shocked him with a passing grade. It pissed Mr. Freemont off quite a bit, Junior overheard. Afterward, Junior met up with Rachel down the hall before heading to sociology.

"Yo, why'd you take the fall for me?"

"I had to. I figured Freemont would've given a Black student less leeway than a white girl," she explained. "So, I outsmarted him. I used his own bullshit against him. What the hell are you doing coming to class ten minutes late, anyway? Dude, I told you the first day. Freemont, ain't the type to fuck around with. Try to be on time the next go-around. Besides, I had an ulterior motive: what happened to you last week? Why didn't you show up to the meeting with the Peace Corps Alliance?"

"It's a long story," Junior sighed. "I got caught up in some dumb shit, and it's just… I lost my job and a bunch of other stuff."

"You still need a job? Why didn't you say so? Parris knows the hiring manager inside the school bookstore. I'll talk to him and see if he can get you on a register—but you really ought to come this time, Junior. We're meeting in the lunchroom at noon with some other members. Please come."

"Well, I'm supposed to be meetin' up with my girlfriend later. How about next time?"

"So, bring her with you," she offered. "Besides, I still want your help on this project I'm working on. I need your insight. What's your girlfriend's name? Does she write?" Rachel asked him. "Maybe she'd be interested. Either way, bring her."

As the two parted ways, Junior went on to his sociology class. He beamed with glee at his new plug-in. Sandy always told him that in life it wasn't always *what* people know, but *who* they know. Not to mention, a job was at stake. Before heading in to sociology, he called Vanessa to share the good news. To Junior's surprise, she seemed barely excited for him.

"Aight-aight, I guess I did say that I was gonna come with you the next time," she giggled. "Yo, sorry about earlier. I had a terrible weekend. I'll tell you more about it after the meeting. What time is it again? Where?"

"Lunch room. About 12:30 or so," Junior told her.

"I'll be there. Yo, wait for me outside, we'll go in together."

After the two hung up, Junior went in to class.

Above & Beyond

Junior was antsy as he waited for Vanessa to arrive at the lunchroom that afternoon. It was 12:42 p.m. The meeting had already started, but Rachel's members had gathered minutes prior to its start time. Rachel arrived on the dot at 12:30 along with Parris. The two stopped to greet Junior at the door before heading in. "Vanessa should be here any second now," Junior told his new friends. "I'm gonna give her a few minutes and we'll be right over."

Junior paced back and forth, waiting for Vanessa to show. Nothing. He checked his watch and even called her phone to leave messages. At one point, he looked over into the lunch room at Rachel. She threw up her hands at him. The gesture made him feel like a leashed dog waiting for its owner to return. Junior left Vanessa a third message. "Yo, where are you, V.? I'm still waitin'. Hurry up before the meeting ends. Peace." Junior went back to pacing and looking up and down the hallways for Vanessa to no avail. He looked back into the lunchroom and noticed Rachel and her team all leaving. His heart tanked. Vanessa had done him in once again. He tried to keep his composure as Rachel passed by him. She tried not to look disappointed.

"Rachel, I am so sorry!" Junior explained. "My girlfriend, she uh... something came up. I promise, I'm gonna make it up to you. You have my word—whatever you need for your mission, I got you. Y'all good?"

Rachel raised her eyebrow at him. She shook her head. "Why didn't you just come in?" She laughed in his face, looking him up and down. "I'll catch you later, Junior."

It was a simple question that Junior couldn't answer, he realized. Vanessa had him so well-trained that he had missed out on opportunity to redeem his finances and fellowship with other writers. Everything he did benefitted Vanessa Bailey, but not Leonard Robinson. Junior brooded with such steam that he left before he could run into Vanessa, afraid he'd do or say something he'd regret. He pushed past his peers through the door and stormed out.

When he got to his car, he flung his bag across the passenger seat and stabbed the ignition with his car keys. He slammed his fist into the wheel, pissed off. Junior closed his eyes and took a deep breath to compose himself. He threw his car into gear and readied to leave when suddenly his phone began to ring. It was Vanessa calling him back.

"Yo, where are you? I'm by the lunchroom," she told him. "Are we still doin' the meeting?"

Junior ripped the phone from his ear and looked at it. He nearly threw it.

"That was a half hour ago, Vanessa! I'm about to leave."

The phone was so quiet, Junior could hear her swallow.

"...Oh," she said. "I-I don't know how I got that wrong, J. I thought you said it was at 1 p.m. Son, where are you? Are you still parked in the same spot from this morning?" she asked him. "I'm gonna come to you. Give me a second, OK? I'm on the way."

Junior hung up on her. He waited inside his car until he saw Vanessa's beautiful face come pacing up the lot. He exited his car, leaned against the hood and folded his arms in contempt. He glared at her as she walked up.

"Juniorrrr," she whined with remorse. "I'm sorry, OK? I don't know how I got that wrong. I really I thought I heard 1 p.m. C'mon, don't look at me like that. It was an accident, J. I swear. C'mon, let's go look for 'em."

"They're gone, V." Junior didn't blink. "They left already."

"*Shitttt*," Vanessa palmed her face. "Son, I am so sorry about that. My head has just been so fucked up. Man, my weekend was a hot mess. I got into it with my parents again. I'm just… I'm sorry, J. I really am. I'm gonna make it up to you. Deadass, yo, the next meeting—I don't give a fuck—I'm there. You still wanna get back on stage?"

Junior had had it with Vanessa's lame excuses and set her straight. His voice fractured as he tried to cycle through his emotions, pulling the plug on their relationship which had been on life support as of recent.

"Above and beyond," he shook his head at her. "That's how far out of my way I've gone for you, Vanessa. But you just keep leavin' me hangin' and I'm sick of that shit!" Junior's lips trembled. "If it ain't one thing, it's another with you. I can't. I just… I don't know about this right now, V."

Vanessa's eyes sparkled. "Jayyyy," she sang, grabbing his hand. "Stop, don't talk like that. What about the pact we made last week? We both promised!"

Vanessa tried to kiss him. Junior grabbed her wrists, stopping her cold.

"No, Vanessa." He took a deep breath. "You've been the mouthpiece for everything we've done in this relationship—everything. And I… I just… I can't let you speak for me anymore. I think from now on, I'm gonna start speaking for myself."

Vanessa gasped.

"What are you sayin'?! What's that supposed to mean?" she panicked. "Answer me, Junior! Son, you tell me right now to my face just what the *hell* that's supposed to mean!"

"It means that," Junior's eyes teared, "I need to start lookin' out for me, and maybe you ought to start lookin' out for you. I can't do this anymore, Vanessa."

Vanessa's mouth hung open as she looked away. Junior could've sworn he heard Vanessa's heart shatter as he laid the axe onto their relationship; it was all over. She stood there, paralyzed with shock and disappointment.

"I gotta go, V." Junior wiped his eyes. "I'll uh… I'll see you around, OK?"

Vanessa grabbed Junior's arm and held it. Her nails clamped down into his skin. As Junior tried to walk away, she flailed at him with sorrow and despair.

"Wait—just wait a damn minute!" she cried, whining. "I know I'm fucked up, but I'm trying, J.," she sobbed. "I'm really trying to be a good girlfriend, but son, that shit is hard, man. I don't even know who I am sometimes. Don't leave me like this, Junior. Son, I swear to God." Vanessa pounded her fist into her hand as she talked. "You are my—yo—oh my, God, J. No. You can't, man. You can't leave me like this."

Vanessa busted into her hands, shrieking terribly. Junior had seen Vanessa cry many times throughout their relationship but never like that. Somewhere in Junior's big heart, he felt sorry for her before remembering that's what had got him into trouble. His heart. What had once empowered him also made him weak. He unboxed the hurt which plagued his weary soul.

"It's not just today or the other day, V. It's everything," Junior explained. "It's Mel's party. The drinkin'. Tony's car—nearly losin' my freedom over that shit. My hand, and everything else that's been fucked up between us as of recent. I'll always love you, but it's too much, V. It's just…too much right now."

Vanessa bit her lip, trying not to lose it again as she processed their ending. "You're right," she cried again. "One thing about me, I own my shit, J. I always…I've done nothin' but get you into trouble. I'm just sorry I couldn't…figure this shit out before it was too late, you know?" She wiped her eyes. "I guess I always knew in the back of my mind that one day I was gonna fuck this all up, and I did it. It still hurts though." Vanessa grabbed Junior's face and kissed him. "Goodbye, Junior," she whispered. Her lips quivered involuntarily. "So, maybe I'll see you around campus sometime?"

"Yeah," Junior exhaled. "I'd like that a lot, V."

Vanessa rubbed Junior's face one last time, turned and left. She squealed as she walked away. Junior stood near his car door, watching as Vanessa climbed into her car. He waited until she drove off before he decided to leave. He slipped into his ride and lost it.

Bittersweet

"Damn. That's all I can think of at this moment."
—LEONARD G. ROBINSON JR.

The ride home was cloudy with a chance of scattered thunderstorms well into Junior's somber afternoon. Everything seemed to remind him of Vanessa Bailey. The public library where they studied for mid-terms during their senior year at Langston. The ice cream parlor. The park bench where Vanessa first showed him how she liked to be kissed. The florist shop where Junior bought Vanessa her first bouquet of flowers. Their breakup was bittersweet, with more bitter than sweet. The city would never be the same without her.

When Junior arrived home, he trudged through the door, bypassing Casey on the couch. "Hey, J.," Casey lit up. "So, how was your day?"

Junior opened his mouth to speak, but nothing came out. He shook his head and went upstairs to his bedroom. Casey's smile collapsed as Junior continued up to his room. Once upstairs, he pushed his door shut.

Junior looked at his wall of collected memories of he and Vanessa Bailey throughout their tenure together. The one and a half years they spent together felt like a lifetime. One by one, with tears in his eyes, Junior plucked down their photos. At the fourth photo of them, he stopped to look. It was a picture of the two kissing on their senior class trip to

Washington, D.C. He took a seat on the floor of his bedroom and held it. Casey then knocked on his door.

"Yeah, Sissy?" he dried his eyes with his shirt. "Come in."

Casey entered her brother's bedroom with two cold Heineken beers in her hand. She took a seat beside Junior on the floor and passed one over to him. His dreadful face half-smiled.

"Thanks, Sissy."

The two gently tapped their bottles.

"Fuck it," she said. "One beer ain't gonna kill ya."

An hour into Junior's pity party, Casey had ordered an extra-large Domino's Pizza and Chinese food. She ate most of it, of course. The two sat facing Junior's wall. His beady eyes scanned his celebrated photos from left to right. At the top left was a photo of he and Vanessa during his 18th birthday party there at the house. To the right, was a photo of them at Central Park.

"We had a lot of fun, didn't we?" Junior sighed as he stared at his wall.

Casey looked over at him.

"Today's a rough one, but it'll get better. I've been there a few times, myself."

"Shit, if I have to feel like this again, I don't even wanna try." Junior sipped his warm beer. "Is that why you're single, Sissy?"

"Maybe," she said. "Look, J., you're a good dude, man. You'll meet other girls. You'll make new friends. You'll get a new job. You've got time to do all that stuff," she told him.

"Someday, hell, you might even get tired of hangin' out here with me and wanna do your own thing someplace else."

"And leave you? Man, that would be so fucked up if I did that."

"No, it wouldn't, shut up! Nothin' lasts forever, J.," Casey told him. "That's what I've been trying to tell you this entire time, man. You're only 18. You've got way more promise in you than I had at your age. Shit, when I was your age, I was already locked up. You'll be fine. Trust me."

"Thanks, Sissy. Man, you always come through," Junior said. "Yo, so, what'd you get locked up for? Knowing you, I bet you beat the brakes off somebody. Who'd you beat down?"

Casey slowly rose to her feet. "Another time, J. Hey, uh, are you gonna eat that last slice of pizza?"

Junior looked down at the box and chuckled. "Nah. You go ahead. I could use another beer though. If you don't mind. You got any left?"

Casey cut her eyes at him. "Don't push it, Junior," she told him. "I let you off the hook today, but tomorrow we pick it back up on my studying. You got it?"

"Yeah, I got it," Junior exhaled. "Thank you."

Casey cleaned up their mess and left.

Junior rose to his feet to finish his job. He headed over to his closet for an old shoe box and returned to clearing his wall.

Sixteen

In your arms was my happy place.
Your tender vessel was my safe space.
Now, I can only dream again of seeing your beautiful face.
What I would give for one last kiss.
I promise I would cherish every part of it.
I miss you. I miss us. I miss a life beside you.
Don't know what to do.
"We" can't be through. I swear this is hard to get used to.

—LEONARD G. ROBINSON JR.

Desperate to find work, Junior busied himself looking for a new job. During his hunt, he found an ad in the paper looking for a sales associate down at the Mart where he used to work. The ad asked for candidates to "email Mr. Wilkinson at DKWilkinson1965@aol.com". Junior shook his head and continued his search. His quest felt hopeless. A restaurant near the college was offering $3.15 an hour (plus tips) to work the graveyard shift as a waiter. Another gig offered $11 an hour to clean its building from top to bottom, five days a week. It was good money except that the hours conflicted with Junior's school time. A woman named Patty was looking for a dog walker. The caption read: "…must be able to walk three St. Bernards! No exceptions! Contact Patty." When Junior showed Casey the ad, she gave him a blank look. "Haven't you seen *Beethoven*?" she asked him. Frustrated, he slouched at his desk, staring at the blank wall where his shrine used to be. He was out of a job and a girlfriend, Junior thought. He reached for his shoebox full of their old pictures that was beneath his bed and looked through them. He sighed again.

When Junior overheard his sissy coming up the stairs, he pushed the box back under his bed. She stopped by to deliver his cell phone bill for the month. Junior had overused his daytime minutes and was on the hook for $201.81 His head nearly came off when he read the amount due. "You'll find something soon, don't worry," Casey told him.

Junior placed his forehead on his desk after she left. Behind him, his cell phone began to ring atop his nightstand. He zoomed his chair across the room to retrieve it. It was Sandy, likely calling to talk his ear off about nothing.

"Junior!" Sandy whispered. "Log onto your webcam. I wanna show you somethin'."

Junior signed into his webcam. It took him forever to load in. When his picture displayed, he saw his daddy sitting at the camera; it made him smile as Senior waved at him.

"Ta-da!" Sandy laughed. "Look who it is! I got him to give it a shot."

"Yoooo!" Junior greeted his daddy. "Welcome to the new era, Daddy."

"New era, my ass," he growled. "I ain't stayin' on but so long—Sandy, why you got me fuckin' with this thing? Them damn gubment peoples probably watchin' us right now."

Junior laughed as his parents bickered.

"Ain't no damn government people watchin' nobody—just talk to your son with your old, dinosaur-ass. Didn't you say you wanted to talk to him?"

"Damn right." Senior glared into the camera. "Junior, why you ain't tell me you got fired from the Mart? You should've told me, man."

"Well, I didn't wanna disappoint you," Junior explained. "I know how big you are about keepin' some money in my pocket. I was gonna tell you; I was just waitin' on the right time."

Senior softened as he looked up at Sandy and back into the lens.

"C'mon, how you gonna disappoint me? I'm your flesh and blood. People lose jobs all the time. I know it don't feel good, but it happens. Just take it and move on."

Junior smiled into the camera. "Thanks Daddy," he said. "Yeah, I'll find somethin' soon."

"Mmhmm," he nodded. "How you doin' up there? Y'all holdin' on? I know things been rough since you and Vanessa split. Things'll get better. Right now, just try to get back on track."

"I got it, Daddy. Yeah, just one day at a time, you know?"

"That's all anybody can do, son. Aight, no more computers. I got to go. Too many boxes poppin' up and shit—I don't know what's happenin'. See you soon, son. I uh…love you, hear?"

"Love you too, Daddy."

"We're gonna head out," Sandy said. "Tell Casey we'll check back in with her later. Bye son. Love you." She blew Junior a kiss. Junior reached out to grab it and placed it onto his heart.

When their cameras went dark, Junior minimized the dormant screen and noticed Vanessa's screen name on Messenger was active. It was the closest he'd been to her since their break-up several days ago. He clicked onto Vanessa's screen name and opened a chat box. He moved his mouse cursor to the "invite to chat" selection and paused. He missed Vanessa dearly but couldn't bring himself to talk to her over IM. Luckily, Vanessa logged off before he could screw up. Junior shut off his computer and headed out.

The Queens Project

On his way out of campus the next day after his classes ended, Junior was headed down to his car when he spotted Rachel in the lot. She was carrying two large tote boxes when suddenly, the boxes slipped and she fell to the ground. He darted over to help her. There was a mound of school supplies scattered across the campus lot.

"Dammit!" she grabbed her knee and bellowed to the heavens. It reminded Junior of the time his old co-worker dropped her change till onto the floor.

"You OK, Rachel?" Junior helped her to her feet then scooped up the spilled items and returned them to her box.

"Ugh! Thank you, Junior." She rubbed her knee. "I swear, I feel like I'm gonna slice my fuckin' throat the way this project has been jerking me around. Now, if I could just get all of this stuff to my car without dying, I'd be OK."

"Well, let's not do that," Junior laughed awkwardly. He looked inside the totes and noticed a stack of journals. He thumbed through a couple and returned them to the box.

"So, you guys donating this stuff?"

"Yeah, I heard about these kids at a high school in Queens and thought they could use this stuff. They barely have Central Air not to mention school supplies for these kids—and these aren't your average high schoolers," she told him. "These kids are writers."

"That's messed up. Why can't they help these kids out?"

"Because the money is tied up everywhere else. That's why I've been trying to get your help with this Queens project I've been on."

Rachel may have been weird and spazzy, but her kindness was unmatched. Her blonde hair covered over her face as she struggled to pick up both boxes. Junior carried them for her.

"I'll get these," he grunted. "So, where's your car?"

Junior followed Rachel up the long lot and back to her vehicle. She drove a faded, ugly '82 Ford Econoline van. It was brown just like Senior's beloved truck. According to Rachel, it had "a gazillion" miles on it. Her lenses fogged when she said gazillion, Junior noticed. He looked up from the large totes and noticed Vanessa whipping through the lot. He slipped his head behind the boxes. His heart did a dance as she passed in the lot one aisle over. If Vanessa even dreamed that Junior left her for a white girl, she'd run him over.

At the van, Rachel searched for a vacant space for Junior to place her tote boxes. His knees wobbled like Jell-O as he waited for her. He gently placed the totes onto the pavement to give himself a break as Rachel attempted to reorganize her supplies. The boxes were all labeled "The Queens Project". The only space that remained was a cut-out for the driver's seat. She swept her hair behind both her ears.

"Ugh! I'm not gonna get a goddamn thing inside of this van," she whimpered. "Why does this all have to be so harrrd?"

"What about Parris, or the other volunteers? Don't they have a car?"

"Everybody's gone but me—little old me. Besides, Parris doesn't own a car and the other volunteers' cars are full." Rachel looked down at her watch. "Shit, now I have to walk all this stuff back to the multi-purpose room."

"Would it help if I were to take it?" Junior offered. "I'm not doing anything."

Hearts aligned in Rachel's eyes. "You mean, you'd take the boxes all the way into Queens for me? It's an hour away in mid-afternoon traffic. I couldn't possibly ask you to—"

"Fuck that. Where do you need me?" Junior stepped up. "Yo, you looked out for me the other day in Freemont's class. So, I'm gonna look out for you. Matter of fact, I'll follow you there. And when we get there. You tell me what you need, and I got you."

Rachel's face filled with admiration as she took a whiff from her inhaler. "I'd totally devour you if I wasn't lesbian." She shifted her glasses. "You're too kind!"

Junior spent the ride into Queens thinking about Vanessa and how much he missed her. The past few nights he noticed her screen name was signed online. Each time she'd log off, it bothered him. The night before, he wrote her a long chat message but deleted it after she logged off. The break-up made him feel guilty.

Junior followed behind Rachel's van with her precious cargo strapped beside him in his car. He'd volunteered to take on some more of her boxes to free up her van. Given her history of spazzy energy, he took it easy. She was as eccentric a driver as she was a person. She used hand gestures to substitute her turn-signal device and was a huge braker, he noticed. She'd brake on the highway and even braked through the intersections although the light was green. Twice on the way there, Rachel got out of her van at the light to double-check with Junior that he was still OK driving there. "I'm good, Rachel, I promise," he chuckled. "Light's green!" He laughed as she sprinted three cars ahead back to her van and drove off. Junior couldn't figure out his new friend, but he liked her. At one point, Rachel mashed her horn at a stubborn cabbie. He laughed so hard his face hurt. Rachel was alright in his book.

At Montgomery Rock High School in Queens, Junior parked behind Rachel in front of the building. Its huge Gothic structure reminded him of an institution from the 18th century. She ran over to his car window. Her breath smelled like menthol cigarettes. "Gonna grab the team. Wait here!" she told him. Seconds later, Rachel, Parris, and other members from the Peace Corps Alliance converged in front of Rachel's van with a flatbed wagon. Junior sprang from his car with Rachel's two boxes and gently lowered them onto the cart.

"Everybody, this is Junior. Junior, everybody," Rachel introduced him. "This is the kid I've been tellin' you guys about from my anatomy class. He saved me earlier."

Parris extended his hand to Junior.

"I remember him." He nodded. "He's the only one who could figure out the last spoken word challenge I put out. Man, you the know the dean called me into his office the day after I did that? He said I was violating campus policy and that if I wanted to perform, I had to do it on stage in an auditorium."

"That's fucked up." Junior shook his head. "People don't appreciate art these days."

"No doubt. So, Junior, heard your shit is dope, son. What kind of lines did you bring?"

Junior looked over at Rachel, confused. "Lines?"

"Shit, I forgot to mention that part." She palmed her head. "Part of our afternoon is doing spoken word for the poetry club. It's totally fine if you don't feel up to getting on stage, Junior."

Junior didn't show it, but the mere mention of performing on stage again made him fraught. With Vanessa still weighing on his mind, he figured he had a lot to clear out from his database. He debated whether or not to perform.

"Earth to Junior," Rachel giggled. "Did you hear me?"

"Huh?"

"Are you OK with performing later?"

Whatever you do, don't say "yes."

"Sure, I-I-I can go," Junior agreed. "I'm a little rusty, but I'm sure I got a few lines somewhere inside of my bag in the car. Yeah, I'm down."

"Great! So, would you mind being the opening act?"

Whatever you do, don't agree to go first.

"No problem."

Are you crazy? What the hell are you doing?

For the next half hour, Junior joked and laughed with members of the P.C.A. as they carried writing materials inside of Montgomery Rock High. It was a good showing considering he was anxious about his upcoming afternoon act. Back and forth, he entered through the school's gymnasium door with boxes in his hands and placed them on a row of tables. The guys did the bulk of the heavy lifting as Rachel and the girls unpacked. It didn't take long for Junior to fit in with the gang. They welcomed him with open arms. He spent most of his time conversing with Parris about life on campus, poetry, and their favorite tracks on Nas's latest album *I am*.

"So, you're from Brooke's Rowe? I used to have a cousin out there."

"What happened to him?" asked Junior.

"Got caught up in some shit," Parris grunted as he hoisted the last box onto his shoulder. "About a few years ago, he got involved in some kind of shoot-out on the north side. Cops were lookin' for him so he slid to Baltimore. Heard some-body split his wig."

The s tory of Parris's cousin reminded J unior of Lawrence's case. To keep from ruining what was turning out to be a good day, Junior switched topics. His nerves prickled as they entered through the gymnasium and noticed a crowd of students had formed in the auditorium. They hooted and hollered as Junior and Parris joined the alliance behind the table of donated writing goods.

Meanwhile, on stage, their program's director took to the mic to encourage his students to thank them. "Let's hear it for the Peace Corps Alliance from Steny College, folks!" The 50 or 60 kids there all clapped in thanks of their generous donation. Junior's nerves began to roast as the event's MC departed the stage, allowing for a short intermission. He reached into his back pocket for a scrap of journal paper he'd torn from his book. He reviewed his lines, hoping to regain the magic he had once possessed. He looked over at Rachel and Parris and noticed they seemed relax. He felt particularly ashamed that Rachel was an odd-looking white girl at a predominantly Black school yet didn't appear troubled about performing. No one else seemed uncomfortable but him. Junior was relieved when Rachel asked to go ahead of him.

"Junior, do you mind if we switch things up a bit? I'm gonna go first, Parris next, and you third. Everybody else can go after us."

Junior sighed with relief.

After their short intermission ended, it was time to perform. Junior huddled next to Parris, hoping his cadence and rhyming ability would rub off on him. The team watched as Rachel took to the stage and approached the microphone. She stumbled on the way up but caught her balance on the railing. A few high schoolers snickered at her misfortune. Junior thought to himself that if he tripped going up, he'd leave and never show his face in Queens again.

Rachel opened with an introduction about the Peace Corps Alliance with Steny and the group's mission. She kept saying "like" and "totally" and flinging her hair from side to side. The kids there all ignored her. Some were playing on their phones or turned to converse with neighbors. It was so bad that the program's director had to twice ask his students to show Rachel respect while she was on stage. Junior grimaced at the tough crowd. It reminded him of Luke's nightclub.

"They're sleepin' on this white girl," Parris told Junior. "That's a mistake. I've done a few shows with Rachel. She's dope on that mic, kid. She's like a female version of Slim Shady."

Junior didn't see Eminem and not even Vanilla Ice on stage. What he saw was his classmate making a damn fool of herself throughout her introduction. He thought to himself that if Parris "The Prophet" gave her the nod, Rachel must be good. After her long-winded speech, she began the group's opening act. She transformed her voice into a broken soul as she ripped into the microphone with style and grace. Her poem was about the life of a stripper:

Dollar bills get thrown at me.
I smile, but inside there's agony. My life is a tragedy.
The crowd validates me.
Dance bitch, keep dancin', they tell me. In the end I feel dirty,
but throughout I felt worthy.
I doubt if you heard me.
I need love. I need care. I need understanding now
more than ever. I can't get it together.
They say tough times never last, but from where I stand,
I'm sliding down the pole of this life pretty fast.
I am mother. I'm somebody's daughter. Someone's aunt.
I am your relative
to those who don't have a fuck to give.
Dollar bills get thrown at me. I smile, but inside there's
agony. My life is a tragedy.

The whole gym erupted in celebration of Rachel. Junior's mouth hung to the floor as she politely bowed and exited from the stage. Rachel was nothing like the dorky, inhaler-using neighbor from his anatomy class back at school. Rachel had soul, and a lot of it. She walked over to Parris and fist-bumped him.

Parris destroyed anything he touched. He had a flow that was seamless. His lines felt more like the bars of a rap verse in a song. The high school crowd connected with him from the moment he arrived on stage. He didn't need a beat or a hook, Junior noticed. Throughout his limited mic-time, he dropped gems of wisdom on the high school crowd:

Buy a gun, put it up to your head. Bang, your dead.
I guess the feds would rather me be dead
than to speak truth to power
with this number-two lead. Money for mass destruction.
Chaos and corruption.
Corporate greed that feeds on the weak which breeds
the need to destroy any who attempts to stop the bleed.
Financial literacy is a subject on campus,
but none of these subjects really give us the answer.
They spend more money killing our community
than they do for unity.
They spend more money overseas than on you and me
and white wash our names from the pages of history.
They give us Black history month as a consolation.
Meanwhile, they own the nation.
From businesses to tanks, property and banks
and leave the little line on our application for justice blank.

Junior wished he had gone first. The bar had been set too high, and he had been off for so long. If the place erupted for Rachel, the roof blew off after Parris's lines. Kids were leaving their chairs and dancing in celebration. "Son is a cold killa! White girl was nice, too!" One of the kids kept saying. Junior waited as Parris passed by the group, high-fiving his way down to the end and stood beside him.

"How the fuck do you do that?" Junior whispered.

"If you're gonna fall, then fall with grace. Stop worryin' what people think."

279

Junior shook throughout the walk, he was so nervous. He didn't have the quick cadence of Parris or the metaphorical genius that Rachel presented. All he had was himself, Leonard Robinson. All of Junior's latest lines had been about heartbreak. He braved the stage and adjusted the mic from its holder. It sent a high pitch throughout the gym which killed the crowd's ears. He closed his eyes and opened them. The crowd was still there. He readjusted the mic and delivered.

Shards of broken sapphire. Since yesteryear,
I shed rain like runny tears.
I used to live in fear for many years.
I used to doubt my presence, but now my soul I revere.
I lounged at the rear—used to hate to awake every morning
and see the sun appear.
Because I lost my brother and felt it was my fault.
Now this onslaught of life is somethin' I endear.
To every pen stroke and every night I choke, for every night
I broke and wrote
lines that enabled my darkness, and I quote.
The sun ceases the day. The day turns to night.
The moon shines bright. The days get better.
The times change.
My rhymes explain. The exchange between life, love
and living through pain.

For once, Junior didn't stick around for the crowd's validation. He exited the stage feeling gratified. The ovation rose

280

slowly across the gymnasium as Junior's heartfelt words touched everyone there. Before he knew it, he received a standing endorsement. He stood next to his new friends and waited for the other members of his group to perform their lines. He thumbed away a tear and stood proudly next to Rachel and Parris, knowing he belonged in the same room. "*Damn*, Junior," Parris whispered. "Looks like I gotta step my game up."

The coronation made Junior smile.

Leave Your Address Blank

"Relieved. That's all I can say in this moment."

—LEONARD G. ROBINSON JR.

After the team's success at Montgomery Rock, Junior hung out with Rachel, Parris, and the other group members at a burger joint not far from the school. The air around him felt whole and lively as he thought about his most recent performance. He zoned at times but was brought back to reality by the warmth of friendship. Junior made his association with the Peace Corps Alliance official and agreed to become a part-time volunteer. Rachel handed Junior an application for him to fill out. "Leave your address blank," she told him. Shrugging, Junior filled out his name, date of birth, and other pertinent info and gave it back to Rachel. She read through it and placed it in her folder.

According to Rachel, the Peace Corps Alliance had over a dozen branches throughout the city. The branch was facilitated through the college via a grant from the federal government. The program had been in limbo for years dating back to the Bush administration and was in jeopardy of being excavated in the 2000 election the following year. With funds quickly diminishing from the program's budget, it created a fierce debate amongst volunteers on where to send help.

Junior couldn't help but wonder why Rachel asked him to leave his address blank on the form. Later, when the remaining members of their group cleared from the restaurant, Rachel left Junior alone at the table with Parris to walk the other members out. "So, why do you think she told me to leave my address blank?" Junior asked him. Parris shrugged at him with a guilty expression. Junior lowered his eyes with suspicion. When Rachel returned to their booth, she took a seat next to Parris. The two sat across from Junior as if to interview him.

"So, should we ask him, now?" Parris asked her. "What if he's not interested?"

"Interested in what?"

Rachel removed Junior's application from her folder and placed it down onto the table. She pointed at the blank spot on his paperwork.

"Not sure if you remember me saying this a while back," she began. "Parris and I rent a house in Jersey City along with a few other kids from the school. It's about six of us total. The rents cheap, and the owner's really cool. The problem we're havin' is that one of our roommates is leaving before the end of the year. Are you interested?"

Junior looked across the table at the two. Neither of them batted an eye.

"...So, y'all want me to move in?"

"If you're interested," Parris co-signed. "Figured we'd offer it to you first before we asked anybody else on the team."

"That sounds dope, y'all, but I stay at my sister's crib already. Plus, shit, I'm not even working," Junior sighed. "I couldn't afford my share of the rent."

"You need a job?" Parris asked him. "I know somebody that might can help. I'll put in a word for you. Dude is solid, he'll hook you up. You're really missin' out though, Junior. We have a lot of fun at the house—good fun. Nothing crazy."

"For real?"

"Oh, my God. Dude!" Rachel peeled her hair behind her ears. "We just got a fire pit in the backyard. We do s'mores. Eat hot dogs. Play board games. We've got two TVs with two PlayStations!" she foamed. "I just bought SimCity and my cousin let us borrow World of Warcraft. All kinds of cool-ass shit to do. On Saturdays? If everybody's free? We take over the fucking city, man! Sundays are for the Giants—no Jets fans allowed. After football, we all meet at the table to study together. We party, but it's real chill. Nothing stupid. You should totally come hang with us a weekend. You'd love it!"

Parris picked up Rachel's folder and started fanning her.

"She gets a little excited sometime," he chuckled. "Yo, just think it over, Junior. We'd love to have you. We're all like

283

family. Everybody gets along. No drama or no shit like that. Son, it's hell findin' good folks to roommate with. We talked it over while you were on stage. Plus, with you on the team now? Shiiit," he laughed. "I'm definitely gonna have to step my game up."

"Thanks guys, but I'm good. I do need the hook-up on the job, though."

"Consider it done."

Junior reached across the table to dap Parris. Rachel tried to do the same but missed target before getting it right. "One more time! Gotta get that good pop in there!" Laughing, Junior dapped up Rachel's hand. She did some weird shit that made Junior pull back. Junior and Parris both looked at her sideways as she tried to explain her awkward shake.

"What? Y'all don't know that one?"

Junior shook his head and left.

Seventeen

Junior's new gig in the college bookstore was a far cry from his dairy days at the Grocery Mart. His eyes widened when he noticed Casey standing in his line. She stopped in to purchase two Steny College hoodies from him: one for her and the other for Sandy. She waved at him with the cheesiest smile he'd ever seen. She was dressed as if she'd just got off from work.

"Good evening there, young man," she greeted him. "I would like to purchase these two items, please." Junior held back his smile as he bagged his sissy's items next to his manager. He handed Casey her receipt along with her change. "Such a wonderful young man," she said, pinching at his chin before walking off. Both Junior and his new manager watched her as she walked out of the store.

"I think she likes you," the manager teased him. Junior couldn't help but laugh.

Junior's new job at the bookstore worked perfect with his schooling. He worked four days a week: Monday, Tuesday, Thursday and Friday. Unlike the Mart, his hours never changed. He also earned a $1.30 extra each hour as well as a 20% campus discount on all merchandise, including his books. He never worked a shift past 6 p.m. which was perfect if he wanted to leave town right after to visit his family in Brooke's Rowe.

One night after his shift had ended, Junior drove by the Grocery Mart to deliver a college mug to his old boss, Mr. Wilkinson. The boss flashed his gold tooth at the boy and placed it on the edge of his desk. "Told you you'd be alright." Mr. Wilkinson smiled at him. "Now, the next time you come back and see me, I want to see you with a degree in your hand. Take care of yourself, knucklehead." Junior shook his boss's hand and left.

Despite new friends, new purpose, and a new job, Vanessa still lingered in Junior's heart. In the passing weeks since their break-up, he'd been lovesick. He rarely saw her on campus but luckily had enough to distract him. If Junior wasn't at the bookstore, he was helping out Rachel and Parris with Peace Corps stuff. Their newest mission was with a rec center in Harlem. Meanwhile, his friends continued to press him about moving in. Junior was also helping Casey put the finishing touches on studying for the placement exam down at her job. Still, Vanessa persisted in his mind. Curious, he'd drive through the lot searching for her car some mornings before classes started.

One morning, Junior decided to look for Vanessa's car and didn't see it. She'd usually park in her same old spot near the sea containers in the back. Junior drove by the next morning and the one thereafter. He drove past her house a few times but didn't see her car there. There was no sign of her. Her phone was even turned off; he called it from a pay-phone on campus.

On his computer at home, Junior logged onto Instant Messenger to look for Vanessa's screen name. Her profile stated she hadn't been signed on in weeks. Vanessa's odd disappearance was unusual. That night, well after Casey was asleep, Junior looked through his old photos of Vanessa. His heart swelled with emotion as he rummaged through his collection of their kissy faces from back in the day. His curiosity later showed up inside of his journal.

It's not as easy as I thought, being apart.
My heart aches for you, Vanessa. I never wanted it to end.
What would you say if I wanted for us to still be friends?
I'm sick without you. My world is empty.
My stars no longer shine.
There's no sun in my sky. There is no purpose in these rhymes.
New York is just another city.
Central Park is just another park.
I guess the hardest part is missing how we used to make love.
The way your leg would tremble and shake,
and the way you'd caress my face.
I miss that. I miss us. Miss holding you
on the back of the shuttle bus.
I miss the way we used to fuss. The way we used
to tongue kiss. It can't be over with.

What's fucked up is I feel fucked up
for doing what I knew was right.
I just hope you're alright.

—LEONARD G. ROBINSON JR.

Late one evening while working at the bookstore, Junior was restocking a section of books on the lower shelf when he overheard a familiar, sweet voice at the register.

"Hi, I'd like to sell these items back to the store, please?"

Junior stood up to look and noticed Vanessa standing there. She was wearing a hoodie with a hat that was pulled tightly onto her head. She looked like a celebrity trying to avoid the paparazzi. Junior called to her from the aisle.

"Vanessa? Yo, where you been?!"

Vanessa ignored him. Junior dumped his stack of math books onto the cart, rushed over to the register and stood behind her. Junior looked onto the counter and noticed Vanessa was turning in her books for school. "What are you doing, Vanessa?" he asked her. Vanessa collected her change and walked out of the store without acknowledging him. Junior followed her out. "V., it's me. Junior!" he tried his luck again. Vanessa continued to walk.

Junior raced back inside to beg the manager for a quick break. Once granted, he dashed from the store out into the parking lot to look for Vanessa. He spotted her trying to leave and jumped in front of her car. Vanessa slammed on her brakes, nearly hitting him. She leapt out of her car to reprimand him.

"Are you crazy?! What if I would've hit you?!"

"Well, fuck it—run me over!" Junior panted. "What the fuck was that back there, V.? Why are you turning all your stuff in like this? Where you goin'?"

Vanessa crossed her arms. "What do you care? What does it matter?"

"C'mon, V.—you *know* I care about you. At least tell me where you're headed. I haven't seen you in weeks—I miss you. You ain't been online and your car hasn't been here, either. I checked," Junior said. "Look, just because we're not together anymore doesn't mean we gotta hate each other. I still love you, Vanessa." Junior's face softened. "Damn, do you love me?"

Vanessa rolled her lips. Her eyes welled with tears. "You know I do," she said. "But that doesn't matter right now because I'm leaving this stupid place."

"What? To go where? Where you goin'?"

"Look, J., I can't talk right now. I gotta go."

Vanessa got back into her car and began to drive off as Junior jogged beside her.

"Well, let's talk later—let's just talk later. Why don't you come past the crib after I get off? Maybe we could meet? I just wanna make sure you're OK and that you don't do nothin' crazy."

"Nothin' crazy? Why do you care so much all of a sudden?"

"I'll always care about you, Vanessa. Even if we're not together. You got me for life," Junior wheezed. "Yo, just come past the crib tonight. For old times' sake, at least. What about your family? Do they know what you're doing?"

Vanessa stopped her car right there. Junior leaned over to catch his breath.

"What family? Fuck my family!" she howled. "Who? My materialistic stepdaddy who thinks money fixes everything? Or my stupid-ass momma who encourages that shit? Yo, fuck all this bullshit, son. Fuck Shannon, and fuck you too, Junior. We made a pact in my parents' basement, and you broke that shit. I don't even know why I'm still talkin' to you. I don't need none of this anymore—and I don't want it! Goodbye, Junior. Take care of yourself."

Vanessa sped off into the night, leaving Junior standing in the parking lot. He watched as her Nissan Maxima turned the corner. He exhaled and returned to the bookstore to finish his shift.

Junior could barely concentrate as he tried to finish up his homework that night after work. He thought of telling Casey of his latest run-in with Vanessa but didn't. Unable to focus, he returned to the shoebox beneath his bed to look at her pictures. She seemed so much happier in the photos than what he'd seen earlier that evening. Vanessa wasn't the type to harm herself, at least from what Junior knew of her. She may have made poor choices in the past, but she was a sweetheart; Junior's sweetheart, he thought. He was sitting by the window inside of his bedroom when he noticed Vanessa's car drive up and park. He threw down his box of pictures and charged down the staircase, bypassing Casey snoring on the couch. It was just after eleven o' clock.

As Junior opened the front door, Vanessa was on her cell phone trying to call him. She hung up when she saw him. "Hey, J." She swallowed back tears as the two warmly embraced. They held each other by the arms and kissed like old times. Vanessa broke down as she tried to talk.

"I'm droppin' out," she wept as Junior held her. "I just came to say goodbye, Junior."

"What are you talkin' about, V.?"

Vanessa dried her eyes with her sleeves. "Been thinkin' a lot these past few weeks since we broke up. I never truly wanted any of this stuff, J. I didn't care about no college, son. The only reason I wanted to go was because I knew *you* were gonna be there. I just didn't want to be alone. Now that we're not together, what's even the point?"

Junior stared at Vanessa's sorrowful face as he continued to listen.

"I realized somethin' about myself these past few weeks. I never...really was happy, you know?" She teared again. "Even though you made me feel good, there was always that hole in my heart, J. I guess I tried to keep you away from doing things that made you happy because I wasn't happy. I didn't want you to love somethin' more than you loved me. So, I uh...I just came to tell you that I'm sorry for being so selfish. You didn't deserve that shit—you really didn't. You're gonna do so well in life, I wish I could be a part of it. I wish I'd been more supportive. I just... I fucked up, J., and I'm sorry. I'm sorry for it all."

Junior grabbed Vanessa's hand and interlaced it with his.

"I guess I wasn't all that perfect, either. Today is all that matters now—maybe we could try again, V. Yo, I'm sick without you. What if we try it again? We'll take it slow this time."

Vanessa smiled as she rubbed Junior's face. She shook her head at him.

"No," she removed her hand. "No, Junior. You had it right the first time. You deserve better. Besides, it's just gonna… like you said, we don't have to hate each other. You'll always have a place in my heart, J.—always."

Junior's eyes filled with tears. "Yeah," he cleared his throat. "So, where you headed, V.?"

"Fayetteville… it's in North Carolina. My aunt lives down that way. I just need to get away from this New York shit for a while. I would've reached out sooner, but I wasn't in a good place." Vanessa reached for his face again as she began to smile. "I'm really gonna miss you, Junior. Maybe I'll call you once I get there?"

A tear swept from Junior's eye down his cheek. He kissed Vanessa's soft hand.

"Please."

Vanessa touched Junior's lips with her finger and left.

As Vanessa walked back to her car across the road, Junior stood in the street.

"Some friends of mine offered me a spot at their crib in Jersey City," he blurted. "It could be a good thing, but I don't know. I kind of like things the way they are here with Sissy. What do you think?"

Vanessa turned around.

292

"I think that no matter what happens, you'll make the right decision." Her face softened. "See you around, Leonard Robinson."

Vanessa fired up her car and drove off, leaving Junior in the middle of the roadway. He watched as the brake lights on Vanessa's car absorbed into the city's darkness. He felt somewhat relieved knowing he had buried the hatchet on his old romance. Junior blew a kiss to Vanessa's car and headed back inside. As he reached the bottom step, Casey opened the door.

"What are you doing out here so late, J.? *Damn*, it's chilly! You good?"

Junior looked up at his sissy and smiled. "I am now," he told her. "Just needed a little fresh air, that's all."

As Junior bypassed Casey at the door, she closed it behind him for the night.

"Keeping ~~Hope~~ Art Alive"

There was a bittersweetness in Junior's heart in the days after Vanessa's departure from New York. The morning after she left, he fetched his shoebox beneath the bed to look through their pictures once more. He cried for a bit, smiling at her lovely dimples and amiable smile. He prayed she made a safe trip down to Fayetteville and that she could find the strength to overcome life's challenges. He kissed her lovely face, placed her photo back inside his box and returned it beneath his bed. He looked down at the sunny spot on the roadway where he had last held her pretty face. Before the sense of loss devastated him, he left out for school.

On campus, Junior kept busy helping Rachel and Parris organize efforts with the Harlem Project. The compassionate deed was soothing to his aching heart. Junior had discovered a new identity to compliment his abilities as a writer: helping others. He penned a letter on behalf of the organization to petition the federal government for more grant money to help disadvantaged high schoolers (like he had once been). He shared his story which began five years earlier in a troubled neighborhood overrun with crime. "...The Peace Corps Alliance at Steny College respectfully requests the urgency of our government to grant us the opportunity to help those who aspire to dream..." the quoted line was included in the school's paper. Junior titled his pleading letter: *Keeping* ~~Hope~~ *Art Alive*. Junior didn't know it until Rachel and Parris came bothering him at work one afternoon.

"Dude, I fucking told you! You're a god!" Rachel came rushing into the bookstore as students scurried out of their way. She cut in line at the main counter and slammed a copy of the article down in front of him. Junior lifted the paper and began to read. He looked down at the article with his school ID picture and grinned.

"*Shit*," he chuckled. "Can't believe they featured it."

"I can," said Parris. "Son, it was a dope line, '...the opportunity to help those who aspire to dream'. Who else would've thought to say somethin' like that? So, have you thought anymore about what we talked about, J.?"

"About what?"

"The roommate thing, duh!" Rachel laughed. "Are you interested?"

"Well, I don't know, guys. Look, I got a lot of shit on my plate right now that I need to sort out. Can you give me some more time to think it over?"

"No doubt. Let us know."

As Junior and Parris reached out to dap one another, Rachel blasted her hand in between them. She was sweet but socially awkward, Junior noticed. He slapped skin with Rachel as she cheesed, showing her gummy braces and left. Parris stayed behind to rap at Junior.

"Gotta love her. Poor thing, she lost her mom recently to leukemia." Parris shook his head as he watched Rachel leave. "I didn't know you lost a brother, Junior. Heard it in your lines at Montgomery Rock. I'm glad you found an outlet."

Junior lifted a pile of unstacked books and began checking them in.

"Thanks. Well, that was a long time ago."

"I had a brother, too. He uh…went to bed one night and never woke up. He was a lot older. Doctors said he had a heart attack in his sleep. I know that's a different set of circumstances—but still," Parris said. "Look, man, I ain't tryin' to push you out of your sister's crib. Don't mind Rachel, she's…a little extra sometimes. If you're comfortable there you ought to stay.

"Thanks, Parris. Mind if I keep this article?" Junior held it up.

"It's yours. Yo, I gotta bounce. I'll catch you later."

As Parris walked off, Junior distracted himself with the article. He picked up his featured piece showcasing his handsome face and smiled. For the next couple days, Junior was a mini-celebrity on Steny's campus. He took his fifteen minutes of fame and ran with it.

Think It Over

"Oh, my Lord. Check *that* out," Sandy gasped in shock upon seeing her son's face featured on the front of Steny's newsletter. Junior held it up to his webcam for her to see before reading the article to her. She clapped and cheered proudly at him. Junior held up a T-shirt with the Peace Corps logo on the front of it. Beneath its insignia was his name written in fancy cursive.

"Be right back!" Sandy told him. She walked away from her camera and returned with the sweater Casey had got for her. She held it up to the camera for Junior to see and put it on. Sandy stood tall in her hoodie looking it over. "So warm and cozy. I'll make sure to tell Casey thank you the next time we talk. Missed you the past weekend. You doing OK up there, Junior?"

"I know, sorry about that. I got caught up on campus with the group. So, where's Daddy?"

"In the room layin' down. His back is bothering him again. I keep tellin' him he's gettin' old and needs to take it easy. He won't listen to me, though."

"Daddy won't listen to nobody," Junior chuckled. "Ma, can I ask you something?"

"Well, can you make it quick? My show's about to come on. What's up?"

No question was ever quick when it came from Junior. He wasn't good at being direct. He'd dance around the point before asking for what he needed. He was still that shy kid who was afraid to speak his piece. Senior called for Sandy in the background which gave Junior a few minutes to think over what he wanted to ask. He jotted his thoughts onto a sticky pad next to his computer. He crumbled it up when Sandy returned to the monitor.

"Lord, that man!" she giggled. "Now, what'd you wanna ask me, Junior?"

"OK, I'll try to make this quick."

"You don't have to repeat what you said earlier, Junior," she laughed. "Just… ask me."

"Sorry, Ma," Junior sighed. "I guess I'm afraid to ask because I don't want to seem ungrateful to Casey or what she's done for me—but I'll just say it, anyway. I been thinkin' a lot lately. About a lot of things. I feel like maybe I wanna spread my wings—I'm not sure about it, though. Just was thinkin'. You remember the new friends I made on campus that I was telling you about?" he asked her. "So, they rent out this house—it's not far away. It's in Jersey City—right across the bridge from Casey. Well, they asked for me to move in. And I've been thinkin' about it."

"…So, like a roommate thing?" Sandy nodded. "Hmmm."

"Yeah! That's the same thing I said," Junior agreed. "Nothin' bad with Sissy or anything. Remember when I told you about Vanessa leaving for Fayetteville? It got me thinkin'. Maybe it's time for me to move on and do my own thing, too. I haven't told Casey yet. But I think it's time for me to start being my own man."

"I'm glad you said that. Because I know *just* the person you can ask this question to. I'm sure he'd love to help you—LEONARRRRD!"

"Ma, no!" Junior waved at the screen. "Don't call him!"

"LEONARRRRD!"

It took Senior a while with his bad back before he humped in front of the monitor. In pain, he sat at the computer screen with a killer's scowl on his face. He had just woken from a nap. He rubbed his eyes and yawned. His hair was wiry and uncombed.

"What y'all want, man? *Damn.*"

Sandy cut to the chase. "Junior's thinkin' about movin' out of Casey's. He wants to be his own man. You know all about that. Why don't you talk to him?"

Junior's heart thumped as his daddy glared at him through the screen. With Senior, the conversation could go either way. Junior might get good advice, or he could take a lashing. Most of the time, it was the latter. It all depended on his daddy's mood. With his back troubling him, Junior braced for the worst.

298

"Yeah, I'm listenin', Junior," Senior yawned again. "What's on your mind?"

"Well, Daddy," Junior began. "Y'all know how I feel about Sissy. But I'm startin' to feel like maybe it's time I do my own thing. Some cats in Jersey City are looking for a roommate. I think it's time for me to be my own man."

Senior stared into the webcam at Junior, not blinking. Even through a computer monitor, the man was still terrifying. His big, black frame took up most of the screen.

"You think movin' out makes you a man, Junior?" Senior asked him.

"No, sir."

"So, what makes a man *a man*? Tell me."

"…Being able to take care of myself? Being responsible and not doing stupid shit."

"Bingo—and being able to make your own decisions." Senior raised his brow. "So, is this a decision you made or did somebody else put you on to do it?"

"It's my decision, Daddy. There's a part of me that feels guilty for even feeling like I wanna move out. But on the other side, it's about making experiences, am I right?" Junior asked. "I just wanna make the best of these opportunities while I still can. I can't stay here at Casey's forever. Even if it's just for a little while, I wanna try somethin' new. Does that make sense, Daddy?"

Junior's parents both looked on at him proudly.

"Well," Senior said. "Seems like you answered your own damn question."

"I did?"

"Leonard and I think so." Sandy placed her hands onto Senior's shoulders. "I think that's very unselfish of you, Junior, wanting to give Casey a little breather and take on new challenges. Why don't you talk to your sister about it? You know it'll be hard because she's been so used to having you around. So, you'll have to find a way to explain it to her. You know how crazy she is about you," Sandy laughed. "But either way, we love you and we support your decision."

Junior waved back at his biggest fans. "Thanks, y'all. See you soon."

Before shutting down, Junior couldn't help but notice Vanessa's screenname, NyCShawty81, was signed onto AOL Instant Messenger. He highlighted her profile box to check her status. She had her hometown listed as Brooklyn, New York and her current city was Fayetteville, North Carolina. It made him smile. She had made it safely. He scrolled his mouse over to the message box and typed a noteworthy note:

Hey V., just passing through. I checked your status and noticed you made it to Fayetteville. So happy for you. Word is bond, I still got mad love for you, miss you and wish you all the best on your new journey, Vanessa. Always and forever, - J."

Junior tapped the "send" button. Before he could log off, Vanessa messaged him back.

[8:16 PM EST] NyCShawty81: ☺ OMG, SON! All of the above! I'm crying right now! Thank you, Junior!

[8:17 PM EST] BRowePhilly: ☺ You're welcome, sweetheart.

Junior thought to write Vanessa some other cute lines but didn't. He had said more than enough. He logged off of his computer for the night.

Eighteen

The thought of moving out distracted Junior for the next several days. He felt guilty for wanting to leave. How could he do such a thing? he asked himself. Casey had been his surrogate guardian for the past four and a half years. She had taught him to drive, how to fill out a job application, prepare for a job interview, pay his cell phone bill, and a myriad of other life skills. When she had got sick with Stage 1 breast cancer, Junior had been there in her corner. They were brother and sister, no doubt. He loved her almost as much as he loved Lawrence. Casey had become a branch on the family tree. The Robinsons had unofficially adopted her.

Junior rehearsed breaking the news to Casey for one week before he decided to tell her that he had planned to move out. In his room, he tried saying it both standing and sitting. He even prepared in case Casey bopped him on his forehead with her palm. "Hold up—wait a minute. Will you just hear me out, first? *Damn!*" he surrendered to her ghost. He positioned his words carefully. When that failed, he tried writing his feelings down and reading it back. He recorded his thoughts on his computer and replayed it, critiquing his delivery. Junior mapped out every possible angle of his conversation with Casey before asking his momma for advice.

"Whatever you say, just say it from the heart," Sandy advised her son. It was the same advice she had once given when he first picked up a pen to write. His mother's words were just as relevant now as they were back in '94.

Junior forewent telling Parris and Rachel of his decision until he first spoke with Casey. He broke the news to her on a Tuesday night after he got home from work. Casey didn't make it any easier for him. The moment he walked through the door, she called him over to the couch. He tried his best to hide his ill look.

"I got somethin' to tell you, Sissy."

"Hold up," Casey stopped him. She reached onto the table and passed Junior an envelope.

"What's this?"

"Will you open it? Stop askin' me dumb shit. Just open it."

Junior opened Casey's envelope and removed her letter. It was the results of her placement exam down at her job. He scrambled to unfold the letter and scanned her document to look for her score. She had passed with a score of 88%. Junior looked over at Casey and noticed her eyes were misty. She put her arm around the boy and pecked him on his head.

"Oh shit!" Junior laughed. "Yo, congratulations, Sissy!"

"I couldn't have done this without you. Thank you, J. So, what'd you wanna tell me?"

"Huh? Oh, uh… nothin'. Just wanted to say that I'm

proud of you and thank you for letting me stay here as long as I have and everything. Congratulations again, Casey."

Casey raised her eyebrow at him. "…Um, OK?" she chuckled. "You're welcome—but you know that already. I'm proud of you, too. Way to make the paper at school, superstar!"

"Thanks, Sissy. So, uh… yeah, I'm gonna head up. I'll catch you later."

As Junior tried to leave, Casey grabbed his arm. "Get over here! Why are you being so weird to me today? What's wrong with you?" she laughed. "Uh-oh. Junior. What'd you do? Did you break something? You still owe me for my rug—I didn't forget. I want my $30, J." She jabbed him. "I ain't playin'."

"Everything's good, Sissy. Just a long day."

Casey released him. Before she could detect anything was wrong, Junior headed to his room and closed his door.

The thought of saying goodbye was too much for Junior to bare. He paced back and forth throughout his room as he tried to convince himself that his decision to leave was right. He thought of dialing his folks to ask for more advice but didn't. It was his decision to make. From now on, every decision was his. Not Mel's, Vanessa's, Mr. Wilkinson's, his parents', Parris's or Rachel's. For years, Junior had relied on the opinions of everyone else. It was time for him to lift himself up for a change. For over an hour, he mulled inside his head before he decided to break the news to her. He left his room and returned downstairs to find Casey resting beneath her blanket in front of the TV. He leaned over the stairway railing.

"Sissy, you busy? I need to talk to you about something. Can you come upstairs?"

Casey rose from her blanket and stretched. She followed Junior up to his room. His anxiety spiked relentlessly as he prepared to drop what felt like a bomb into Casey's world. He entered his room and took a seat on the bed. He motioned for Casey to sit beside him. She sat cross-legged with her big, chunky legs folded beneath her. Her fists were beneath her chin.

"You know better than to mess with me when *X-Files* is on," she laughed, swatting at him. "So, what's up? We good?"

Junior's head slumped forward. He reached for Casey's hands and held them. Junior noticed her palms were just as sweaty as his. She was just nervous as he was, if not more. He raised his head and look into her worried eyes. Telling Casey that he was moving out was proving harder than ending things with Vanessa.

"Casey." Junior squeezed her hands. "There's really no easy way to tell you this, so I'm just gonna say it," he sighed. "I've been doin' a lot of thinkin' lately, and uh... I think it's time for me to... you know... spread my wings a bit and maybe... move out at some point... soon."

Casey's hands went limp. She stared right through him, not offering a reaction. Junior held her hands even tighter.

"Living with you has been an absolute *dream*, Casey. You taught me so much these past four—almost five years we've been together. I couldn't ask for a better friend... sister." His eyes fizzled as he corrected himself. "I don't want you to think that me leaving means that this New York thing didn't work. It did, in my book. Because it gave me the opportunity to experience things. A new school. College. Love. Commitment. Responsibility. *Shit,* I've grown so much under your wing, Casey. But now, it's about time that I move on and make my own way in the world," Junior explained. "My friends with the Peace Corps have a house in Jersey City across the bridge. They offered me a room, and I've decided to take it."

Junior leaned forward to kiss Casey on her warm cheek. Her eyes sparkled.

"Thank you for everything. From the bottom of my heart, Sissy."

Casey's mouth hung open. "Wow!" She used her finger to dab away her tears. She tried to giggle it off, but more tears fell as she wept inside her small hands. She got herself together and grabbed Junior, hugging him. "C'mere, little brother," she moaned. "I always knew this was gonna happen, just not as soon."

Casey let him go. She giggled as she dried her eyes with her T-shirt. Junior did the same.

"Sorry," she exhaled before rejoining hands with her brother. "So, I don't want you to see me cryin' and think you did anything wrong—you didn't. These are happy tears, OK?" Casey's eyes pooled again. "You know how much I love you, J., and I *know* you love me just the same. It's all good, OK? But damn, J., you sure know how to touch a person's heart. Can I have another hug?"

Junior grabbed Casey right away and pressed her. Casey pecked him on the side of his head. Junior pecked her right back. As Junior latched onto her, the two fell clumsily off the bed and onto the floor together. *Boom!* Casey winced in pain.

"Fuck, you're heavy!" she strained. "Get off-get off!"

The two laughed together as Junior helped Casey onto her feet. They hugged again.

"Yo, you better not forget about me. I'll come find you, and when I do, I'm gonna blow your new house up and kill everybody inside of there. I'll do it. Can I at least meet these folks, first?"

"After you've threatened to blow up their house? Sure, why not?" Junior laughed. "We'll still be together, Sissy. No matter what. We're family, now."

"Now? We've *been* family, knucklehead!"

At the door, Casey looked at Junior with an awestruck expression. "I gotta be honest with you, Junior. Before you came along. My life was just…" Casey shook her head at him. She pulled Junior's door mostly closed before a good cry came on. "Never mind. Forget it. Yo, I'm proud to be your big sister, that's all."

Junior placed his hand on the door and kept it there after Casey left.

Life Is a Journey

Life, death and taxes, my mother said was certain.
They'll be there even after they lower the curtain.
Live your life. Make new friends. Laugh 'til it hurts.
Never look back.
Picture that. Jump on a plane and explore the map.
See the world.
Experience real love. Send a prayer high up above.
Make a wish. Share a kiss before it's all over with.
Before you know it, you'll be asleep for eons.
Live your life above and beyond.

—LEONARD G. ROBINSON JR.

Junior was the last to finish Mr. Freemont's latest exam. A week had passed since he and Casey had talked about him moving on. She'd arranged to meet up with Junior and his soon-to-be roommates for an early lunch after his test. Junior could barely focus anticipating what was to come of their experience. The idea still felt surreal to him. Junior hadn't yet told Parris and Rachel of his big decision. He wanted it to be a surprise to them.

Junior was midway through a grueling semester that had seen a lot of changes happen in his life. He and his former best friend from Langston, Mel Roberts, had fallen out. He'd lost his cushy gig down at the Mart and burned his bridge with Mr. Wilkinson. He'd lost his passion for writing before ultimately regaining it. He'd nearly lost his freedom (and his life). He was also on the verge of moving out of Casey's, a change which was still hard to process at times. Last but not least, he had lost the love of his life, Vanessa Bailey. Despite his shortcomings early on, he was still standing and had found new purpose through the Peace Corps.

When Junior placed his test packet facedown onto his teacher's desk, Mr. Freemont eyed him skeptically. Junior gave it all back to him and returned to his seat. The professor graded every exam right there on the spot. Junior took his seat next to Rachel and waited in wonder. He tried to read Mr. Freemont's expression, but his teacher wore his best poker face. He called out his students' grades aloud; he could give a shit who he embarrassed. Once they received their score, they were free to leave. With each grade, he added his own colorful commentary.

"Kirkpatrick, 79—and I wouldn't be so happy about that if I were you," he said. Rachel stuck her tongue out at him and waited out in the hall for Junior. "Franklin, 64. Are you kiddin' me, Franklin? All that tutoring? Posey, 45—c'mon Posey! Winslow. Stay behind. Graham. Stay behind. Jones-Parker... stay behind. *Robinsonnn*," he sang with delight as he read the scores out of order. "91, but stay behind."

Junior and Rachel both looked at one another in amazement. Neither could believe it.

After class, Junior stood in front of Mr. Freemont's desk waiting for his teacher. The professor re-scored his exam twice. He compared Junior's test scores with the other students in the class. From what Junior could tell, he had the third highest score out of everybody. Meanwhile, Mr. Freemont continued to scratch his head.

"I can re-take it if you want me to?"

"Forget it, it's nothing." Mr. Freemont waved him off. "Congratulations."

As Junior turned to leave, he stopped himself. "Is there any reason why you double-checked only my test score, sir?"

"Look, you got a good score. You should be happy."

"Well, I'm not," said Junior. "Seems like you got a real issue with minority students doing well in your class—I think this point has been brought up before. You double-checked my work, but you didn't check Lisa Reeves's work, the white girl who sits behind me. She got a 94."

Mr. Freemont slammed his hands down onto his desk. "Are you trying to insinuate that I'm a racist?"

"I ain't insinuating nothin' because you are!" Junior barked. "You been on my back since day one. Yo, you might not be used to Black kids doin' well on your tests, but you better get real used to me scoring high on *all* of your stuff. Because I will not be dragging my ass back in here ever again once this semester is over."

Junior gave his professor the peace sign and left. Out in the hallway, Rachel trolled beside Junior as he angrily strode down the hall.

"Goddamn! You fuckin' blew that bitch up—boom!" She pumped her fist. "You scored a 91 on the test but scored a perfect on him. What a dick. So, where's lunch?"

"Actually, I got a surprise. Why don't you and Parris meet

me downtown at BuBoy's Café and Lounge in about an hour? It's on the corner of West 44th and 7th Avenue."

"Why? What's there?" she asked him. "You must make some pretty good cake at the bookstore, man. Are they still hiring, by the way?"

"Will you just meet me there? You and Parris," Junior laughed. "It's a surprise."

Rachel stuck out her hand at Junior to try to dap him again. Junior looked down at her hand and back up at her. She failed every last handshake they tried. He spared his friend the embarrassment and gave her a sturdy hug.

"*Damn*. Did I get it wrong, again?"

"Yeah, we'll work on that," Junior laughed. "See you soon."

Casey was already at BuBoy's when Junior arrived. She was on her lunch break. The café didn't have the same ambience as when Junior had first visited in '95, but the glass elevator which overlooked the city was as remarkable as he last remembered. Once upon a time, Junior had conned Casey into taking him to New York. It came at the heels of her losing her job at Medgar High where the two first met. To celebrate the holiday, Casey got them bus tickets. For Junior, at the time, it was the furthest he'd been away from home, and the first time he'd gone ice skating at Rockefeller Plaza. Their joyous day ended with a trip to Langston High where Junior would eventually enroll before Casey adopted him as her brother. The rest was history.

At the door, Junior greeted the host and looked through the lounge for Casey. He spotted her sitting in a booth next to a window where'd they sat the last time. She stared out into the city as she sipped from her steamy cup. Junior observed Casey before approaching her. It was hard to fathom leaving her behind. He thought about what she meant to his life, and all the hell that they'd gone through since they first met. Regardless, she was still there. Junior slid beside her, butt-bumping his Sissy as she scooted to the window.

"If I was to bump you back, I'd knock you into Brooke's Rowe!" she giggled. "So, where are your little idiot friends so I can tell 'em to fuck off?"

"They should be here soon. Yo, don't be all evil and shit, either. I know you."

"Mmhmm." Casey drank from her cup.

"Why you gotta be a hater, Sissy?"

"I'm just sayin', I'd like to know who my brother's friends are. Give a sista a break, J. Do you remember this place? This is where I brought you a few years back. Before you nearly got both of us *murdered* after I drove you home. I was scared for your life!"

Junior leaned his head onto Casey's arm as he hugged her. "I know you was. That's why you'll always be my Sissy."

"Mmhmm."

Just as Junior and Casey finished reminiscing about their iconic day, Parris and Rachel appeared at the door. Casey nearly spit out her drink at Rachel's foggy, crooked glasses. Junior waved his new friends over as Casey looked on, stunned. Junior hoped that his new friends didn't notice Casey rolling her eyes at them.

"What the hell is this sideshow-ass shit, J.? Who the hell is that?!"

"C'mon, Sissy. Be nice—these are my friends." Junior muttered. He stood up to greet his new crew and introduced them to Casey. She wore her fakest smile as she rose to her feet and extended her hand for a shake. She introduced herself as Junior's sister—not his friend. Parris looked at the two, trying to find the resemblance before taking his seat. Junior and Casey both looked at each other and laughed. Rachel, as expected, was awkward. She gasped as if Casey was a celebrity.

"So, you're Junior's sister?"

"That's right. And let me guess. You're Junior's friend?" Casey joked.

Rachel nodded her head, refusing to let Casey's hand go. "That is *so* cool. Your brother is awesome."

"He's aight," Casey laughed. "Mind if I have my hand back?"

"Oh, sure. Sorry, I always do that!"

Junior and his friends all took their seats but Casey didn't, he noticed. She slipped over to the Ladies' room, leaving Junior to mingle with his friends. Junior thought of his sissy the entire time, wondering if she had run off to the restroom to hide that she was emotional about him leaving. In the days since telling Casey about his plans, he barely slept a full night. He admired their old pictures of them together back at the house and reminisced on the times they shared. The many times they laughed and cried together as a family. Now, he was a young man, set to write a new chapter in the story book of Leonard Robinson Jr. Someday, he hoped to write a novel about their time together. Minutes passed before Casey returned to the booth to join them. Junior carefully studied Casey's face to look for any sign of tears. Although he thought he saw a few, he knew they were happy tears.

"Well," Casey said, putting on her scarf, "I guess I ought to get back to work. It was really nice meeting you all."

"Wait a minute, Sissy!" Junior scooted from his booth. "Yo, what about lunch? I thought you said we were all gonna grab a bite? C'mon, you can't leave us now. We haven't even ordered yet."

Casey placed a $100 bill onto the table. "So, enjoy." She smiled and winked.

Junior excused himself from his friends and walked Casey over to the glass elevator inside the café's lobby. Casey straightened her brother's collared shirt for him as she waited for her elevator to arrive. Junior straightened his sister's scarf.

"I'm good. I don't need to interview your friends." She flicked away a string of lint from atop his shoulder. "I'm gonna head back to the office and try to finish up some paperwork. You guys enjoy lunch, and I'll see you back at the house tonight."

As Casey went to get on the elevator, Junior leaned against the shaft.

"Just so you know, I might be a little late gettin' in tonight. We're headed to the Harlem Project this evening. After that, we'll probably kick it somewhere until late."

"Late? Well, what the hell time are you gonna be in? Can you at least give me a time?" Casey questioned. "It gets so crazy at night in the city when…"

Junior looked at Casey with a look of admiration. Casey stopped herself.

"Like you don't already know this stuff, right?" she giggled. "Have a nice time, J."

"Don't wait up." He smiled. As the elevator closed, Junior returned to his friends at the booth.

The End

Epilogue

HAPPY TEARS

The walls inside of Junior's old room at Casey's were bare as he stuffed the last of his valuables into an Adidas gym bag. The rest had already been loaded onto a small U-Haul truck which awaited him outside. He sat in the corner against the wall next to his shoebox with Vanessa's pictures. He traced his fingers along her elegant face and stopped at her lips. The last Junior had heard from her was on Instant Messenger months earlier. They chatted often at first, the two. Eventually, their messages got shorter until Junior seldom heard from Vanessa at all. "That's life," Sandy told him. Junior covered the box with its lid and stood on his feet.

Junior tossed his carrier onto his shoulder and looked around. The moment was surreal to him. His old room there at Casey's was so empty that it echoed as he walked throughout. Junior removed his new phone from his pocket and snapped a grainy photo for safekeeping. His heart filled

317

with nostalgic memories. Junior had once wanted out on his grand opportunity, believing New York was too big for him, but Casey had thought otherwise; he was glad she'd convinced him to stay. Junior broke in slowly before eventually finding his stride along the way. He'd faced setbacks but ultimately overcame them to emerge into a young man. His writing had soon evolved as well as his love life—which had since withered away. Perhaps someday he would love again. Life was an experience, Junior had learned.

He walked over to his window and overlooked his neighborhood, bypassing his moving truck beneath him. Outside, Senior and Parris loaded his work desk along with a box labeled "fragile" up a metal ramp into the back. The two pulled the bay door close, solidifying that Junior's time there had come to an end—at least for now. Meanwhile, Rachel and Sandy were checking off Junior's items on a clipboard. Casey soon entered her brother's old room to bid him farewell. The sound of her footsteps grew louder as she approached him by the window.

"Wow," she gasped. "It's so empty in here."

Junior reached for Casey's hands. "No, it isn't. You filled this room and this house with so much joy during my time here," he told her. "I can't thank you enough, Casey."

Casey smiled warmly at Junior. "Well, you, young man, have filled *my* heart with so much joy these past four and a half years. You made an old dog used to being kicked around start to believe again. Thank you, Junior."

With the sun peeking at them between the venetian blinds, the two hugged.

318

"Oh, shit! I almost forgot." Junior pulled himself away. "So, you got a special friend now? Don't try to play it off, either. I saw you get out the car the other night. You ain't slick, Casey! So, what's his name?"

"Actually… it's a 'her', J." Casey cheesed, covering her face. "Yeah… we're taking it slow."

"Oh… well, love is love, right? No matter who you are."

"Exactly—and I'm serious about this whole Jersey City thing, J. You better not forget about me. I'm still gonna need you to look over all my papers for school."

"You know I got you. So, what's next for you, Sissy?"

"Well, little brother," she paused. "You're gonna think this is so silly, Junior, but I was thinkin' about writing a book—about my life. Yeah, me and books! I barely like reading the ones I got for school—and now I'm gonna try to write my own. Ugh! Maybe I'll let you pick the title."

"Just as long as I get to be in it."

The two hugged again before Casey pulled herself away.

"OK, get off me!" she giggled. "So, no crying, right? We've done enough of that."

"Yes, we have. This isn't goodbye, Casey. This is more like… see you again real soon."

"No doubt, J. So, you ready?"

Junior hoisted his bag onto his shoulder and followed Casey out. In his hand was his shoebox with Vanessa's old pictures. He walked over to the closet and placed it onto the empty shelf as Casey looked on.

"Now, I am," said Junior. The two left out, pulling his old

door closed behind them.

Downstairs, Junior and Casey met up with his moving crew consisting of Senior, Sandy, Parris, and Rachel. They lounged near the foyer, waiting for him. Senior glowered at Junior as he sipped an ice-cold beer to cool off. He gave Junior the blues.

"Why you ain't call some real movin' people, Junior?" Senior growled. "You know I'm gettin' too old to be movin' your ass 'round all over the place. Now, c'mon and let's get goin' before I leave all that shit out there on that truck and go home."

"Oh, stop!" Sandy flailed at him. "Don't mind him, y'all. He's just a grumpy, old man."

"I ain't grumpy," Senior pouted. "You see how big that boy's dresser was, Sandy? I don't know why you bought that boy that big-ass dresser, *knowin'* he don't need it."

"Actually… I bought it." Casey slowly raised her hand. "I got it at a yard sale. The neighbors helped me bring it in. I didn't realize it was so heavy. Sorry, Pops."

Senior threw up his hands and walked out. The room roared with delight at his frustration.

"Well, I didn't think it was all that heavy," said Rachel.

"That's 'cause you ain't lift it!" Parris clapped back. "You been on the clipboard, Rach. Matter of fact, you drive."

Rachel and Parris said their goodbyes to Casey before climbing into the U-Haul truck, leaving Junior, his momma, and Casey behind. Sandy turned to face Casey and joined hands with her. Casey held in place.

"I'll see you later, Casey." She squeezed her. "Maybe we'll

320

do Thanksgiving, if not, definitely Christmas or somethin' before the new year. I'll be in touch."

Sandy went out the door. Junior's momma wasn't one for long-winded goodbyes. She didn't believe in them. In her book, there was no such thing. She hobbled down the staircase with her cane in her hand as Junior and Casey looked on in awe. The two were alone again. Before Junior left out, he reached inside of his bag and handed Casey a white envelope. She opened it and discovered $500. She looked up at him, confused.

"Whoa! What's all this, J.? Why the extra bread?"

"Yo, sometimes you gotta pay back what you owe, right? Later, Sissy."

Junior pecked Casey on her cheek and walked off. Halfway down the sidewalk, he turned back to look at Casey and noticed her eyes were misty. Junior wiped his and smiled. "These aren't sad tears. These are happy tears." He winked at her. Casey grinned at Junior. She shook her head at the boy and closed her door.

Out on the roadway, Junior bypassed his daddy's truck along with Rachel and Parris in the U-Haul and headed to his car parked at the front of the line. He turned back to wave at his convoy, pressing on his horn.

"Try to keep up, y'all," he called out as he waved.

Junior fired up his loaded car and drove off as his procession followed behind.

Life, death and taxes, my mother said was certain.
They'll be there even after they lower the curtain.
Live your life. Make new friends. Laugh 'til it hurts.
Never look back.
Picture that. Jump on a plane and explore the map.
See the world.
Experience real love. Send a prayer high up above.
Make a wish. Share a kiss before it's all over with.
Before you know it, you'll be asleep for eons.
Live your life above and beyond.

—LEONARD G. ROBINSON JR.

Acknowledgments

Thank you for reading *Beyond Poetry: Above & Beyond*. The creation of this work would not be possible without an outpouring of support from family, friends, and the many fans who helped to make this series special. Thank you all so very much!

About the Author

Nathan Jarelle is an indie author and poet from the Washington, D.C. metro region. He is the creator of the *Beyond Poetry* series; a collection of African-American and young adult literature combined with poetry and retro storytelling. In his spare time, Jarelle enjoys reading, fishing, family time, traveling, and of course, writing. To learn more about Jarelle's works, visit or subscribe to his website at:

www.natejayreads.com

Thank you for reading *Beyond Poetry: Above & Beyond*. For autographed copies or business inquiries, be sure to visit his website.

BOOKS BY
NATHAN JARELLE

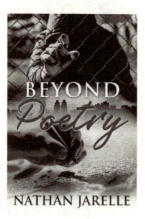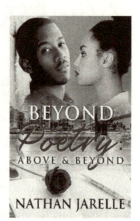

If you haven't done so yet, grab a copy of the original title, *Beyond Poetry*. Follow Junior's pathway to poetry and discover how he and Casey Haughton first met. *Beyond Poetry* is carried by most online book retailers. For signed copies, visit the author's website at www.natejayreads.com.

Did you enjoy the book? Help me to spread the word by leaving a kind review with your retailer or telling your friends about *Beyond Poetry*. Thank you for your support!